# ONE BECOMES A THOUSAND

## The ArchAngel Missions

### Book IV

# JOSHUA LOYD FOX

Published by Watertower Hill Publishing, LLC

Copyright © 2022 JLFoxBooks, LLC
www.jlfoxbooks.com

Cover and internal artwork by
Copyright © 2022 JLFoxBooks, LLC



Author's Note
All character and names in this book are fictional and are not designed, patterned after, nor descriptive of any person, living or deceased.
Any similarities to people, living or deceased is purely by coincidence. Author and Publisher are not liable for any likeness described herein.

Library of Congress Control Number:
ISBN: 979-8-9855562-3-0

This book is dedicated to my big brother,

Jason L. Daughrity.

The guy who encouraged my addiction to Fantasy, starting in the eighth grade, like a crack dealer in Detroit.

First taste was free.......

*"A little one shall become a thousand, and the smallest a mighty nation. I, the Lord, will hasten it in its time."*

Isaiah 60:22 NKJV

**What is, what was, what will be**
**Will always be corrected**
**By a few that never knew**
**What sacrifice had then decided.**
*Book of the Tower and the Traitor—Strophe Four*

# Prologue

"Gabriel Fairchild? Is there a Gabriel Fairchild here?"

The rotund black woman with the leopard print colored glasses perched on her nose, held to her head with a short gold chain, called into the large room.

She yelled the name into the room again. Gabe looked up from where he sat and raised his hand like a second-grader being called on to answer a math problem on the blackboard.

" Ri-right here," he stuttered quietly.

The woman saw him and motioned for him to approach the desk she sat behind. A barrier of tall, bullet-proof glass separated her from the rest of the waiting room.

Gabe didn't take his eyes off the woman's face as he shuffled toward her. He held in his hand a perfectly clean and crisp manila folder, gripping it tightly as he approached the woman behind the glass.

The receptionist thought the man walking toward her window looked scared. She could see it on his face. She couldn't place an age on the man behind the large, black, horn-rimmed glasses.

She looked him up and down, noticing the lanky, greasy blond hair falling to his shoulders under a flat twill hat. His clothes looked dirty and slept in.

The receptionist casually looked at the other four families sitting peacefully, and much more clean than the homeless man before her, and sighed loudly.

She mentally shrugged his appearance off. She had seen hundreds of people approach her desk with the same look on their face. There was wildness in their eyes. She understood that all too well.

"Please present your claim form and signed ticket to the man standing there," she told the nervous man, and pointed.

They both watched as Jose, the overlarge security guard, approached the man, one hand held out, the other unconsciously hovering over the black pistol on his hip.

Gabe flinched. He held the manila folder tighter to his chest. Gabe looked back at the women behind the glass.

He then looked back and forth between the two employees several times. Jose saw this and smiled.

He, too, had seen this very scene played out many times. He looked into the homeless man's eyes and smiled again.

"It's okay sir. We're just going to verify the claim form. You can sit back down while we take it in the back."

Jose had often had to placate nervous, panicked people in this man's situation.

It always started out tense here. The celebrations came later.

Gabe handed the security guard the manila folder. He didn't take his eyes off it as Jose walked with it to a solidly built wooden door with a keypad next to it.

Jose pressed a quick series of numbers, and the door opened for him. He walked though, and the door shut behind him with a loud bang. Gabe flinched again.

No one looking at him could tell it was all an act.

Gabe sat down nervously and wondered at the life that was going to unfold when the contents of the manila folder were analyzed by someone behind that big door.

Exactly twenty-one minutes later, according to the simple digital watch on his left wrist, Gabriel heard the commotion coming from behind the door to the left of the now empty waiting room.

The other four groups had each presented their own tickets and scratch-offs to the same guard Gabe had surrendered his folder to. Each of the groups went into the back room for exactly three to five minutes, then left, all with their arms around each other and grinning broadly.

He had heard different amounts, but they were all less than ten thousand. Gabe chuckled. His ticket was worth slightly more than that.

He looked around at the waiting room of the Virginia State Lottery Headquarters in Richmond.

He was happy to finally be in this room. He had been planning this day for thirteen long years, and now that all the changes in his life were about to begin, he felt a dizziness he didn't expect.

After all the careful preparation, all the long nights praying and planning, it was all about to start. He quietly went over his mental checklist for the meetings about to happen.

He was confident his plans would all work out. He had meticulously planned every minute leading up to this day. He adjusted the wig on his head, reached into the pocket of the over-

sized sweater he was wearing, and drew out a pair of dark
sunglasses.

He slipped them on his face as three men and one woman
in dark suits and fancy shoes came through the door and walked
up to him.

They were all smiling broadly. He stood up, took a deep
breath, squared his shoulders, and thought to himself, *Well, here
we go.*

The first man who to approach him was the oldest. He
was holding out his hand and had a bigger grin on his face than
Gabe thought was possible.

"Wow! We've known for a couple of months that the
winner would show up any day but are we glad to see you! Can
you believe it? 305 million dollars! The largest jackpot in
Virginia history! Are we glad to finally meet you!" the older man
said, all in one breath.

Gabe shook his hand vigorously, smiled behind the dark
sunglasses, and was ushered into the back, where, he knew, they
would change his very existence with a couple clicks of a
keyboard.

Gabe thought back thirteen years to the day this whole
journey started. He sighed and walked toward his future, feeling
more scared than he had thought he would.

He saw it all again in his mind, as he had first seen it
thirteen long years ago.


A tall Being, with dark purple wings outstretched, a violet
aura surrounding him, and a jovial grin on his angelic face stood
looking down on a man's life.

The life he looked upon was on the brink of change, but
in order to facilitate that change, the Being must go back to the

beginning, and move some pieces on the chess board of this particular world, and this particular man's life.

If the ArchAngel Jeremiel did not make those changes, the man below would never become that which would be needed the most.

He would never become the Fate Maker, a man destined to be able to wrap reality around his very fingers and allow his visions to manifest into the real.

As it stood, the man below, whose countenance was stoic and strong, was yet brittle. He would crack and break with but the lightest breath of testing.

*No*, the ArchAngel thought to himself.

*This man would need to be much, much stronger.*

And so the ArchAngel chose a point in time in the man's early life, his childhood, and stood to intervene.

Jeremiel's last thoughts before leaving the Spiritual Plane were that he would change this man, and his life, as many times as needed to make him the person Creation needed him to become.


The Creator, the Father of All, looked down on his Child as the ArchAngel started to manipulate a man's life.

And then the Creator watched his Son fail, repeatedly, until the man was who Creation needed him to be. *And that was okay*, the Creator mused to Himself.

Failing was not failing. Only giving up was failure. It was another of His Laws.

Contemplating the Fate of the man below, the Creator worried.

This man would be needed like no one else who had come before him.

Not the lovers, not the killer, not even the army of evolved human beings that the Creator had worked for so long through two of his Children to create.

No, this man, this Fate Maker, would be needed in the coming Heavenly cataclysm like no one else in all of Creation.

# Part 1
# Fits and Starts

# Chapter 1

"Gabe, hey man, you okay? Gabe!" The look of concern on his best friend's face was the first thing Gabriel remembered seeing after his vision returned.

"Yeah, yeah, I'm okay. Sorry. Blanked out there for a second, I think," Gabe said in a shaky voice.

He glanced around. He and Danny were standing on top of a B-5 maintenance stand next to the number 2 engine of a C-130. Tail number 196526. It was an R-model KC-130.

They were replacing the constant speed drive on the engine. It was a straightforward job, but it didn't help that Gabe had lost focus and seemed to spaz out for a few seconds.

"What happened, man? One second you were holding the torque wrench, and the next, you just went completely blank. You almost hit your head on the side panel, dude," Danny said in a worried tone.

Gabe thought back on what he had just seen during the blank spell.

His vision had narrowed to a tiny pinprick for a second, and then he was in a completely different place.

*He saw himself, standing on a stage of some kind, with huge posters behind him in a lot of bright colors. There was confetti falling in different streaks of color, and Gabe saw himself holding a huge white cardboard check. He looked around at the room, and there were lots of people clapping and hollering.*

*There were two more people up on the stage with Gabe, neither of which Gabe recognized. He saw himself smiling broadly and felt an overwhelming feeling of peace and joy. It was not a feeling Gabe knew well.*

*As the clapping and yelling reached a crescendo,* Gabe snapped back to himself, standing still on the B-5 stand, next to his best friend. He felt the hot sun beating down on the Cranial headgear he was wearing.

Sweat was beading down his back, and he glanced over at his friend as Danny voiced his concern.

Gabe looked around, shook his head, and grinned away Danny's concern. He clapped his best friend on the back, and picking up the torque wrench where it had slipped from his hand, went back to the job of changing the CSD on the engine.

He would think about his daydream when he got home.

Right now, he needed to finish this job, get inside, and get some water. He had paperwork to handle, and at least one more job to do on another airplane before the day was over. He again grinned at Danny and started re-torquing the nuts on the engine in front of him.

At the end of the day, Gabe walked out to his car in the parking lot across the street from the hangar where he worked. He had been working as a civilian contractor for the Navy for just over a year. It was demanding work, but it paid really well, and he was happy with his career for the first time in his life.

He enjoyed the people he worked with, and even though the work was difficult, and he was constantly out in all kinds of weather, it was still fulfilling. And he also knew his wife would never have married him if he didn't make the kind of money he was making now.

She was like that. It was all about the bottom line with Karan. She was all business.

He loved her but worried every day that he had to change his needs to be happy with her. He sighed as he got in his car. He looked up and saw several of his friends and co-workers walking to their cars in the full parking lot.

He waved and was waved back to in return. He really did like these guys, and what they were doing.

Starting the car, he remembered back to his daydream on the maintenance stand earlier in the day. He felt emotion catch in his throat. What did it mean? This kind of daydream had never happened to him before, and the first thing he thought was that something was wrong with him.

Was it a tumor? Was he going to have a stroke? He had just turned thirty at the beginning of the summer. All his friends told him it was all downhill from there. Were they right?

Only after he was on the road home to take a shower and get ready for the evening did he think about the actual contents of the daydream. And as he thought more about it, he started having a conversation with God about it. He prayed under his breath about the contents of the dream.

*God,* he said in his mind, *what is this that you are showing me? Is this the future, Lord? Is this going to happen to me? Am I going to win the lottery? Please Lord, give me guidance in this.* He got a gut feeling at that moment, still in his car, turning onto his street, that what he had seen was not a daydream.

It was a full-fledged vision from God. He was sure of it.

He was convinced, and calm came over him as he turned into his driveway. He put the car into park and sat idling while he bowed his head and thanked God for the vision. He didn't know when it would happen, but he now knew, beyond any doubt, that God had revealed his future to him that day. He assumed it would happen soon and was excited to tell Karan all about it when she got home.

He hurried inside the house, took the quickest shower he could, and started making mental plans on what to make for dinner that night. After his shower, and getting on his clean clothes, he felt like a new man. He drove to the grocery store and bought fresh salmon and asparagus as he knew they were Karan's favorites. He then drove to the daycare and picked up his baby daughter.

Getting back home, he opened a bottle of Chateau St. Michelle Riesling. He cooked the salmon and asparagus to perfection and waited patiently for his beautiful wife to get home. He was bursting with happiness and wanted to share it with her.

At that moment, he didn't know that she would ruin the night, as well as any preparation he made for his vision. At that moment, the vision still fresh in his mind, and with the baby happily playing in her highchair, he was on top of the world.

He smiled, took a swallow of the cold wine, and planned out how he was going to break the news to his happy – he assumed – wife.

"I don't care if you think it's a vision from God. We are not playing the lottery! Have you lost your mind?" Karan practically yelled from the bedroom.

Dinner had been enjoyable up until Gabe happily told his wife about his vision. He tried to explain to her how he just knew it was a vision of the future, and how it would make everything so much better. But he didn't expect her response.

She was practically vicious about it. She told him over and over that he lived in a fantasy world, and that he needed to wake up. They had bills to pay.

He should have known not to say anything to her about his vision. How would she understand? She wasn't even a Christian. She didn't believe in anything that she couldn't see, feel, or touch. She was just too practical of a person to understand his happiness at the vision that the Lord had given him that day.

He stood washing the dinner plates in the sink and feeling like someone had kicked him in the chest.

From that day on, two things happened simultaneously. Gabriel started playing the lottery in secret, while Karan publicly rebuked anything that had to do with her husband's "fantasy life."

Gabe would go to the grocery store every day, and as he paid for that day's groceries, he would get five or ten dollars back in cash, which would not show up on the bank's online digital banking app. He would use that money to continuously play the Powerball, or the Mega Millions, at two dollars a ticket.

His wife had no idea, but Gabe knew in his heart that one day, and hopefully one day soon, he would hit the jackpot, just as the vision showed, and his unbelieving wife would for once have to agree that Gabe was right in his faith, and they would live happily ever after.

Unfortunately, that day would not come while Gabe was with Karan. But early on, he would lay awake at night and make his plans. Plans within plans. He was a man who made plans.

But he had no idea in those early days just how involved his plans would become.

Or how futile.


Two splendid Beings looked down on a life that wasn't quite right for their needs.

The taller of the two was calm. The other, agitated.

"Father, this won't work. I need to go back and start again. There must be a way to make him stronger," Jeremiel said to the Creator.

The Creator looked down on His favored Son and smiled. Calm lit up the area of the Spiritual around them. Jeremiel basked in the warmth of his Father's love.

"Yes, my Son. Begin again. This time, change more than circumstances," the Father said.

Jeremiel knew that this was not going to be an easy Mission.

# Chapter 2

Gabriella Fairchild was malnourished and strung out. But she was crafty and strong. She knew both things, simultaneously.

She was twenty-two years old and had been homeless for the last five. But it didn't bother her. Most things did not. She would get through it, or this life would finally take her. She didn't care either way.

Covered in layers of dirty clothing to hide the fact that she was a female, she lay under her makeshift tent and pallet under the overpass of I-10 East. Hearing the cars cross over her head every night was like the soothing song her mother used to sing to her to calm her enough to sleep.

That was a million years ago, and a thousand miles from where she lay, trying to stay warm and dry.

Her mother's face appeared in her mind, and she wondered why she didn't hop a train or bus, or hitchhike home. Her mother would still be frantic about her only daughter and wondering if Gabriella was still alive.

*I am alive, Momma,* Gabriella thought to herself, for the millionth time.

When Gabriella's father had left them both, six years previous, Gabriella had blamed her poor mother. Since then, and after seeing the darkest side of humanity's underbelly, she knew her mother had had nothing to do with Gabriella's father abandoning them.

He had been a shit husband, father, and human being. But Gabriella had run away from her mother, and her only home, before she realized that. She just hadn't had the guts to go back since she had figured out the truth. She was too dirty now, too broken.

Her mother would never love her again if she saw Gabriella's face.

Or her broken and battered body.

But Gabriella was made of stronger stuff than this world could throw at her. She could get through anything.

And just as she thought those things for the millionth time, a long, dark car pulled up on the side of the road under her overpass.

"Shit," she said under her breath, looking out from her tent and pallet. It was Anton.

The pimp got out of the back seat of the long Cadillac. He was wearing his rings. And his fedora.

"Shit," Gabriella said again. Only louder this time, making Anton smile at her.

"This is where my best girl got to?" the large black man said to the pile of blankets, pallets, and thrown together tarps.

And that's when Gabriella decided to make a run for it.

She bolted out of her makeshift home of the last two months, after her escape from the man who was goading her at the moment. She would rather have died than to go back to working on her back for the deranged pimp.

But she hadn't eaten in days, and she was weak and slow.

He caught her easily, before she even broke out into the drizzle coming down from the dark, overcast sky.

She turned around, aiming a savage kick at the large man's shins, but she wasn't even given the opportunity to do that.

Out of the shadows, and before either of them could do something about it, a large, dark, and teeth-filled dog-like creature bounded toward them, jumped, and flew into the two humans standing still in fear and panic. The pile of flesh, claws, teeth, and a gun pulled from Anton's shoulder holster rolled out into the road.

And as the oncoming tractor trailer hit the spinning mass of once-living creatures, at the same time Anton's gun sounded loud in her ears, Gabriella's very last thought was of her mother's face.


Jeremiel the ArchAngel of the Younger Ilk was too slow to reach Gabriella in time to save her from the Dark Dog, as the Spiritual Realm had started calling the creatures that were hellbent on interfering with the Creator's plans.

She was gone, but so was the Dark Creature, dispatched by the ArchAngel himself.

Jeremiel looked down on the girl's life he had been trying to guide and strengthen for more than two decades.

"What a shame," he said aloud.

And with that, the Material Realm dissolved around the tall ArchAngel, and he descended back through time, and worlds, to try, once again.

He could not fail in this Mission. The outcome of the Final Conflict that they all knew was to come hinged on him succeeding.

Gabriella Fairchild was malnourished and strung out. But she was crafty and strong. She knew both things, simultaneously.

She was twenty-two years old and had been homeless for the last five. But it didn't bother her. Most things did not. She would get through it, or this life would finally take her. She didn't care either way.

Covered in layers of dirty clothing to hide the fact that she was a female, she lay under her makeshift tent and pallet under the overpass of I-10 East. Hearing the cars cross over her head every night was like the soothing song her mother used to sing to her to calm her enough to sleep.

That was a million years ago, and a thousand miles from where she lay, trying to stay warm and dry.

Her mother's face appeared in her mind, and she wondered why she didn't hop a train or bus, or hitchhike home. Her mother would still be frantic about her only daughter and wondering if Gabriella was still alive.

*I am alive, Momma*, Gabriella thought to herself, for the millionth time.

When Gabriella's father had left them both, six years previous, Gabriella had blamed her poor mother. Since then, and after seeing the darkest side of humanity's underbelly, she knew her mother had had nothing to do with Gabriella's father abandoning them.

He had been a shit husband, father, and human being. But Gabriella had run away from her mother, and her only home, before she realized that. She just hadn't had the guts to go back since she had figured out the truth. She was too dirty now, too broken.

Her mother would never love her again if she saw Gabriella's face.

Or her broken and battered body.

But Gabriella was made of stronger stuff than this world could throw at her. She could get through anything.

And just as she thought those things for the millionth time, a long, dark car pulled up on the side of the road under her overpass.

"Shit," she said under her breath, looking out from her tent and pallet. It was Anton.

The pimp got out of the back seat of the long Cadillac. He was wearing his rings. And his fedora.

"Shit," Gabriella said again. Only louder this time, making Anton smile at her.

"This is where my best girl got to?" the large black man said to the pile of blankets, pallets, and thrown together tarps.

And that's when Gabriella decided to make a run for it.

She bolted out of her makeshift home of the last two months, after her escape from the man who was goading her at the moment. She would rather have died than to go back to working on her back for the deranged pimp.

But she hadn't eaten in days, and she was weak and slow.

He caught her easily, before she even broke out into the drizzle coming down from the dark, overcast sky.

She turned around, aiming a savage kick at the large man's shins, but she wasn't even given the opportunity to do that.

Out of the shadows, and before either of them could do something about it, a large, dark, and teeth-filled dog-like creature bounded toward them, jumped, and flew into the two humans standing still in fear and panic. The pile of flesh, claws, teeth, and a gun pulled from Anton's shoulder holster rolled out into the road.

And as the oncoming tractor trailer hit the spinning mass of once-living creatures, at the same time Anton's gun sounded loud in her ears, Gabriella's very last thought was of her mother's face.

Jeremiel the ArchAngel of the Younger Ilk was too slow to reach Gabriella in time to save her from the Dark Dog, as the Spiritual Realm had started calling the creatures that were hellbent on interfering with the Creator's plans.

She was gone, but so was the Dark Creature, dispatched by the ArchAngel himself.

Jeremiel looked down on the girl's life he had been trying to guide and strengthen for more than two decades.

"What a shame," he said aloud.

And with that, the Material Realm dissolved around the tall ArchAngel, and he descended back through time, and worlds, to try, once again.

He could not fail in this Mission. The outcome of the Final Conflict that they all knew was to co

# Chapter 3

"I just feel, every single day, that I cannot do anything right. It doesn't matter what I do, or how I do it, she makes me feel crazy. I walk on eggshells every day, and she doesn't even see it. If I tell her how I feel, she turns it around on me, and I'm the crazy person. I can't take it anymore." Gabe was practically weeping as he answered the therapist's questions about his marriage.

Gabriel was at the Maryland Veteran's Clinic. He was attending one of his monthly therapy sessions. He had caved into his wife's demands that he get help for what she called his "manic behavior." He felt extremely lucky to qualify for VA healthcare, but he did not like the medicine he was forced to take for his diagnosis.

"So, you're increasingly frustrated at home. Are the pills helping you relax?" the therapist said.

"No. I hate taking them. I feel like a robot, and all my friends at work comment on how I act on the meds. There is such a difference when I skip a pill that they can all guess correctly when that happens. They all hate when I'm drugged out," Gabe said, dejectedly.

"I think playing around with the doses and making your own decisions on when you take the meds and how much is what is triggering your episodes. Your wife seemed fine when I spoke to her earlier. I'm sorry I asked to see her without you, but I wanted to get her take on your behavior." The therapist wasn't even looking at Gabe as he said this.

He was writing notes on his yellow legal pad, and Gabe was getting frustrated at how he felt teamed up on by his therapist and his wife.

When he scheduled this appointment at the mental health clinic, his therapist had asked him to bring Karan. He didn't want to, and she complained about it the whole hour-long car ride earlier in the day. She didn't want to take off work just for his appointment. She flat out told him to handle his problems himself, but to be sure to tell the doctor when and why he was skipping his meds.

"I'm sorry, Doc, but I really don't think I should be on medicine. It makes me feel so uncomfortable. And I'm gaining a lot of weight. I think it's a side effect of the meds."

"Well, I disagree. You're making great progress, and please stop skipping doses. In order to get the full benefits of the medication, you have to take it as prescribed. And you have the pill for when an episode comes on, so use them as you need to."

"That's the thing, Doc, she makes me take that pill every time I even tell a joke, or play with the kids, or show any kind of emotion. Why can't I have emotions? This all feels wrong to me."

"Your wife cares about you and loves you. She doesn't want to see you get any worse." With that, the therapist put his pad and pen on the desk next to him, stood up in dismissal, and ushered Gabe out of the office.

As they walked down the antiseptic-smelling hallway, the therapist put his hand on Gabe's shoulder, and with what Gabe thought was a fake fatherly way, told him to just try and relax, trust the medication, and make sure to make another appointment for the next month.

They shook hands at the heavy door leading out to the overflowing waiting room, and the therapist turned on his heels and marched toward his next vet to help.

Gabe found his wife's glare from the middle of the waiting room and walked over and sat down next to her.

"You should get your own insurance and see a doctor closer to home. I am not going to take an entire day away from work to come up for this again."

Gabe sighed for the hundredth time that day, got up, and walked with his wife out to their car. The entire car ride back he was quiet as Karan discussed what the therapist told her to watch out for and let him know if certain things happened and he needed to increase the dosage of psychotropic medication Gabe took every morning.

Gabe was promising himself deep in his own thoughts, while his wife rambled on and on about his "mania," that he was going to stop taking the medication. He hated it with a passion. He hated it almost as much as he was starting to hate his life. Not for the first time he started a list and a plan in his mind on how he could run away from all of this, and what the consequences of following through with that plan would be.

A deep well of anger was burning inside of him to put his foot down and stop taking all of this abuse. And glancing over at his wife, he knew in his heart that it would be forever futile to try to get her to realize that she was as much an abuser as the ones who hurt him so much as a child.

She thought that she was the one sacrificing to be with him and take care of him. She was the victim here, and he sighed deeply as he realized that she would never see the truth of things.

He felt like slamming the car into a tree just to stop the pain. And he knew if anyone knew he had those thoughts, then he would really be labelled the crazy one. How was he ever going to get out of this? Another plan started spinning in his head. A bold, hard plan. A plan that would label him the biggest bad guy, but one that he knew he had to follow through with if he was ever going to be free and be healthy.

He felt like there was a sun shining above the dark, murky water he was currently drowning in. If only he could break the surface. Break it and save his own life.

He reached over and turned on the radio. Karan gave him a dirty look but took the hint and stopped bitching at him for once. He turned on his favorite Christian music station, knowing he only had a little time to listen to it before she turned it.

There was a commercial on that was a regular on this particular station. It was one of the popular morning disc jockeys giving the verse of the day. Before Karan reached over angrily and turned the radio to her favorite rock station, he heard the last of the verse of the day. He knew it by heart. Jerimiah 29:11. "For I alone know the purpose I have for you. A plan to prosper you, and not to harm you." Gabe smiled, even while listening to his wife once again complaining about his love of Christian music.

He had almost forgotten it in his gloom from this day.

The plan God had for him.

Thinking about the vision from the year previous gave him a spark of hope, and he knew that he shouldn't have been thinking about how, with that dream coming true, he would be vindicated in his decisions and dreams.

That finally, Karan would have to say "thank you" for all he did for her.

That finally he could see that smug attitude that made him feel like a failure every day evaporate from her face.

He wasn't thinking about being a blessing for others with that daydream. He was thinking about how he would finally have freedom from this abuser, and the life he hated. He didn't know it at the time, but that dream would not happen until he put the other plan into motion, and saw fruit from it.

The other plan he was formulating to escape his present life, for his own good, the plan that would teach him lessons that would make him whole and healthy.

He had no idea, driving through the beautiful trees in middle Maryland, oblivious to the beauty around him, that he would have to seek his own freedom first. He had no idea, on that beautiful sunny day, that he would have to go through hell before God blessed him with his real purpose.

A purpose to help others, not to seek vindication and finally approval from his chosen life partner. If he could have seen what was ahead for him, he would have gladly driven the car right into a tree without delay.

He had no idea he should have been thanking the Creator that on that day, he did not see the whole picture.


The ArchAngel Jeremiel didn't like where this man's life was heading, and he knew, deep in his own angelic soul, that the man was the most brittle he had ever seen.

*There goes another four decades*, the ArchAngel thought to himself, as he once again decided to go back and start again.

But Time meant nothing, nor did Space or Energy.

The ArchAngel Host had been manipulating all of those Laws of Nature for millennia.

So, gathering himself together once again, from the Realm of Dreams and Visions, of which he was the master, he moved, once again, to a time deep in the past, on a world far away.

He was tired of failing. But Creation would not let him give up quite yet.

# Chapter 4

Little Gabe, as his father was keen on calling him, sat in the front pew next to his mother, happily munching on cereal out of a Ziploc baggie she had handed him while his father spoke from the pulpit.

He looked up at his strong father, proud of the man that Gabe had looked up to his entire five years of life.

His father was everything to him. And so, as his father often asked him to do, he listened to the words his father spoke from his pulpit, explaining the love God had for us all.

"A man married his high school sweetheart. *Never before has there been a stronger love story*, the man thought, as he placed the ring on his new wife's finger," his father, the Baptist preacher, was teaching his flock.

"And as most love stories go, they lived happily together for many years, working, planning, raising a family," the sermon went on.

"Until earlier in life than they should have needed to worry about such things, they got a medical scare. The beautiful wife and mother got a call from her doctor that she had cancer.

"The man was distraught, didn't know what to do. And so, like all good Christians, he got on his knees," Gabe's father told the rapt audience around the young boy.

"On his knees, the man begged God for a cure. 'Please, loving Father, please, send healing and a miracle to my lovely wife, the mother of our children,' he prayed. But God was silent," the preacher said.

"But the man never lost his faith, and knew it was God's blessing when the doctors came into the hospital room, and explained that there was a new, radical treatment that they felt the woman would benefit from," he preached. The congregation around young Gabe hung on every word.

"The only problem, the doctors explained, was that the radical treatment was not covered by insurance, and would cost the couple half a million dollars out of pocket," the sermon went on.

"The couple didn't have that kind of money; they didn't even know how to raise it. No one they knew had any money like that, and so the man, the distraught husband and father, did the only thing that he knew how to do in times like this. He got back on his knees," the preacher said. Gabe could feel the tension in the air around him, although, at five years old, he didn't know what it meant.

"Back on his knees, the man asked God for the half a million dollars. He told God that he had no idea how it would be done, but it wasn't his job to know the 'how,' just the 'what,' as most of us put our prayers up to God, don't we?" the preacher asked the church.

"But God, once again, was silent. And the man became angry at God," he told the congregation.

"The man got so angry at God for not showing him a way out of this danger, this cancer that was eating his wife away every day, that he stopped praying altogether. Isn't that what we do, church? When God doesn't give us what we ask for, exactly as we want it?" he asked.

"And so, this man started losing hope that he would ever have a future with the love of his life, and he became bitter, blaming God for not answering, for not caring, for not being an ever-present heavenly father to the man," the preacher went on.

"One day, not long after the man lost his faith, he was sitting in a dark room, hearing the machines upstairs practically breathing for his wife, and there not being a thing the man could do about it, and he saw a commercial on the television," the preacher intoned. The congregation knew that the climax of the story was coming. There were many sitting on the edge of their pews.

"The commercial was advertising a local lottery of sorts, a fund raiser. The prize was exactly half a million dollars," the preacher said.

The congregation believed they knew where this story was going. Faith in God even when you lose your most precious gift. *God would never condone gambling*, they thought.

But the preacher had a different kind of message this morning for his flock. And as he finished the story, he looked down on his precious son. *No*, the preacher thought, *this story was for young Gabe the most*.

"So, the man got back down on his knees, and he prayed like he had never prayed before. Pleading, begging, giving ultimatums, angrily blasting words of defeat at his God, at the same time he sent up words of love and obedience," the preacher told the church.

"And a few more days went by, and nothing was happening. The man could not feel the presence of God. He was still distraught, still frightened, still so incredibly angry at God," the preacher said.

"Finally, it was the day before the drawing. The lottery prize would be handed out to some lucky soul the very next day. The man got on his knees again. Begging God, cajoling God, pleading with God," the preacher said.

"And that's when the man finally heard the voice of God. After so many days, and months, of nothing, and the man was at the very end of his rope, ready to lose his beloved wife, God spoke to the man, and it shocked the man to his core." The preacher had the congregation right on the edge of their seats, breath held.

"The voice of God came down to the man, the evening before the drawing of the money that would save his wife's life, giving them years more together. The voice came down into the man's feelings and the man's mind, with a single, clarifying statement, which changed the man's life forever afterward," the preacher said. The congregation still held its collective breath.

"The voice told the man, 'You have to go, and buy a ticket!'" The preacher spoke the last line in a booming voice.

Gabe looked up at awe at the man who held so many around him in sway. He knew, even for an incredibly young boy, that what his father had just told the room would stick with him for the rest of his life.

*How very blessed he was*, young Gabe thought to himself that day, *to have such a loving and nurturing family around him.*

He felt that way for many weeks and months, right up until the day that a dark presence drove the family car off of a cliff, during a peaceful vacation the family took, driving up the coastal Route 1 in the beautiful state of California.

As the car crashed down the rocky cliff, screams loud in Gabe's ears, he thought once again, how incredibly lucky he had been in his short life.


Two Beings looked down on a devastating scene that they had been too slow to stop.

"Well, start again, my child. And watch for these Dark incursions against these plans. We MUST bring up the Fate Maker. There is no other choice," the Father told his Son, the beautiful ArchAngel Jeremiel.

Jeremiel simply nodded, knowing that he was going to have to keep working at bringing about just the right set of circumstances and challenges to raise up the Fate Maker.

All of creation depended on it, no matter how long it took.

# Chapter 5

"So, the numbers of the drawing both add up to eight. The jackpot is 314 million, and the cash option is 212.3 million. Three plus one plus four is eight, and two plus one plus two plus three is eight.. Angel number eighty-eight, what does that mean?" Gabe was mumbling to himself as he sat in the car outside the liquor store where he was about to play his most recent prayed-over numbers.

"Eight plus eight is sixteen. One and six is seven, God's perfect number. So, aspects of eight, and seven. It all adds up. Perfect, perfect," Gabe continued to mumble, and started scratching notes in a secret notebook no one ever saw.

He got out his cell phone and googled angel number eighty-eight. It meant financial freedom, and a tremendous change. *Perfect, perfect,* he thought to himself.

Passingly, he wondered if he was starting to get a little carried away with his thoughts concerning winning the lottery. He knew his friends thought he was a bit obsessive about it.

But no one could sway his belief.

*This was the only way*, he thought, *that his life was going to change for the better*. He started to believe that God owed it to him for giving him such a shitty life. *His whole life,* he thought, but his thoughts quickly turned to the money.

He didn't care about the money.

The money was a tool, he knew. He was actually getting tired while thinking of all the steps after the win. But he knew he had to keep going. He couldn't give up. Too much depended on this.

He got out of the car holding his notepad and slipped on his sunglasses. He looked down at himself and made sure none of his tattoos were showing, or anything else distinguishing enough for a video camera to pick up and the media use to determine his identity.

Satisfied that he wouldn't give anything away to digital media, he walked into the liquor store where he enjoyed buying his tickets every week.

Gabe Fairchild was not aware of the dark, hidden, dog-like creature waiting for him in the walk-in refrigerator, nor did he see his death in the sudden and instant attack of a nightmare creature outside of anything that he could ever have imagined.

Before his last breath left him, and he was given the vision of what his life was, and what it should have been, he saw himself in the Lottery Headquarters, wearing a fake wig, and glasses, and knew that somehow, something much larger than himself had intervened, and changed his Fate, forever.

Two Beings looked down on the man, from the Spiritual Plane. An aura of calm surrounded the Beings, but conflict crackled in the air outside the calmness.

The entire Spiritual Plane was preparing for conflict. And the plans the Father had made to assure chaos did not reign were not panning out as expected.

At this very moment, in a place where Time and Space was not factored, the Father was not pleased with what He was seeing.

He froze Time in the Material Realm in which they watched the man below being attacked by the dog-like creature.

"It's not going the way it should go, my Son. You need to go back to the beginning. He must be stronger," the Father told his Son, Jeremiel.

And so, Jeremiel, looking down on the man who was supposed to be able to shape the very existence around him, agreed with the Father, and chose a place in the man's life to interfere.

The man, Gabe, would not enjoy this.

"Also, my Child, I am changing his name. HE WILL NOW BE KNOWN AS KREO," the Father commanded.

The ArchAngel Jeremiel winced slightly at the Command Voice of the Father.

"And make sure that Dark Dog doesn't live outside of this Time Freeze."

Jeremiel simply nodded his understanding, disappeared in the Spiritual, and materialized in the boy's life, at the moment he was born.

Taking the boy's mother on this day of celebration would strengthen the boy dramatically. And taking his father a few years later would put the boy on the road that the Spiritual Realm would need him on.

The coming conflict would need someone made of steel, sharpened by iron, and hardened in fire.

The ArchAngel Jeremiel felt deep sorrow for what he was about to do to a young boy's life.

And he knew with all of his heart, that now, he would need some help.

So, he sent out the call, deep from within his aura, to his brothers and sisters all.


And the entire Host answered him, as he knew they would.

# Part 2
# The Fate Maker Begins

36

# Chapter 6

Kreo Fairchild looked down on his father's shiny black coffin being lowered into the wet ground, and wept.

He felt like he had done much more weeping than was normal for an eight-year-old boy.

But, he sniffed up his final tears, and vowed to himself and to the world that he would never cry again. The boys at school said that crying was for girls. And now he wasn't going to be going back to that school. No, his father was gone now, and so the state was putting him in a boys' home. They were taking him there right after the funeral.

His single suitcase was already in the van waiting for him in the parking lot of the funeral home.

He sniffed again and looked up at the counselor that had placed him in the home. She was the only other person at the gravesite. And she was looking at the ground. Kreo figured she was impatient to get him out of her hair.

*So be it*, he thought, wise for an eight-year-old boy.

A few hours later, he sat in the very back seat of a large, white, eighteen-passenger van. He watched out the window as the lush Northern California countryside turned into large brown fields full of twisty vines and wooden stakes. He had heard of Wine Country before but had never seen it.

No, his life had been spent on the streets of some of the roughest parts of the Bay Area. And he was tougher for it. But this land outside the windows scared him in ways that he couldn't quite put a finger on.

Soon, the van rolled through a large gate, which was standing open and seemed inviting. The road wound through large, open grassy areas, and Kreo could see boys playing soccer and a game with sticks on one of the fields to the right. His heart quickened a bit. He loved sports.

Very soon, the large black man who had driven Kreo out to the boys' home in Sonoma, California, pulled up to a large white building, and without saying a word, cut the ignition and looked at Kreo through the rearview mirror. Kreo met the man's eyes.

"Listen, kid, this is going to be tough, but you have to be tougher, got it?" the man asked the small boy.

Kreo simply nodded, surprised at the man's voice. It was the first time that he had heard it in the two-hour drive. It soothed him, and he couldn't understand why. He shrugged off the feeling and gathered his backpack and single suitcase, ready to find out all he could of his new home.

The large black man – Kreo had never learned his name – led him up the stairs to the side of the building, and into a large, dark foyer. There was a pretty woman sitting at a desk to the side of the large room, and a wide, modern-styled staircase ran up the into an overhang above their heads to the other side. Straight ahead, Kreo saw, was a set of double glass doors leading to what looked like offices.

"Kreo Fairchild, from San Pablo," the large man told the pretty girl.

She smiled at Kreo and asked him in an overly sweet voice to have a seat on the benches underneath the staircase. Kreo's shoulders hung low as he walked toward the benches to sit down. He was dreading the large man's departure. The driver was the very last link to the life that Kreo had known.

The man followed Kreo over to the benches and said the last thing that Kreo thought he would say before leaving.

"Chin up, son. Your life is just beginning. And don't worry, we will be here with you, watching you, and protecting you," the man said. He winked at Kreo, and quickly left the building.

Kreo had no idea what the man had meant, but it had made him feel tremendously better. He was still scared, but his heart, at least, beat a little slower, and the day didn't look quite so gloomy anymore.

Jeremiel stood next to the white van, door open, and in the guise of the large black man. He pondered the small boy he had just dropped off at the Catholic boys' home in California.

Floating in the air around Jeremiel, colored in all colors in eternity, and with the strength to upheave whole worlds, the entire Host of ArchAngels hovered with him, watching the child inside the building, protecting him, and making sure that nothing would stop this final iteration of the Fate Maker's life.

*This was going to be tough on the kid,* Jeremiel thought to himself as he, and the van, suddenly vanished in the hot California sunshine.

The Host of ArchAngels vanished as well.

A last Angelic thought hovered in the air where the van had stood seconds before, like a glimmering mirage, heat strokes in the air, echoed by fourteen other, like-minded minds.

"This was going to be so very hard on that young man, but we will protect him, this time."

# Chapter 7

"Kick him in the balls!" the taller of the two teenage boys yelled to the other one.

Kreo was on the ground, and he tasted dirt. He could hear frogs croaking nearby. *That was a weird thing*, he thought, as the shorter boy aimed a kick at Kreo's mid-section.

The kick connected with the young boy's stomach, and the dirt taste in his mouth was washed out as the air in him left his lungs and wouldn't return. As he struggled to breathe, the bullfrog croaking grew louder in his ears. *At least the bullfrog could breathe*, he thought, right as consciousness left him.

He woke later that day in the infirmary. He was in a clean bed, covered with a white blanket, and there was a can of Sprite and some crackers on the table next to him. Other than that, he was completely alone.

His body hurt, and tears came to his eyes as he remembered the two boys jumping him. He had not done anything to deserve the beating. Or any of the others that he had received since he was dropped off at the boys' home. But he knew that crying over it wouldn't solve his problems. So he wiped his eyes, snorted the snot threatening to drop out of his nose back into his throat, and reached for the soda.

He didn't get soda very often.

The nurse came in soon after and *tsked* over him. She checked the bruises and scrapes on his upper body and unwound a tightly bound Ace bandage around his midsection that he had not really noticed. As soon as the binding was loose, his ribs felt like they re-adjusted, and pain flared in him. He sucked his breath in sharply, and the nurse looked at the small boy with concern.

"I think you have a cracked rib or two, young man," she said to him as she prodded and poked him, gauging by his facial tics and sharp intakes of breath where it hurt the most.

The concern deepened on her face. And after she re-wound a new ace bandage back around his ribcage, she looked down on him. He met her eyes and saw the sorrow in them. He smiled through his pain back at her.

"Be careful, Kreo," she said. "You aren't invincible."

"I will," he promised her.

That evening, they let him leave the infirmary with a handful of ace wraps and some pain pills. He was only nine years old, but some days he felt like he was fifty. He walked in the growing darkness back up the hill to the dorm that he had called home for the last year.

As he walked over the short bridge covering the quickly running creek below, he heard the bullfrogs again. It made him pause in the gloom of the late summer evening and listen. He looked up into the sky, seeing the stars shining brightly over his head, and knew that there was so much more to this life than what he was experiencing.

He said a quick prayer in his mind as his father had taught him to do.

He suddenly felt a *leaning*, a snapping, and the world shifted around him.

A sense of peace and warmth settled into his mind. With that, the sound of nature around him, the warm breeze ruffling his rather shaggy hair, and the pain in his body slowly dissipating, he felt better.

For the first time in a long time, he felt better.

Later that night, snuggled under his covers, and hoping another late-night beating wouldn't come from the two older boys in his room, he remembered his prayer. He had simply asked the Universe to feel better.

And then he did feel better.

*He needed to remember that*, he told himself, as he drifted off into a deep, healing sleep.

# Chapter 8

The soccer pitch between the two slanted concrete walls was really only half a field, but it still looked monstrously large to a small ten-year-old boy.

And there were about ten other boys between Kreo and the net at the end of the shadowed recess made by the large concrete wall behind the goal. He didn't know why this area had been built above the swimming pool, but the boys often gathered in the half-field to play soccer, and generally cause a loud ruckus and not a few skinned knees or bloody lips.

Kreo was at the open end of the half-field, and he had the ball. He looked down at it, sitting innocently on the low grass in front of his shabby tennis shoes. *The ball was just a ball. Of course it was not mocking him*, he thought.

He looked back up at the boys standing between him and the small net standing a million miles away. He had never made a goal during these early evening games.

And he wondered if he would ever make a goal his entire life. But then he chided himself for that thought. *No*, he said in his mind, *this was his night*.

So, he said a quick prayer to the Universe, and started toeing the ball toward the first boy. In Kreo's mind, the boy stood seven feet tall and that made Kreo feel even smaller.

But then at the last moment, as the tall boy ran toward Kreo, intent on stealing the ball and taking his own turn at the net at the far end of the sheltered field, Kreo juked to the right, and the boy went to the left. Which left Kreo open for a short few seconds before two more boys ran at him.

*He could do this*, he thought to himself. *He could finally score against the big kids!*

He ran right through the two boys who were watching the ball and not Kreo's fast-moving feet. And then Kreo was past them both. He gained a confidence at that moment that shocked him. Scoring a goal against all the boys on the half-field was inevitable.

He hardly saw the rest of the boys coming against him to steal the soccer ball. He felt light. He felt invincible. He felt like nothing could stop him. It was a very heady feeling.

And before he knew it, the ball was through the goal, against the net, and had fallen down to the grass. It sat still once more, looking innocent and innocuous, and not at all mocking Kreo now.

Kreo was stunned. He had never scored a goal before, and he had no idea how he had gotten past at least ten boys, all of whom were bigger and faster than him.

He had a sneaking feeling that the adult onlookers had somehow told the older boys to let Kreo score. But the looks of shock and disgust on the faces of the boys he had scored against bolstered him once more.

He really had scored the goal on his own.

And that made him, once again, suspicious that he had somehow caused the miraculous event to happen simply by *leaning* against the reality of impossible, and making what he saw in his head happening, real.

Later that night, he sat on the hard, carpeted floor of the Big Room of his dorm. The large room was walled in large windows that looked down the hill at the rest of the campus. The furniture was old, but sturdy, having been used by scores of boys for years. There was an area where old books were kept, barely touched by most of the occupants of the room, and an enclosure parallel to the library area that held a long shelf that served as a desk area, with eighteen sturdy plastic and metal chairs lined up against it.

He was surrounded by other orphan boys as they all watched the weekly movie. The campus administrator went into town to rent a movie every week and played it on channel three for all of the dorms on the campus.

When asked ahead of time what the movie would be, he always replied to each boy with the same answer.

"*Gandhi*," he would say. It was never *Gandhi*, of which all of the boys were glad.

The movie that night was a Disney movie. *Swiss Family Robinson*. Kreo remembered watching this movie with his dad, in a rare moment of sobriety for his father.

He had loved the movie, and the memory brought pain to his chest. But he held in his tears. It wouldn't do for the boys around him to see weakness in him. These boys pounced upon weakness like a stray lamb, and they were all ravenous wolves.

And so, sucking up his tears and wiping his nose, he thought back on the day. He thought back on the soccer goal that he had scored against all odds.

His being a very inquisitive mind, he wanted to explore the few instances where he seemed to make things just happen.

He wanted to try it again.

He would do so the next morning, as it was a Saturday, and after chores, the boys usually had the day to themselves. He would get to experimenting this phenomenon right after lunch, he promised himself.

Saturday morning, things went right to hell, fast.

His Saturday morning chore was to vacuum the long hallway carpets. Every boy in the dormitory, all eighteen of them, had a chore to accomplish every Saturday. As soon as their chore was complete, they would have the rest of the weekend for their own activities.

The morning started out well enough. Breakfast was filling. Pancakes this time. But on the walk back to the dormitory from the chow hall, one of the older boys in his room, Ronald by name, ran up behind Kreo and whispered to the much smaller boy that he was going to 'get it' that morning.

Kreo, who had been the victim of multiple beatings by the larger black boy, grew angry at the threat. He was so tired of being too small to protect himself, and always being at the mercy of the older boys!

He started to see red hot rage behind his eyes, and all thoughts from the previous night for practicing his newfound abilities flew right out of his mind. He only saw red.

He was so fucking tired of being afraid.

As he returned back to his dormitory with rage and hate in his heart, he didn't want to vacuum the hallways and clean the dorm with everyone else. He wanted to find the two older boys who incessantly picked on him and bash their brains in with a baseball bat.

And that thought shocked him out of his anger for a moment. It was as if a voice whispered in his mind, encouraging the hate and the rage.

With that thought, he realized that a voice had been whispering in his mind since his father had died suddenly.

He needed to figure this all out.

"There are things that still need to be vacuumed in this area. I'm not going to tell you what I want to see gone, so what does that mean?" His houseparent that day was Ms. Gross. That was her real last name.

"It means that I'm going to have to get it all to make sure to get the thing you want gone," Kreo answered her. She had been inspecting his work, and he wanted to get the chores finished so he could have some time to himself.

"Exactly. You are so smart!" Ms. Gross told him. He didn't care what she thought. He had other things on his mind.

Kreo hurriedly finished the vacuuming, and while listening for the other boys who were all cleaning various parts of the large dormitory, he went to the bathroom before heading outside to ponder the last few days.

He finished up in the stall, and moved across the large, tiled bathroom to wash his hands. He didn't want to run into anyone before he could make it outside and get his mind right.

But the quiet around him was too good to be true. Just as he turned off the water faucet, shaking the excess wetness from his small hands, he heard the bathroom door open.

He turned to dry his hands on his towel, and in walked Ronald, followed by Kreo's other roommate, Kim. Both boys were taller than Kreo by a head and outweighed him by at least thirty pounds. Both of them appeared together, and Kreo knew he was in for some pain.

Kreo moved toward the door as quickly as his little feet could carry him, but the boys grabbed him from behind, and threw him down on the tiled floor.

As he fell, hitting his back on the hard tile, the breath leaving his lungs in a great rush, he wondered just why the hell these boys hated him so much. And then the voice whispered in his mind again, telling him it was because he was worthless, and even his parents didn't want him.

As the kicks and yelled obscenities rained down on him, the voice in his mind was cut off mid-sentence, and Kreo wondered why that was as he lost consciousness, once again.

Jeremiel watched from the Spiritual Plane as the young Fate Maker started pondering the powers that he had received from the Father.

And he watched as the young boy turned into a rage-filled creature with the whisperings of the large boy.

The large boy's threats, and something else.

Something on the edge of both the Spiritual and the Material.

So the ArchAngel of visions and dreams moved closer to the presence he could barely feel but couldn't see at all. He needed to understand for himself what this was all about.

Jeremiel, in all of his seven-and-a-half-foot splendor, moved to a crack in Creation and saw darkness whispering to the mind of his young progeny.

A large, double-bladed halberd formed in the tall ArchAngel's hands. It whispered of violence, and gave off wisps of cloudy, purple aura.

Shining in the light of Creation, it had been forged of Heavenly Steel, and diamonds, sharper than razors, adorned both blade edges at the ends of the five-foot-long staff.

The blades faced in different directions, and the ArchAngel had wielded the large weapon for all of eternity.

The ArchAngel Jeremiel swung his Heavenly Weapon, nicknamed 'Visionary,' in a wicked blur, aimed at the Crack in Creation.

A loud, painful scream, like the hissing of hot steam escaping from a broken pipe, issued from the crack.

Jeremiel smiled. He knew he had scored a mortal wound against whatever it was that had whispered in Kreo's mind.

*Not on his watch*, the ArchAngel thought, as the Crack closed up. He pulled his double-bladed halberd from the unnatural Crack before it closed. He was satisfied once again as he looked back down on Kreo.

A sizzling sound could be heard in the Spiritual plane, and Jeremiel looked up from where he stood, following the noise.

Half of the diamond-sharp blade, made from the most indestructible metal in all of the Heavens, was already missing, and the rest was slowly dissolving, right above the ArchAngel.

The metal of the large blade had melted from the blood of the creature from the Crack.

*That wasn't good,* he thought, dropping his weapon before the acidic blood could drip down onto his own countenance.

*That wasn't good at all.*

# Chapter 9

"I don't know the piano well enough to play that song," Kreo said to Ms. Fogg. Another funny name for a beautiful woman.

"Kreo, we can play a tape. You just pantomime the music, and lip-sync the words," the music teacher told the young, growing boy. She looked up at him now, which she couldn't do a year ago. He was really getting tall for an eleven-year-old boy, that was for sure.

Kreo just shrugged, forgetting about playing the piano for the school talent show for long enough to worry about how they were going to make the moon head.

When he had heard news of the talent show coming up in three weeks, he and his best friend at the Boys' Home, Brian, wanted to sing a new song they had heard just recently. "Hazard" by Richard Marx. But the music teacher in charge of the production said no to their song selection. It had murder and hate in it, she had said.

So Kreo did not know what he wanted to do now, but she had a ready suggestion for him.

"Do 'Mac Tonight,' Kreo!" she exclaimed loudly.

"The commercial on TV for McDonalds?" he asked. "With the moon guy?"

"Exactly! We can get a blank tape made with the music, and you can play on the piano on stage. We can even make you a big moon head mask, and scrounge up some big sunglasses to wear," she said. Ms. Fogg was a lot more excited about the silly song than Kreo was. She finally talked him into doing it, much to his embarrassment.

That had been two weeks earlier, and he had diligently learned the silly jingle from the TV commercial. He felt like an idiot doing a stupid TV commercial song when other boys were doing Guns N' Roses, his new favorite band, or doing jokes and magic.

Kreo walked off the stage at the end of the auditorium with his shoulders hanging low. And then he heard music coming from the classroom off the left side of the large room and had to investigate. A litany of musical notes played on an acoustic guitar caught his attention.

The song was captivating. Thrills of notes from the guitar made his spine tingle as he approached the half open door. And then he heard Christian's voice start singing the lyrics of the song, and it all hit him in the stomach like a brick.

He walked into the large music classroom as Christian, a large senior, was singing and strumming his guitar. Kreo had often heard the older boy play his favorite guitar in his room at the end of the hallway of Kreo's new dormitory. *Christian was really, really good with music,* Kreo thought distractedly.

The other boy playing the enchanting song was a boy named Chris. Chris, Kreo knew, was the most musically talented boy at the Home. He could play any instrument and could sing like an angel.

Kreo's attention went back to the song. He had no idea what it was called, or who sang it, but he would find out as soon as the two teenagers were done singing it.

He sat on the floor, right to the left of the door leading into the large, airy room. Windows high up on the walls let sunlight shine into the room, and it seemed the rays of light lit the two boys sitting in chairs, facing each other, like angels in a movie.

The song continued on as both boys strummed their acoustic guitars, both singing the refrain. Both playing along together.

Chris suddenly broke into a picked solo on the guitar. The notes were hauntingly beautiful, and Kreo couldn't take his eyes off the boy's hand picking each note. Kreo had never been moved by a song more in his young life.

Christian broke into a finality of lyrics and Kreo knew that the song was almost finished.

He kept repeating the same phrase of lyric. "Patience, just a little patience," he sang. Chris broke into his own lyrics at the same time. "The streets don't change, but maybe their names, and I ain't got time for the pain, oh, I need you. Yeah, oh yeah, I need you…" the boys sang together.

And very soon after, it was finished. The two musicians sat in the middle of the sunlit room smiling at each other. They turned and saw that they had an audience of one.

And the tears streaming down Kreo's face told both boys that the song was the perfect song to sing at the talent show. They would win for sure. And that made Chris and Christian incredibly happy.

Kreo finally found his voice. The song's lyrics didn't mean much to him, but the notes played together on the two guitars had awakened his soul.

"What song was that? Please, Christian, what song was that?" Kreo asked in a shaky voice.

"Kreo, you okay, bud?" Christian looked concerned. He had taken the young boy under his wing when Kreo was moved into his dorm a year ago.

"Please, Christian, what was that song?" he repeated.

"'Patience', by Guns N' Roses," Christian answered the boy.

And then Christian and Chris both watched as the young boy ran from the room. They tried not to think much of it and turned back to each other to practice the song one more time. They were facing each other just like Axl Rose and Slash had done in the MTV video for their new favorite song.

As the opening notes of the song started behind him, and he could hear Christian whistling the opening notes, Kreo broke into a large grin and wiped the tears from his eyes.

"'Patience,'" he said out loud as he began his walk back up to his new dorm, lovingly called 'Rosary Hill.' His day got brighter, and he couldn't believe it was all because of a song. But it was going to be his new favorite song, he already knew that. He just had to get his hands on a tape of it.

That night, when he walked into Christian's room at the end of the hall to tell the older boy how much he had loved the song, and couldn't get it out of his head, the tall, older boy threw Kreo a black cassette tape.

"Keep it, Kreo, I have the full album. That's just the single," he said.

Kreo looked down at the precious tape in his hand and felt tears coming to his eyes again. It was like he held the most precious thing in the world in his still small hands. He would treasure the tape for the rest of his life.

He ran from Christian's room, while the older boy watched him go and shook his head. *That kid was really weird sometimes*, Christian thought to himself. *But he sure had been through a lot*, he finally decided before turning on his radio, and turning the tuner knob to the best radio station in the area, 97.9 KXXX.

As the beat of "Pour Some Sugar On Me" from Def Leppard started playing, the large boy, ready to become a man in a few short months, forgot all about Kreo, and the weird way the boy loved that GNR song so much.

Kreo, meanwhile, ran back to his room, and to his most prized possession, a small boom box he had saved up for and had bought for himself the Christmas before.

He reverently placed the cassette into the radio, put his overlarge headphones over his ears, and lay back on his bed, as far as the headphone cord would let him.

The same opening notes of the precious song started playing in his ears, and tears leaked out of his eyes. But these tears were ok. Crying over a GNR song was not a wussy thing to do. On the contrary, it was 1989, and crying over a love ballad was *the* thing to do.

*If only the other boys knew*, Kreo thought, listening to words that didn't mean anything, but hearing the notes played expertly on acoustic guitars.

If only they knew that Kreo could see the future when he listened to the chords and picked, ringing notes.

If only they could see what Kreo saw.

# Chapter 10

Kreo Fairchild was on cloud nine.

He had found his calling, and he had found it early. Kreo was only fourteen, but he knew what he was going to do with the rest of his life already.

He was going to be a rock star.

Music was everything to him. It brought him out of any funk. It sang to his soul. He wanted to create his own songs, give back to this world that had taken so much from him. He was beyond passionate about his music and making a dent in the world.

He wasn't exceptionally good at any particular instrument, but he tried to learn them all. His music teacher for the last three years, Ms. Fogg, was extremely patient with him, but he insisted that he was going to change the entire music world. She was skeptical but kept it to herself. Inside, she often told herself to give the young orphan a chance, and not to ruin his dreams.

But he really wasn't particularly good.

"Push the strings against the frets harder, Kreo. You'll never make the right notes if you can't press the strings harder," she was telling Kreo, who was learning the acoustic guitar at the moment.

They had recently switched from the piano to the guitar in the hopes that Kreo's enthusiasm would make him a better student.

But Kreo didn't care that he didn't pick up playing instruments naturally. He was determined to work as hard as he could at this. This was his future, and his passion, and *damn it*, he thought, *he was going to be the best*.

So, he kept at it. Day in, day out. To the detriment of the other boys in his dormitory, he played his chosen instruments at all hours of the day and night. And he played them badly. Everyone could see it, hear it, and understand it. Everyone, that was, except for Kreo himself.

"Gotta give him credit," Brian told a younger boy in Rosary Hill. "He sure as hell tries hard."

It was a Saturday afternoon, once again. Kreo, like the other boys around him at the boys' home, had the afternoon to himself. And that's how he found himself sitting at the top of a large, grass-covered hill behind his dormitory.

He sat in the early summer sun, enjoying the warmth of the day, and thinking about the future he could see so vividly in his mind.

He looked down at his growing body. *Being fourteen was such a weird experience,* he thought, for the millionth time. He had felt an almost daily sense of déjà vu his entire life. As if he had been this age before, but in another place, and another time.

It was like he knew what to expect, yet at the same time was experiencing it all from a new perspective.

Looking at his body, he knew he was getting taller. Stronger. His skin was dark, thanks to his father's Pacific Islander heritage, but he knew nothing about it. He had dark, lanky hair, and bright green eyes. He thought he was handsome when he looked in the mirror, but he also suffered from a deep insecurity.

He hoped as he got older and became what he could envision so very clearly in his mind, that the insecurity would go away. He was sure it would.

The other boys in the dorm called him 'pretty boy,' so he knew he wasn't ugly. Although, if he thought about it too much, he figured they were being sarcastic, and then he was hard on himself again.

*Teenage angst*, he thought, smiling to himself. He should write a song about it.

So, that night, after his long afternoon of thinking about his future up on top of the grassy hill, he did just that.

He sat at one of the desks in the Big Room and took out a piece of college ruled paper and a pen and began to just write words. He could almost hear the music in his mind.

The words flowed easily. Almost too easily. He merely had to *lean* into the project, and it unfolded in front of him like magic.

Words, and accompanying notes and chords, were jingling around in his head the next day when he had his music lessons with Ms. Fogg.

"Ms. Fogg, I wrote something last night, but I don't know how to get the music out," he blurted out to his music teacher the minute he saw her.

Ms. Fogg, bless her, took it all in stride, and knew to build the young orphan up, rather than dash yet another dream of his.

She took the sheet of scribbled words from the boy and put her reading glasses on the edge of her nose. What she saw surprised even her.

"And here is the tune that has been in my head all night," he told her.

He hummed a thrill of notes in quarter tempo, and as they sprang from his lips to her practiced ears, she could see the song as clearly as the young boy could the night before.

She sat on the hard bench of the piano and tried to find the same expression of notes that Kreo had hummed for her. And her fingers found them quite naturally.

Ms. Eugenie Fogg, a master musician of almost half a century, finally felt what she had always heard of, but had yet to experience. The feeling that what she had just played had always been in the world, but which she had just played for the first time. It was a dizzy, déjà vu feeling, and she quite liked it.

The image of a sculptor came to mind, chiseling marble from a tall slab. She had seen an article once where the artist had described his work as "having always been there, I just had to chip away the excess rock to expose it."

That's how the song felt to her ears and her heart. It had always been there, she just had to peel away the excess to expose it.

She excitedly got her own paper and pen, and with the boy who had a new definition and standing in her mind, worked on the song for the rest of the day, ignoring all of their other responsibilities.

Late that afternoon, right before the boy would need to go to the chow hall for dinner, the song was finished, and on several clean pieces of lined music sheets.

She looked at the opus that she and the boy – well, really only the boy – had created, and for the first time in her long life, heard the whisperings of evil in her ears.

No one knew about this critically amazing song except her and the young teenager.

She decided without delay, with the whisperings of dark fate in her ears, not to come to work the next day, or for any day after that.

*No*, she thought, driving home that evening, after promising the boy that they would get other boys to play the song the next day, and hear it in its entirety, *she was retired from that day onward.*

The blessed pages clutched to her chest the next morning; she didn't pull up to the music building at the boys' home like she had done for thirty years. Instead, she pulled up to a tall white building in downtown Los Angeles, changing her life forever.

# Chapter 11

"And that was the new smash hit from Guns N' Roses, 'November Rain,' folks, running the charts, and landing at number three of the Top 100!" the disk jockey on the station in San Francisco blared over Kreo's boombox.

He swore under his breath again, for the thousandth time. She stole his song, but even worse, she had sold it to Geffen Records, in LA, who had given it to GNR to record.

That really ate at his soul.

But there was nothing a fifteen-year-old orphan could do about it except scream into the cosmos his displeasure in his life, his choices, his inability to do anything, because he had zero support, and now, his loss of what he wanted to do with his life.

He was utterly lost.

So, for more than a week, he withdrew into himself. He didn't talk to anyone around him, and even his teachers got worried about him. They all knew his story, and that he was a bit bitter and depressed anyway, but this was a new low for him.

The nuns prayed for the boy, the teachers tried to pull him aside to chat, and even the priest of the boys' home got word that Kreo was withdrawing into himself more than ever.

So, Father Johnson, a newly frocked priest, and having only been at his new station for a few months, went to the chapel on a Saturday afternoon that was overcast and raining, cold for the late summertime, and prayed on his knees for the poor boy who was like so many other poor boys, but who had stolen the hearts of the adults at the home.

And the Creator of all heard the priest's prayers, and the nuns' prayers, but even more than that, he heard Kreo's prayers, and gave permission to his child, the ArchAngel Jeremiel, to speak to the boy in his dreams.

So, Jeremiel did just that.

The same night of the day that Father Johnson was praying for the young boy, Kreo went to his bunk as depressed as he had ever been.

He knew that sleep would be restless, but he went nonetheless, as the rules of the home was lights out at nine p.m..

His eyes closed, his breath deepened, and his body movements ceased. He was asleep in seconds.

And the dream found him.

*Kreo found himself at the gravesite of his late father. The sun was bright overhead, but as he looked up into an azure blue sky, bright with white fluffy clouds and chirping birds, the sunlight threatened to blind him.*

*But he was happy.*

*Until he looked down at his father's gravestone. It was lying flat against the ground, the only proof that his father had ever existed staring up at the same blue sky that had threatened to blind Kreo seconds before.*

*Kreo's heart sank. He had not visited his father's grave since the day the man had been buried right here in this spot, and that made Kreo sad.*

*And as his sorrow sank into his heart, the bright, sunny sky above him turned dark with ominous clouds and stormy wind. The sun was obscured by darkness, and the day turned gloomy and cold.*

*Kreo looked around himself, seeing that the day had turned dark with his mood, but he was in no mind to bring back the sunlight.*

*However, a beam of light hit him square in the face, making him take a large step backward, away from his father's gravestone.*

*A voice sang out from the middle of the beam of light, and it took all the courage within the young man's heart to look up at the source of that voice.*

*"Kreo Fairchild, I have been watching you," the voice rang out from a Being that was larger than anything the boy had seen in his life. The Being must have been the size of a large building, and it hung in the air, its giant, wide-spread wings causing air to stir all around Kreo.*

*And as the young man watched the giant being, it began to change, morphing into a man, right before his eyes.*

*The man was tall, still, dressed impeccably, in what Kreo would describe as prep clothes. Pressed khaki pants, a tight, flowing, almost sheer white shirt, and boat shoes with no socks. Kreo thought the man looked right off the cover of a romance novel.*

*The man was still over six and a half feet tall, and had long, flowing blond hair.*

*But it was the man's face that made Kreo suddenly comfortable with all that was happening around him. The man's face radiated kindness and joy. And Kreo couldn't help but to share in those feelings, as he took in the man's countenance.*

*Kindness and joy. Two things that Kreo had seen extraordinarily little of in his short life.*

*Suddenly, a table and chairs appeared, standing next to his father's grave. The table was covered in a pure white tablecloth, as pure as the man's shirt and smile.*

*The tall man, who had yet to speak, gestured to the chair nearest Kreo, indicating that he wished for Kreo to take a seat.*

*And so, Kreo did. He sat down at a table, within a dream, standing next to his father's grave, with clouds and wind all around, which seemed to not touch the pair of them.*

*The man spoke first.*

*"As I said, Fate Maker, I have been watching over you, all of your life, and we felt it the right time for me to introduce myself," he said.*

*Kreo had not found his voice yet, and so, taking his silence for assent, the man continued talking.*

*"You, Kreo Fairchild, are the culmination of decades of work and planning. Well, centuries, actually," the man told him.*

*Kreo finally found his voice.*

*"W-what are you?" the boy stuttered.*

*The man's smile broke even larger, and he suddenly laughed as if Kreo had told a great joke.*

*"Look at me, trying to be so serious, to leave an everlasting impression on you, and I didn't even tell you who I was." The man literally slapped his knees in laughter.*

*"Allow me to introduce myself, young Fate Maker. I am the ArchAngel Jeremiel. I am one of a heavenly Host, sent to watch over you, and make sure that you become all the Creator of the Universe needs you to be," the man explained.*

*"Why do you keep calling me 'Fate Maker'? What is that?" Kreo asked the ArchAngel.*

*"Well, Kreo, because that is who and what YOU are," Jeremiel told him, pointing a stern finger at the boy as he punctuated the last two words of his statement.*

*"And we have been protecting you," the ArchAngel told the boy, as he lifted his arms, and looked to the air.*

*Suddenly, directly above Kreo's head, and reaching up into the cloudy sky as far as Kreo could see, flashes and images started flickering into existence. In each, a large ArchAngel, colored in more colors than Kreo had ever seen in his life, were fighting darker beings that Kreo couldn't quite see clearly.*

*The flickering became more intense and was as widespread as Kreo's mortal eyes could see. The flickering intensified and grew even larger, if that were possible, until Kreo could see clearly a massive battle surround him in all directions.*

*The tall ArchAngels, covered in glowing armor and wielding massive weapons, each one different, but all of them something out of the greatest Hollywood movie, were fighting for Kreo himself.*

*And as the boy watched the fierce and vicious fighting around himself, tears sprang to his eyes.*

*They all fought, just for him.*

*He turned back, tears streaming down, obscuring the man sitting serenely across from him, as if a massive battle weren't being fought around them both, and listened to what the ArchAngel had to say to him.*

*"This fight has lasted already for millennia, and we have no idea who it is we even fight. But something is coming. A war that we have never seen before in the Heavens, or here on the Earth," the man said.*

*"And the Creator of all has decreed that you, young Fate Maker, are going to be a very large part of all of this," Jeremiel said, his arms raised again, indicating the fighting around them both.*

*And now, Kreo could hear the sounds of the battles above him. Steel ringing on steel, screams, and yelled curses filled his ears. The cacophony was more than he could take.*

*In fact, all of it was more than he could take. He started to panic.*

*And yelling a single word back at the man, at the ArchAngels around and above him, at the entire scene, noises of war and all, Kreo awoke back in his bed, the single word still echoing in his mind and his ears, as if it had come from outside of himself, but which all in the Vision knew to come from within him.*

*"Noooooooo!!!"*

The entire Host looked down on the boy, sweating in his bed, lost amongst so many other lost boys around him, and sighed to a one.

But Jeremiel had watched and directed this boy from birth. He alone of all the Host knew the truth of Kreo's reaction to the Dream.

Jeremiel knew deep within his soul that Kreo was truly the Fate Maker, and that he would be fine.

This dream had been but a seed, planted in the very fertile soil of the boy's mind, and it would grow mighty indeed. Jeremiel had no doubt at all.

It would take a few more years for this seed to grow, and a few more years after that for Kreo to realize just what he was to do, and why.


Standing above all of the Host, and looking through two Planes of existence, the Creator watched the boy's reaction to the Dream, and could see down the long road of the future.

And that gave the Creator the doubt within Himself that His son, Jeremiel, so strongly felt in the opposite.

# Chapter 12

"But I really like my own company. The conversation is always good, although the sex can get boring," Kreo laughed.

"That's not what I meant, young man, and you know it," the large man behind the battered and over-cluttered desk said to Kreo.

"You've been alone all your life. Why don't you try to make friends or even find a girlfriend?" the social worker asked the young man sitting uncomfortably across from him.

Kreo just looked at the floor. He focused on the light beige tiles under his uncomfortable chair. He didn't want to answer the man's questions, but he knew he should. After all, this was the very last time he was going to have to talk to the man who had made sure that Kreo was taken care of for many years.

And now, on the verge of Kreo's eighteenth birthday, and his emancipation from the State of California's Child Welfare division, he knew he should be forthright and open.

But he couldn't. And he really never could, through all the many conversations he'd had with this man since being placed in the boys' home so many years previously.

Kreo looked up into the kind man's eyes, noticed the care there, and said the one thing that was really on his heart.

"Because God hates me," he told the man. "And I don't need anyone but me."

The older, kinder man just shook his head. *If only this boy knew his talents, and more importantly*, he thought, *if he only knew himself.*

Kreo sighed deep in his soul and rose to leave the office. The older man stopped him before he could get out the door.

"Son, God doesn't hate you. He loves you more than you could ever know," he said.

Kreo just nodded his head. He had heard it before, but that didn't change anything in his life. It certainly didn't give him a family, nor his parents back.

Deep in his heart, he wanted to stay in the office. He wanted to unburden his heart to the man who wanted the same thing. But Kreo was too scarred. He was too brittle, thinking it was strength.

He just shrugged once again, while looking the man in the eye. He felt a tear fall but wouldn't let it unburden his soul. He just turned and left.

And, as always when he was feeling down, he remembered that dream from when he was fourteen, and shivers ran up and down his spine.

As he walked back toward his dormitory, those shivers didn't seem to want to leave him. It had been one hell of a dream, and he was happy that he had not had it again. But for some reason, it did always seem to do the trick of cheering him up on gloomy days.

He looked up as he walked into the Big Room of his dorm to see the house parents preparing for the upcoming winter trip.

Every year that he had been at the boys' home, the dorm had taken two road trips a year. One in the summer, and the other in the winter. He had always been excited for the winter trip more. He loved the cold.

And this year's trip was going to be extra special. They were actually leaving the state of California, and it would be the first time in Kreo's life that he left the state in which he had been born.

He had always wanted to see the Rocky Mountains in Colorado. He felt like this trip was going to change his life, and he had no idea why.

And that's how Kreo found himself, two weeks later, sitting in the back of the same old eighteen passenger van, staring out the windows at the highest mountains he had ever seen.

They were snow covered and seemed to rise from the flat lands they had driven through for two days like impossible sentinels, guarding the entire world.

The van was approaching the city of Pueblo, Colorado, and Kreo could not take his eyes off the view to the west. He couldn't wait to get up in those mountains the next day, to go to a place his house parent, Mr. Dorty, had told him about from Mr. Dorty's own life.

They were going to see some castle made by a man over the last couple of decades. Kreo didn't care about some tourist trap. He wanted to sit and stare at the mountains all day.

But he had no idea how his very life would be changed forever by being in that castle, the very next day.

# Chapter 13

Father Johnson happened to be needed to drive the boys on their winter trip that year, and was as excited as the children to see the Rocky Mountains. And as he parked the passenger van across the street from the large stone castle deep in the Green Mountains, he, too, could not take his eyes off the tall mountains around him.

He disembarked from the white van almost as fast as the boys. He was excited, and marveled in the majesty of God's creation.

But he didn't let it distract him from keeping the boys together as they crossed the two-lane road high in the mountains.

It was tough to see both ways down the road, and everywhere was covered in a thin layer of snow and ice. He tried to make a head count as they crossed the road as a single unit.

Someone was missing.

After getting the group of twelve young boys across the street safely and leaving them in the hands of the two nuns who had accompanied the group, Father Johnson turned back to the van, and through the glare from the gray and overcast sky reflected on the side window, saw the silhouette of a boy still sitting in the rear seat.

He knew it was Kreo, and he felt like he knew why the boy had remained in the van.

Father Johnson said a quick prayer to God before crossing back over the slick and ice-covered road, and climbed back into the driver seat of the large white van.

"Don't want to see the view from the top, Kreo?" the priest asked, looking into the rearview mirror.

Kreo just shrugged and kept looking out the left-side window of the van, toward a line of snow-covered pine trees, still green in the deep winter chill.

"For all of the change in your own life, son, you still hate new things, don't you?" he asked.

"I guess so," Kreo answered.

"Then I'll tell you what, son. Why don't you think of this castle as yours?" the priest told the boy.

That got the young man's attention.

"Yeah, go up into this castle like you own it. Feel what that feels like. You're the king of this castle. Why would you be uncomfortable going into your own castle?"

Kreo's head shot up. He had not thought of that before. And so, he agreed with the priest, smiled, and got out of the van, practically running across the ice-slick road and up the snow-covered hill toward the castle that he now saw in a whole new light.

Father Johnson smiled at the back of the young man who had often been in his prayers. He wondered what God had in store for Kreo.

He wondered if Kreo was going to just be another statistic, like so many others like him.

He prayed for the boy, and he prayed even harder for the fallen world that would take such a sweet boy and bury him under mountains of agony and fear.

The day got a little darker for the middle-aged priest.

Kreo didn't stop moving until he was in what was called the Grand Ballroom of the hand-hewn stone castle on the side of a Colorado mountain. He almost lost what breath he had within his lungs as he witnessed the sheer awe of the space around him.

The room was quite large. Several doorways led to other wonders surrounding the large room, but Kreo's eyes could only take in the splendor of the Ballroom.

The ceiling was made of transparent plastic or glass. There were large, arching, spanned-steel girders between Kreo and the clear ceiling. The entire loftiness of the space made Kreo swallow loudly. He had never seen anything like it.

And he could see the mountain scenes around the castle through the large stained-glass windows that made up the front and the rear walls of the Ballroom.

The sheer audacity of the builder to construct something so beautiful, and so high up in the mountains, moved Kreo. He wondered at the man for a fleeting moment.

But then his eyes looked at the floor and the colors swirling around the wide planks from the sunlight beaming weakly through the glass walls.

He wondered what this castle would look like in the middle of summer, with the full sun beaming through the colored glass, and the bright green trees fully leafed-out around the castle.

Kreo knew that he would do everything he could to find out what that vista would look like in the heat of the middle months.

Kreo couldn't seem to get his feet moving. He wanted to explore the rest of the castle. He wanted to follow the more daring boys up onto the cages on top of the castle made of the same wrought iron as the spanned girders of the ballroom.

But he couldn't move a muscle. Something kept him rooted to the spot he was in, his eyes wide in wonder, embarrassment leaking into his thoughts as his friends ran around him, calling to him to come and climb the thin staircases above and around the room in which he was rooted.

But he still couldn't move.

And as Father Johnson finally made it up the steep staircase into the Grand Ballroom, and their eyes locked in the serenity of the space, Kreo's mind expanded almost painfully.

His friends and fellow orphans ran and played around him as he stood stock-still in the middle of the Grand Ballroom, not able to take his eyes off the black steel girders, the stained-glass windows, and the beautiful brown stone that made up the walls of the room.

He could sense Father Johnson's eyes taking in the same wonderful sight.

The wide wooden planks under Kreo's feet were sturdy, and the whole castle felt more solid, more real, than anything he had ever witnessed.

Only one thought took up his mind, as all of the emotions, the feelings, the awe and wonder stormed within him. That thought was a simple command to the Universe.

Kreo, his eyes still on the wonder around him and the solid ground under him, *leaned* into the single thought.

*One day, I will live in a castle just as solid, just as beautiful, just as REAL, as this one*, he commanded in his thoughts.

And the Universe *shifted* around the young Fate Maker.

Two tall, glorious Beings, standing together high above the young man below, both smiled.

The taller put his strong right arm around the other.

'Well done, my Son," the Creator told Jeremiel.

"We have created a Fate Maker."

*Yes, they had*, the younger ArchAngel thought quietly. He was marvelously pleased with that fact, after so many fits and starts, spanning decades of watching and protecting.

But there was still so much more to do.

The young man below, coming fully into the Favor on his life, was strong and able.

But he still wasn't ready. Not really.

He would need so much more pain. And Jeremiel felt remorse and guilt for what would have to transpire next.

The Father felt the ArchAngel's trepidation.

"Don't fret, my Son. It will all be worth it in the end," the Creator of All told the young ArchAngel.

Jeremiel sighed deeply in a place which had no air, and no sense of time or space.

"Yes, my Lord," Jeremiel told his Father. "But he may not see it quite that way."

The Father of All Creation simply nodded.

*No*, the Creator thought to Himself. *The young man below would not understand at all.*

# Part 3
# Losses

# Chapter 14

Kreo had forgotten how beautiful the Bay Area of his childhood was. And now, he was pretending to be an adult in the same place where he had lost everything.

It was not a comfortable situation, and the expected feelings of excitement at being on his own, had not manifested.

He was actually quite terrified, almost every day.

Kreo had graduated from the school at the boys' home that he had lived at for nearly eleven years.

And ever since they released him from the home, as well as the State of California's juvenile custody system, he'd had zero direction to what he wanted to do with his life.

And so, he was merely surviving.

He had saved up a bit of money working jobs throughout high school, but that was slowly dwindling. He needed a job, and he needed one fast.

Kreo knew that implicitly.

So, he was quite motivated to find a waiter job, or at the very least, work in fast food, and start making a bit of money before he went off to college in the fall.

He found himself becoming motivated to be more responsible and make good, adult decisions, until the day he was sitting in a park in Berkeley, minding his own business, reading a Stephen King book.

And his life was changed completely.

The most beautiful girl he had ever seen jumped, reaching for the Frisbee thrown in her direction, her fingers just missing the rim; the flying disc sailed past her, hitting Kreo square in the side of the head.

"Oh, no. I'm so sorry!"

Her voice, sounding more amused than worried, spoke up behind him.

He looked up at her as the sunlight filtered down through the trees behind her, silhouetting her body, and couldn't utter a single word.

All he could see was her smile, and the aura of light surrounding her, like an angel that he had manifested out of thin air.

"Um, um," was all he could mutter. He berated himself for not being cooler in that moment.

"Are you ok?" she asked, her voice like a song, her long, dark hair blowing around her face in the light breeze. She blew the stray hair out of her eyes, smiling down at him until he felt his heart was going to burst.

He finally found his voice.

"Yes," he said. "I'm okay. Are you okay?"

He felt stupid again. Why would she not be okay? He silently berated himself again.

She only smiled down at him.

"That's a really good book," she said as she reached out her hand. He was confused at first, but then figured out that she wanted her Frisbee back.

He could only grin stupidly up at her.

He handed her back the white Frisbee that had fallen nearly in his lap, and she gave him one more smile as she turned to throw the disk back to another girl that Kreo had not noticed until that moment.

The girl who reminded him of an angel turned her back on him.

His book was suddenly forgotten, as was the whole rest of the world. He had to find out her name. He had to find out who she was. He had to have her in his life.

He devised a plan. He couldn't speak straight to the girl of his heart now. She had already dismissed him. So, he would go through the friend.

*That's perfect*, he thought, as he watched the pair, hatching his scheme.

He was sitting on a blanket that he had been given in the boys' home. His book was hardly noticed next to him, and the sun shone brightly through the trees, still lighting the sky a deep, nostalgic blue.

*Everything was perfect*, he thought, as he picked up his things, and moved to the only entrance to the small park near the university's campus.

He would wait until the two came out together, and then ask to speak to the plain and slightly gothic friend of the girl.

*Perfect*, he thought again, as he got to the entrance and casually leaned up against a tall and sturdy light pole. People were moving all around him, but he only had eyes for the pair of teenage girls still tossing the Frisbee.

Their pauses were getting longer and longer between tosses, and he knew they would be winding up soon, as the sun was sinking lower in the sky, and he knew they would set out for wherever they lived.

He sincerely hoped that the girls would go separate ways upon leaving the park and give him an opportunity to speak to the friend.

And then finally, as the street lights around him, including the one he leaned against, came on against the encroaching darkness, the girls gathered their belongings and headed toward the entrance where Kreo still stood, waiting expectantly.

He watched as they hugged at the entrance to the park, and as he had hoped, turned and started walking in separate directions. The friend started walking toward him, and he felt like Lady Luck was shining down on him at that moment.

"Excuse me, excuse me," he said, jogging up to the girl. He noticed that the green streaks dyed into her dark hair sparkled in the fading light.

She turned suddenly, clutching a blanket, purse, and the offending white Frisbee that had started this whole thing in the first place.

He stopped a distance from her, his hands outstretched in front of him. He didn't want to frighten the girl away.

"I'm sorry, I'm not trying to scare you," he said. A slight laugh helped the girl relax visibly.

"No, no," she said. "You just startled me."

He wanted to blurt out his desires for this girl's friend, but he knew he needed to be casual. He needed to act cool.

"Is that the Frisbee that hit me in the head earlier?" he asked, nodding his head toward the toy she still held to her chest.

She smiled.

"Oh, was that you?" she asked in return.

He nodded.

He was suddenly standing there for too long without saying anything. The situation became awkward. And as he shuffled his feet and couldn't speak further, the awkwardness fully on his mind, the saint of a girl broke the silence with a question.

"You want to ask me about Charlie, don't you?" she asked.

He looked up sharply. This girl was more intuitive than he thought.

"Well," she said, looking down the street at where her best friend was disappearing in the growing darkness, "we better go get some coffee and talk."

# Chapter 15

The coffee shop was busy, even this late in the still, summer evening. The smell of strong Columbian coffee beans permeated the air and mixed with the affable laughter and din from the boisterous college-aged crowd.

Kreo felt right at home and didn't know why. This wasn't his usual scene. *But then*, he thought as he looked around the richly decorated shop, *he didn't really* have *a scene*.

"So, you didn't even ask me my name," the girl sitting across the small round tabletop from him said.

He looked over at her sharply. He felt like his mind had been clouded ever since Charlie had spoken to him hours earlier.

The foggy feeling was how his friends had described being high on grass. He didn't like it, but at the same time, it made him ponder the significance, while perversely enjoying it.

"Umm, I'm sorry," he muttered. "What's your name?"

"That's better," she said, nodding her head. *Her smile made her look ridiculously cute*, he thought distractedly.

"My name is Mya Green."

He smiled back at her. That was a pretty name.

"My name is Kreo. Kreo Fairchild," he said in response.

"Salutations and well-met," she said.

She was a dork; he knew that at least. It made him more comfortable as he settled into his chair, his hot latte, and the warm and boisterous surroundings.

"So, are you guys both students at Berkeley?" he asked her.

"Charlie is," she replied. "I go to the culinary school at the bottom of the hill."

"You're a cook?" he asked her, confused.

"I'm going to be a chef," she replied; kind of snooty, he thought. "A five-star rated chef, to be exact," she finished.

"No offense, no offense. I've just always been told never to trust a skinny cook," he said with his most affable smile. She relaxed visibly.

"I couldn't gain weight if I was force-fed marshmallows for a year," she smiled in return.

She was very skinny, he noticed. Well, as skinny as he was. They were both what people would call gangly.

He wondered if this girl was struggling with adulthood as much as he was.

"So, Charlie…." he said.

"Charlie, Charlie. The girl that all the boys drool over," she said with a touch of wistfulness to her tone. Kreo caught it right away.

He knew that he looked like a lovesick puppy that needed attention and treats, but he couldn't help it. Looking at Charlie as she played in the park, and the few words that they had shared together made his heart want to leap from his chest.

He knew that he would do anything, be anything, say anything, to be with her. He didn't like the weakness of it, but he knew in his heart of hearts that he was meant for her, and she for him.

He had never felt anything more real.

And so, he told this wisp of a girl sitting across from him all of that and more, as she rolled her eyes, felt sorry for him, and promised to help him gain Charlie's trust, her love, and finally, Charlie's whole heart.

And Mya made those promises all while her own heart melted every time Kreo smiled, or when his eyes twinkled in the lights of the coffee shop.

Or when she thought about the boy, later that night, lying in her bed, while he snored out on her couch. She made the promises knowing who Charlie really was, and that she would tear Kreo's own soul out of his body if she could.

And how Mya Green, future five star rated chef and destined to be lonely forever, hated herself for it that night, and thousands of other nights to come.

# Chapter 16

A loud booming brought Kreo out of the deepest, darkest unconsciousness that he had ever experienced. And as he was about to succumb to the darkness once again, the booming sounded even louder.

His body hurt. And he didn't know where he was. He could barely open his eyes. They were caked with eye boogers so thick he wondered suddenly if he had pink eye.

*How was his mind both working, and not working, at the same time*, he wondered. He could hardly feel his body.

But everything hurt all at once. *His life, at whatever time of day it was on this day, was in a state of complete yin and yang*, he mused. Everything and nothing, all at once, and not at all.

That thought made him smile until the booming sounded behind his eyes once again.

The loud, staccato sounds wouldn't stop. It was causing loud, bright lights to blossom in his mind and behind his eyes with every pounding. He wondered why someone was banging on his front door. *Wait*, he thought. *He didn't have a front door.*

Where the fuck was he?

And then the booming cut off with a silence even louder than the noise had been in the first place.

*There you go*, he thought. *Back to sleep.*

Until glass broke somewhere close to him, making him jump, and realize that he was on a hard, cold floor, covered in sweat.

"Kreo, man, where the fuck are you dude!" A loud, feminine voice came from the broken window near him.

"Kreo, wake the fuck up. You idiot, you god-fucking idiot. What did you do?" the voice said again, closer this time.

He thought he recognized it. Slowly, his mind was coming back to him from the deep abyss he had allowed it to succumb to.

It was Mya. *What the hell was she doing here?* he wondered, as he tried to pick himself up off the floor and at the same time, to wipe the crust from his eyelashes.

Then he felt a small yet strong hand under his armpit. He realized that he didn't have a shirt on. Where the hell was his shirt?

His closest friend, who had picked him up and saved his life more times over the last three years than he had known, was lifting him up off of the cold concrete floor and moving him toward sunlight.

*Where the fuck was he*? he thought again.

"You goddamn idiot. I can't believe I found you here!" She was screaming into his ear. It was both too loud and muffled. Yin and yang again. He suddenly thought of the tattoos on his chest showing just that very black and white circle.

At one time, he had been a philosopher. That thought made him laugh.

It hurt his chest to laugh.

He woke again, and this time, his face was pressed up against the cold, wet glass of the passenger side window of a car. Mya's car.

She was cursing him again. And it suddenly started all coming back.

His sweaty back stuck to the leather seat of her new SUV. And he was cold. Contradictions once again. His whole life was a contradiction.

When she eventually fell silent, and he could hear her pain in the absence of sound, he finally came back fully to himself.

And he was ashamed. And he needed his fix. That made him even more ashamed.

His fix. Sweat broke out all over his body when he thought of the drugs that he had been addicted to for over a year now.

And in that time, he had lost everything. Absolutely everything that had ever mattered to him.

And he had no idea how Mya had found him this morning, and why she had him, stinking, sweating, hating life, in the passenger seat of her genuinely nice new car.

He cracked open one crusty eye and glanced over at his friend. His only friend, if he thought about it too hard.

The only other person he knew in this entire world anymore was his dealer. And Kreo wished to see Cadillac, his dealer, more than anyone else at the moment.

He also did not want to see the big man, ever again. More contradictions.

His life was one big contradiction.


It had begun earnestly enough. He had crashed on Mya's couch that night, and for many nights after.

He finally agreed to be her roommate after her other one had suddenly moved out, the girl's parents forcing her to move back home when she failed a semester of college.

And Mya had fully and completely brought Kreo and Charlie together, young love blossoming between them like fireworks.

The love affair started off fun, exciting, and full of passion and flair. It turned into pure hell within a few months, however.

Charlie had the proclivity of enjoying the attention of several guys at once, and Kreo just couldn't quite handle that. No one could, he figured, the way she acted towards the end. And it was that end that brought him into contact with Cadillac, and his very first high.

It was not his last. Not by a long shot.

It had been a weekend. He remembered that.

Saturday, he had tried to take Charlie out on a date. He had received his tax return from his waiter job and had been surprised with the amount he had gotten.

He didn't really understand how taxes worked, and being a waiter, and working mostly off of tips, he didn't know about things like earned income credit, or California tax breaks for working wages. But he had a chunk of money in his pocket, and he wanted to treat his girl.

She had been excited about the date at first. He had borrowed a buddy's car and wanted to drive up the PCH with the top of the old Volkswagen Beetle down, letting Charlie's beautiful and shiny hair blow in the wind.

But she had other plans.

He had told her how much he had gotten back in his tax return, and she had asked him to take her to a concert in the desert. He couldn't remember the name of the festival, but it had seemed like a really promising idea when she told him about it.

Until he had paid the exorbitant entrance fees for them both, and within an hour of arriving, had lost Charlie, and didn't know anyone there, nor anyone within 350 miles.

But Charlie had known several of the musicians there, and when he came upon her, rolling around naked with four or five other men and women, all with tattoos, funky hair color, and a don't-give-a-shit attitude about the love he felt for the girl, he had lost himself completely.

As he drove back to the Bay Area alone, tears streaming down his face, and his soul shattered into a million pieces, *his fate* led him to a seedy bar, a back table with a large man with the Cadillac logos tattooed on the back of each hand, and his first taste of illicit drugs, as he snorted a line of cocaine.

And the cocaine was the only thing that could take his mind off Charlie and seeing her with all those naked musicians.

Which meant that the cocaine became his daily companion, and the escape from his reality.

But it still wasn't enough after a while. And after he started following Charlie and seeing what she did on a daily basis. He didn't think that she meant to tear his heart out every single day, but she did a really excellent job at it.

The men who had money, who had families, who had prestige, that she spent time with, and made love to, and laughed with in expensive restaurants as he watched through the foggy restaurant windows, were all better than Kreo.

And them being better than him made him realize his lot in life, and that drove him deeper into his hole of depression, shame, and chemical dependency.

He followed her, stalked her, was driven almost mad with thoughts of her and how she had hurt him. He could do nothing else but wallow in his pain and the lot he had been given unfairly in life.

*Why?* he prayed. *Why did God hate him so?*

The day that he halfway came clean, and could think, realizing that he had not followed or seen Charlie for quite some time, he approached a newspaper stand in downtown Berkeley, and saw on the front page of the Bay Area Gazette that Charlie was engaged to the son of a prominent local politician and business owner, he spiraled down all the way.

The picture on the front page showed Charlie, his Charlie, arm intertwined in the tall, handsome rich boy's arm, smiling up at him like he had brought the sunrise just for her that day.

Kreo got sick in his spine, brain, and soul, whispers from a dark presence close behind him, telling him he didn't deserve to live.

He had gone straight to Cadillac's ground floor apartment, banged on the back sliding glass door, and when the big man answered it, Kreo said the only thing he could utter in such pain.

"I want something stronger."

Which led to his first taste of shooting heroin, more months than he could count of not being aware of his surroundings, and a final weeklong bender that landed him, shirtless and close to death, on the cold concrete floor of an abandoned flop house.

And his only friend in the world finding him in the worst shape he could be in while still breathing.

He looked over her on their way to the hospital.

All the while Mya cussed him, and he knew, in his addled state, and with his mind almost gone deep within, that the curses she sent his way were all true.

He had no idea why he was still alive. And he felt deep inside that he didn't deserve even that much. His shame was deeper than even his convictions.

He was ready to die.

What he didn't know in that moment, as he sweated the drugs into the new seats of Mya's beautiful SUV, and shivered in the light of a bright, cheery sun that he couldn't even see, was that *Fate* had a different future for him than he could even fathom.

The Fate Maker was at the bottom of the hole he needed to be in, and the tall, splendid Being who watched over him, keeping his heart beating while it was shattered in a million pieces, smiled down on his charge.

The strength Kreo would gain from his recovery and being brought back to himself would see him through what was to come.

Jeremiel looked down on the broken, battered man, and smiled more broadly.

Kreo was finally ready to come into his full power, and finally find out just why it all had to happen the way it had.

Creation would need him more than ever now.

# Chapter 17

Kreo hurt again.

From the tips of his individual hairs, down to the hard calluses that he had developed on the bottoms of his feet from walking, homeless, and shoeless, on the streets of the Bay Area.

The only solace he had from the pain was that he was warm, comfortably ensconced in a soft hospital bed, and he wasn't being rained upon.

He was dry for the first time in what seemed like ages, and he was grateful for it.

He could hear the rain and thunder coming from outside the dark windows next to his hospital bed. It was almost soothing. The pain in his body, and in his soul, took away from the enjoyment of listening to the harsh storm outside.

And all he could think in his still fuzzy mind was that he was lucky to not be caught out in the freezing rain, under an overpass, or trying to stay warm inside a pile of dirty blankets and cardboard cover.

He lay his painful head back into the soft pillow, his eyes closed, and allowed himself to feel the pain in his body.

That pain, mixed with the gratitude of not being cold, and lonely, caught in the rain falling outside, allowed his mind to fall back into a restful, healing sleep.

Sometime later, he woke again, still hearing the storm raging outside, but this time, his room was well lit, and nurses and a doctor was hovering around his hospital bed, talking to each other, seemingly ignoring the young man, still full of pain, his mind's eye seeing the world through the haze of opaque reality.

His mind did not become sharp and clear until he head Mya's voice beside his bed. She made him jump, shocking him once again, like she had done in the flop house.

And shame overcame him again as she stood next to his bed and took his dirty hand, holding it tightly in her own angelically clean one.

He couldn't hear what she was saying through the rushing of blood in his ears. His shame and sorrow were threatening to overcome him again, and all he wanted was to shut out the voices and the pain in his head.

His hearing soon cleared up, and she was shushing him like a baby, trying to give him comfort when he didn't deserve it, nor want it.

He wanted nothing more than to apologize to his friend and ask her forgiveness for not living up to how she had always seen him.

Kreo knew that Mya loved him. He and Charlie had laughed about it at the beginning.

And thinking of Charlie once again made the tears come rushing back into his pained eyes, and he once again wanted his life, and the pain, to be gone. He needed a fix. Or he needed a miracle.

He couldn't understand the difference between the two, in that moment.

Soon, his emotions abated, and the overwhelming physical need for a fix subsided, and the pain went down in his mind a few ticks.

And he could still feel the soft, firm, and loving hand of his best friend within the shameful folds of his own hand. He opened his eyes and looked up at her. And saw her for the very first time.

The two of them were alone in his low-lit room. The storm raged outside the dark windows behind her, lightning exposing the harsh reality he found himself within, but he couldn't take his eyes off his friend.

And he transposed this scene in his mind with the first time he had met both girls, and for once, he was okay with the memory.

But only because, for the first time since it had happened, he did not allow his focus to settle on Charlie within the memory.

No, this time he saw Mya as she was three years prior, with her green-tipped hair, her punk rock t-shirt over holey jeans, and her black eye makeup making her seem darker than he knew her to be.

And his heart *shifted* around the memory, and the pain in his body lowered a few more ticks.

He wasn't out of the woods yet, but at least in that dark hospital room, with its stark white walls, the insistently beeping monitors surrounding his bed, and the deep and dark storm raging outside the windows, he found a reason to leave those shadowy and lonesome woods and find the easy sunshine.

As his eyes closed again to a healing, restful sleep, he saw her, and the buzzing and screaming pain that had been a constant squatter in his soul settled down for the first time in two years.

*It was enough*, he thought, as the healing darkness closed in, finally allowing him to rest.

# Chapter 18

"So, you're twenty-two years old, are strung out from a drug overdose, and you think your life is now over," the therapist was saying.

"And you have zero idea what to do now," she finished.

Kreo wondered how many times he had been in a similarly appointed office, with degrees on walls, books on shelves, and some therapist or other sitting across the desk trying to guide him to a future he, himself, could not see.

"Pretty much," he whispered, not taking his eyes off of his bony legs under the hospital gown.

"Kreo, your life has only just begun," she said.

She sounded exasperated. Like she had given this spill to wayward youth for a long time.

And she had.

She had uttered the same words so many times, only to watch the majority of them slide right back into drug use, promiscuity, and ultimately an early death. It was getting tiresome, she felt.

He knew what she said was true. But he couldn't help feeling like he had ruined his entire future, and that he should just take his life now.

He had no reason to live.

But her next words shook his entire world and set off what would happen after.

"Kreo, get the hell out of here. The Bay Area, California, hell, walk away from everything and everyone you know," she said.

He didn't know where it came from, but the idea of getting the hell out of his own life, and the muck and mire of it, was just what he needed to hear.

Six months later, a new, energized, and fully healthy Kreo found himself on a bus with thirty or forty other wide-eyed youth, each clutching the only belongings they had in the world, and listening to the drill instructor at the front of the sickly-green painted bus screaming orders in their faces.

Parris Island, South Carolina.

All the way across the United States from all he had ever known.

The United States Marine Corp Recruit Depot, or as the recruiter had called it, "the Depot," "the Suck," or basic boot camp.

Kreo had lied to the Marine recruiter about his history with illicit drugs, but his high school grades and his high score on the ASVAB had made the recruiter look the other way on a full background check.

And therefore, Kreo found himself on an ugly bus that smelled of fear and trepidation.

He was nervous as hell, but also excited to see the rest of the world and leave California behind him forever.

His only regret was having to leave Mya as well. Her last words to him still reverberated in his mind, and a tear escaped his eye every time he remembered her standing at the gate of the airport, waving to him as he marched off to his future.

"Take care of yourself, Kreo," she had told him.

"Don't die. And come back and see me sometime. You know where I'll be," she had said.

She had hugged him tightly, and he felt horrible that he didn't feel the grief at that moment like she had. He only felt excitement to be disembarking to his future.

"I love you, Kreo, you big goofy dumbass," she said. And then, to his surprise, she had pulled his head down to her level, and had kissed him square on the mouth.

That had shocked him more than anything, as did the stirrings he had felt in what he had thought was a dead, black heart.

And now, facing the horrible crucible of boot camp, he felt overwhelming fear, excitement, a bit of anger, and a burgeoning yet bright emotion in his heart when he thought of Mya standing at the gate, waving to him, her kiss still vibrating on his lips, and the tears streaming down her face.

He squared his shoulders, took a deep breath, and focused forward, as the bus drove through the front gates of the Recruit Depot.

His bright and shiny future awaited him, along with a yelling drill instructor, telling him to move his ass.

He smiled and ran headfirst into an unknown fate.

# Chapter 19

"Keep your fucking head down, Boot!"

The Staff Sergeant screamed at Kreo over the sounds of heavy gunfire and the moans and groans of dying Marines around him.

Kreo wondered briefly why the sound of bullets whizzing over his head was so very much like the buzzing of horseflies and hornets from his childhood summers.

He pulled his flak helmet closer to his head as his desert goggles fell into his eyes. He scrambled behind some rocks, the sun threatening to burn his thoughts away, if the enemy towelheads didn't do it for him.

Everything was happening too fast, and way too slow.

*More contradictions*, he thought.

He had wanted to get away from his life and see the world. *Well, a desert stint in fucking Afghanistan was doing just the trick*, he thought sarcastically.

He just had to keep his damn head down like his platoon leader had screamed at him. Finally opening his eyes, he looked deep into the fear showing in the eyes of his squad leader crouched next to him behind the big rock.

*Not a good sign,* he thought.

Being the newest PFC in the field, everyone close by outranked him. But that didn't make them any more knowledgeable of what to do in an ambush than he was.

Kreo took in a deep breath, and following his squad as they jumped up running and attempted to make their way through the ambush they had walked into, he started yelling and firing his military issue automatic weapon toward the enemy.

Just him and his weapon. An army of one. A fucking Marine.

And a big bag of flesh and goo that bullets did not, in fact, bounce off of.

His brothers were falling around him. They had walked into a heavy pile of shit, and they were trying to force their way out of it.

He could hear the platoon leader yelling orders ahead of him, and he ran towards the sound like his life depended on it.

Because in that moment, it did.

He was praying under his breath for the enemy to miss him, not see him, hell, of being so scared of seeing a platoon of US Marines coming at them that they all threw down their weapons and ran, screaming for their own lives.

He felt the world around him *shift*, and miracle of miracles, just what he had been wishing would happen really did.

The enemy, who had the high ground a few seconds beforehand and had been firing AKs down on the trapped Marines in the narrow valley below, literally threw their weapons to the ground and ran back the way they had come - to a man.

"What the fuck," he muttered to himself.

The new silence around him was more deafening than anything he had ever witnessed.

All he heard were the sounds of the gentle desert wind, the Marines moaning behind him, and felt the heat from the oppressive sun overhead bouncing off the light tan rocks all around him.

He looked around him, desert-camo-clad Marines lying on the sandy road, bleeding and moaning, but he himself was unscathed.

*What in the holy fuck of warfare had just happened?* he asked himself. He went to the man laying closest to him. It was Ramirez. His squad brother and best friend in the world.

They had done bootcamp together, and infantry school. Ramirez had taken a bullet to the knee, looked like.

Kreo's short battlefield medical training came to the front of his mind, and he began rummaging through his pack to get out the bandages and meds that they all carried.

"Fairchild, man, what the fuck happened? Why did they stop?" Ramirez said through gritted teeth. He was hurting bad.

"Don't know, Ramirez, but thank God they ran. Probably saw your ugly mug coming, scared them all off," he told his fellow Marine.

"Shit, this hurts," was all Ramirez could utter as Kreo went to work trying to stop the bleeding.

After tying the field dressing in place, Kreo took a bottle of water out of his pack and held it to his friend's lips. Ramirez took a deep drink, wincing.

Kreo checked his buddy all over again.

It didn't look like any arteries were hit. A mere flesh wound. Kreo promised himself that he would make the joke from Monty Python when Ramirez was stabilized.

"Medic!" he yelled, seeing the corpsman working on a Marine close by.

The corpsman nodded at Kreo, seeing that Ramirez was well cared for, but signaling that he would come as soon as he finished with the Marine he was stabilizing.

Kreo nodded back and added another field dressing pad onto the bullet wound in his brother's leg.

He cringed at the fear, and more so at the pain, in his battle brother's eyes, and wished the corpsman would hurry the hell up with the morphine, so Ramirez would lose the look.

And that look is what tore at Kreo's heart the most.

It wasn't concern for his best friend, as he knew Ramirez would make it.

It was more that the fear was replicated in his own heart, and it took him back to the abandoned flop house where Mya had found him, almost a year earlier.


Later that day, as Kreo found himself back at the Forward Operating Base, or FOB, and sitting on a sandy hill above the bustle below, he remembered that look, and how it had made him feel.

He looked down at his hands and started scraping dry blood from under his fingernails. His brother's blood.

But he knew that he had done all the right things, and his battle brother would live.

That didn't change the fact that he felt at odds with himself, and that he was on the verge of a breakthrough on top of that dirty hill.

His thoughts were all over the place.

He really had no idea what he was doing, all the way around the world from all that he had known, getting shot at, watching friends suffer and die.

But he really had no place in this world, and staring off into the slowly sinking sun, setting behind the dirty tan mountains to the West, he was slightly all right with that.

Slightly.

*Sure,* he thought to himself, *it sucked, but when you didn't have a place in the world, the world tended to put you where it needed you.*

Kreo watched below him as Ramirez was lifted into a Helo for flight to a military hospital in Germany.

And he concluded that this was where the world needed him at that moment.

On top of that dusty, brush covered hill, in a region of the Middle East that he couldn't pronounce, he felt his body, his spirit, and his mind all connect, and he was finally at peace.

For now, he knew, he was ok.

He was alive, against all odds, and he knew that he would be fine. Better than fine, actually.

Because it was time to take his own fate in hand and become all that he could be.

The slogan from the Marine's TV commercials back home made him smile.

And his grin grew as he felt the health and wholeness of his body and mind meld, and he knew he could do anything.

It was time to test his mettle and see just what kind of man he could be, as he took control of his fate, and wrestled it out of the hands of chance and luck.

That night, after chow, prayers, and some low-key grab-assery with his Marine brothers and sisters who had made it through the ambush, Kreo fell into a fitful sleep, and for the first night in more years than he could remember, he did not dream of the Celestial Battle around him, that the ArchAngel had showed him so long ago.

His body settled deep into the cot he had for a bed, and his dreams that night were of home, and parents he had never really had. And Mya, cooking for him.

Always of Mya from that night forward.

Kreo had taken control of his dreams from whatever Beings had held sway over him, and his dreamworld *shifted* around him, marching to his own drumbeat.

He knew deep in his sub-conscious mind that he had done that.

And the next day, during patrol, he took control of a light within him, that had always been there, and he had never really noticed.

He made the same *shift* in his waking world as he had in his dreams, and he finally knew the truth of what had eluded him all of his short life.

He could somehow control his own fate, and the fate of those around him. He didn't know where the power had come from, only remembering the dreams that the ArchAngel had given him as an answer.

He really did have control over his life, and in some small ways, the world around him.

He would never be the same again.

# Inter-Mission I

Jeremiel was standing amongst the Younger Ilk, but close to the front, near the Eldest of all ArchAngels, Gabriel, and he felt like a child.

The golden light emitting from his Eldest Brother was glorious, and Jeremiel was ashamed of his own purple aura. As if his aura was dirty, and his Eldest Brother's was pure and clean.

Gabriel was the one who had yet to smite the Enemy, but at the same time, had done it Eons ago.

Jeremiel felt small next to the drastic age and wisdom of Gabriel, and he hung on every word his Brother was speaking to the Father.

"Father, we know not what we face, still," Gabriel said.

He stood tall, clad in gleaming Celestial Armor, his Demon-vanquishing sword, Glory, strapped to his broad back, facing the Father without the normal awe and fear held by the rest of the Host.

"I was able to get close to the Tear in Creation, where the fighting was heaviest," he said. "We almost lost two of the Younger Ilk in the battle."

That alone concerned Jeremiel the most. They had already lost one of their number for the first time in all of existence.

The fact that more of them could die, to be re-made into something lesser, was a horrifying thought. Jeremiel tried to remove the thoughts from his mind and focus on what Gabriel was telling the Creator.

But the second ArchAngel ever created, Michael, was standing just as tall next to Gabriel. His aura was changing back and forth between the brightest white and the deepest red. Anger rose from him like a heat mirage.

Michael's matching sword to Gabriel's own, named Mercy by the Father Himself, was also changing colors, seething in anger, hanging in a metallically clear scabbard against Michael's left leg.

Jeremiel felt himself join in with Michael's wrath.

Jeremiel's eyes went back and forth between the two Eldest. He knew he wasn't the only member of the Host baffled by the words spoken into existence by the Eldest.

"As I approached the Tear, Father, I could discern the other side," Gabriel said.

The entire Host perked up at this news. This would be the first time any one of them had seen what was on the other side.

"It was confusing, to say the least," Gabriel said with exasperation in his heavenly voice.

"But I could make out another Creation, another Existence. Just like this one, yet darker. Almost the exact opposite of your own Creation, Father-of-All."

Even the Creator sat up straighter on His Throne. His brilliance expanded around the entire Host, and all the levels of Angels surrounding the Throne Room.

Curiosity was not a reaction they normally received from their Father, but on this day, it merely joined the rest of the Host and the Heavenly Bodies of Angels rising and descending from the Throne.

"And I felt one last thing, Father," Gabriel said.

His voice, golden and splendid in both battle and in peace, lowered to a level where even the Host could barely hear him.

Gabriel lifted his golden head, cascading amber hair falling down his broad back, and his usual golden aura dimmed perceptively.

He looked at the Father of All straight in His face, a feat most in this Creation could not, nor would not, do.

And his words rang around the Throne room for millennia after. The Host heard the words for eons to come.

"Father, I felt the presence of Another," Gabriel said quietly.

"It felt like you, Father, only…" He paused.

Attentive faces, and Celestial Auras were poised on the final words Gabriel spoke into existence in the Throne room, the very center of all Creation and Reality.

"Only… it felt your very Opposite, Heavenly Father," Gabriel finally said.

"It was another God. But not You, Father."

The silence of the statement reverberated around the Throne, and Jeremiel could swear he heard Creation itself break open, and nothing could ever be the same again.

# Part 4
# Findings

# Chapter 20

The room was cold, and goosebumps arose on First Lieutenant Kreo Fairchild's arms, under his dress blues.

His Mameluke sword at his side felt just as cold against his leg as he tried to keep from making a sound with his shivering. It wasn't every day that an enlisted Marine rose to a battlefield commission and became the executive officer of his very own company, a role usually reserved for a higher-ranking captain. Officer Candidate School had been nothing compared to the stress he currently felt.

So, to say that he was nervous was an understatement.

To keep his mind occupied during the speeches and honors given to him, along with his old platoon, he thought back over the four years that had gotten him to this podium, on this prestigious day.

It had begun in Afghanistan, as most recent military stories went these days.

His first deployment, where the ambush had changed him and his life forever, was well behind him. He had become accustomed to the daily marches, the intense fighting, and the acts of humanitarianism that had brought the US military to this god-forsaken country.

Kreo was getting really good at dodging bullets, Taliban raids, roadblocks, IEDs, and suicide bombers. He was also honing this ability he seemed to have, to make things just… happen.

He didn't want to think too much into that stuff. He was afraid it was just going to disappear one day, when the universe figured out it had made a mistake.

And so, he thought of the men and women he had lost in that time as well.

The faces swam in front of his mind as he half listened to the speech the commandant was giving, outlining several of the skirmishes and battles he and his platoon had fought in.

The Marines he had lost along the way distracted him as the speech went on and on.

And the guilt of still being alive ate him up as they handed him his medal, and took pictures of him and the commandant, hands clasped together, the shiny blue box holding his medal between them.

Hernandez and Cox. Lt. Griffin. Shakes, Dog Balls, and Ace.

His best friend, Southpaw.

Men and women he had fought next to, and had lost along the way, their blood on his hands, or their dead eyes staring up at him from the floor of a Helo as he felt like shit for still being whole and unwounded.

But he still had a job to do, and as he was congratulated by everyone in the room for being the pivotal reason his men came home, he knew that soon he would be back over to the sandbox, and had to keep fighting.

He suddenly felt lightheaded as his commission was read aloud, and he took command of his platoon.

The platoon colors were transferred, salutes were given, and suddenly, he was morally and physically responsible for up to fifty Marines.

He stepped off the podium and started down the line of people lining up like they would at a wedding, ready to congratulate and offer kind words most of them didn't mean. But it was military protocol, and he kept his military bearing about him.

His sword still hung heavy at his side, and his hands sweated in his crisp white gloves. But he made the necessary responses and smiled when he was supposed to smile. He could feel his new medal slapping against his left breast, right over his heart.

As he got to the end of the line of people lined up to shake his hand and tell him how amazing he was, he saw Mya standing against the back wall. She was dressed smartly and had a smile on her face just for him.

And his heart leapt in his chest like he was a schoolboy again, and not a war-hardened Marine, just home from battles that should have ended his life many times over.

He walked up to her and stopped a few feet away. She smiled up at him, almost shyly. No words needed to be spoken. He knew how she felt about him now. She had voiced them at his apartment early this morning, and late last night, and the day before as well.

He smiled back, and knew that in his heart, his life was whole, and right. But he had a job ahead of him, and Mya's smile faltered as she saw the look in his eyes, and she knew instinctively where his mind was.

But she had to be okay with the man she loved having to go back to the fight. He was a soldier now, and she was prouder of him than she could express.

But her fear of and for Kreo had never quite left her heart, and the man certainly had done nothing to assuage that fear. *But that wasn't his fault*, she thought as she took his arm, and allowed him to escort her to the dinner being thrown in his honor.

He really had no idea of the world around him, she knew. And she loved his innocence. But it wasn't an innocence born of naivety.

*No*, she thought as she took her seat next to him at the head table.

*It was because he was too strong for the world to affect him.*

And that strength frightened her more than anything else. Because she knew with all of her being that when he came fully into himself, he would take over the world.

And remembering the boy she had saved in that abandoned flop house so long ago, she wondered just what kind of man he would be when he took over that world.

Would he be the good man she knew him to be?

Or would the things that had made him so strong be the very things that turned him evil and hard?

The light in the room dimmed in her imagination, as the man she loved smiled at her, and she could see the coldness reflected in his eyes. Her heart dropped suddenly.

She loved Kreo with all of herself. But she had no idea who he was.

No one really did. Not even Kreo himself.

And that was the scariest thing of all.

# Chapter 21

"What we are teaching here, gentlemen, is leadership. And leadership starts in mindset," the woman told the group of young officers gathered together.

Some of the young officers snickered behind her back.

Kreo turned in his uncomfortable plastic seat, and glared a hard stare at the young officers behind him. They instantly stopped laughing and turned serious. Kreo nodded his head at the group and turned back around to listen to the instructor.

He knew, more than the men and women behind him, how retaining the instructions, like the class they were in, could save lives in the field. Unlike the other officers in the room, he had actually been in combat.

And he had gained all of their respect because of it.

The stories about his exploits over in the sandbox had made the rounds at Cherry Point, the base he found himself at, in North Carolina.

He didn't do anything to stop the exaggeration of some of the stories, as he knew the stories would boost his reputation, along with the respect his men would give him.

He was willing to let it go, as long as it made his troops trust him.

"And mindset, ladies and gentlemen, will keep you and your soldiers fighting long past the time most people would give up," the instructor said.

Kreo agreed with everything the young woman was saying. He knew you had to be strong in the mind first before the body. One without the other made for a dead soldier.

He had learned that the hard way. Fear on the field got you killed much faster than unpreparedness or fatigue. It often locked you up. Froze you in your tracks. Made you do stupid things. Things that got people killed.

His mind was suddenly lost again in memories. Memories from long ago, and the more hurtful ones, most recently.

Later that evening, Kreo sat, alone again, on the couch in his apartment.

The room was dark, and rain beat against the windows. Lightning lit up the room suddenly and made Kreo flinch with the sounding boom of the thunder that followed right after.

The light of the storm lit up in his mind as well, like grenade flashes or mortar fire. He found himself flinching, again, from the brightness. His mind wondered briefly if this was going to be a permanent situation.

And so, with that, he let his mind finally let loose, and he allowed the pain to come.

He was walking on a dry gravel road. His desert-color boots crunched the hard, foreign rocks under him, and he thought once again of the differences between this god-forsaken country and his home.

The land around him was raped of nutrients after so many thousands of years of farming and planting. He missed the dark, soft dirt of home. But he had a job to do here.

All of his Marine brothers and sisters did.

The radio operator walked beside him, and they both carried M-16 long guns, sidearms close by if necessary. You didn't go anywhere in this country, especially outside the base, without being fully armed and in pairs.

Southpaw, as they called the tall radio man, was over six feet tall, and wore a ready smile as well as a quicker jab than any that Kreo had ever had the privilege of being on the receiving end of.

They were in the Kandahar province of Afghanistan. Their mission was daily perimeter patrols, protecting the US base against enemy Taliban operators.

They were a part of a compliment of pairs that patrolled the inside and the outside of the base fence twenty-four hours a day.

For now, Southpaw and Kreo had drawn the swing shift, working the evening hours of patrols.

And so, the sun was setting behind the mountains surrounding the deep valley they found themselves in, and the shadows were long, and dangerous.

It was the drowsy, hot part of the day, and Kreo made sure the pair of them stayed alert.

They were integral in protecting the base from the enemies, and even more integral in protecting it from friendly fire. The Taliban enjoyed recruiting US military-cleared Afghanis and turning them into bomb-vest carrying weapons against the soldiers from the West.

The two of them, Kreo and Southpaw, whose last name was McCallister, talked easily as they walked the beaten path outside the fence.

They had been patrolling together for months now. Kreo enjoyed the taller man's northeastern accent, from the 'Bas-ten' area of Massachusetts, and Southpaw felt at ease in the normal, brooding, silence Kreo surrounded himself with.

It was an easy camaraderie, and Kreo was glad he had found a battle brother he could have a good relationship with.

"And so, I go's around the side of the school buildin' and wouldn't you believe, this wicked pussy of a guy had my sista up against the wall, hand up her shirt already," Southpaw was telling Kreo as they passed the northeastern corner of the tall chain-link fence surrounding the rigid collection of tents and weapons depots of the base.

"Well, I grabbed that goobah from behind, and beat his face in the concrete right in front of my sista." He said.

"Tha hole time, my sista was eggin' me on, and Kreo, get this, she got in the last kick on that piece of filth before we headed to the house," Southpaw finished, laughing at the memory.

Kreo smiled up at his tall friend. He believed the story the tall man was telling. He had felt a few of those same left hooks during hand-to-hand drills or the mock boxing matches the Marines routinely put on.

Kreo had heard so many stories of the man's sister, he felt she was now his own sister. Her name was Grace and Kreo hoped to meet her the next time the pair of them were stateside.

He looked forward to seeing the two siblings re-unite once this tour was over. His smile deepening, Kreo's mind went to the fact that he had already made plans with Mya to meet in Boston and have a small vacation with the people who meant the most to him in all the world.

The smile drained from Kreo's face as they looked up ahead and saw a beat-up station wagon behind old debris on the northern border of the base, right outside the security fence.

The car was not supposed to be there.

He alerted his tall friend with a nod toward the out-of-place car.

They were both instantly on alert.

A car this close to the perimeter was something they were supposed to report, but Kreo grabbed Southpaw's hand before he could call it in. He wanted to check it out first and didn't want to make any noise.

Southpaw nodded his understanding.

They both crouched down, to make smaller targets of themselves, and Kreo used standard battlefield hand signals to have Southpaw move around in a flanking direction. Southpaw nodded his understanding once again.

This wasn't their first enemy contact.

Kreo watched his tall friend double-time around the back side of the debris and blown out buildings, and moved himself into a pincer position. He knew that Southpaw was awaiting his signal from the other side of the car that was not supposed to be where it was.

So, Kreo moved toward the car in a run, yelling for hands to raise, or weapons to be thrown to the ground.

He heard Southpaw's louder voice yelling from the opposite side of the debris, moving toward the car, and closer to Kreo.

And that's when all hell broke loose.

As Kreo and Southpaw ran toward the beat-up old station wagon, weapons trained forward, years of training kicking in, they both saw a familiar face, and pulled up short of the car.

Samir, a local man whose wife made small finger food – rolled up friend bread filled with different meats and served with spicy ketchup – got out of the driver's side door of the car.

Southpaw was grinning from ear to ear as they approached, but Kreo kept his face stoic.

Because Kreo saw it first.

He tried to yell at his battle brother, his best friend, his favorite person on the planet besides Mya, but it was too late.

The look of horror and fear on Samir's face told Kreo everything, but Samir's back was toward Southpaw, and so he didn't see the whispered apology come from Samir's lips as he pressed a hidden button on a makeshift box he held in his left hand.

"No!" Kreo yelled, just as the straps of C-4 adorning Samir's tunic exploded, obliterating almost everything within a few hundred meters' space.

The world went fiery bright around Kreo, and then suddenly went black as he felt it *shift* around and through him.

It had been the last thing he felt for a long while, except the pain that was now a constant companion.

# Chapter 22

As Kreo sat on his soft, expensive couch, alone with his thoughts and fears, the thunder crashing outside his apartment, his mind was on the funeral, the condolences, and the look on Grace's face, more than anything else.

The look of blame and hate on the face of his best friend's sister still made his stomach churn, a year later.

As well as the fact that Kreo walked away from the fray with hardly a scratch, against all odds, in an escape that people were calling miraculous.

But he knew what it really was, and the fact that Southpaw's body could barely be recognized as having been a living, breathing human after the blast made his pain intensify tenfold.

Kreo knew that he had survived when his best friend had not because of this power he seemed to have over his life, and the lives around him.

Almost as if he could change things by wishing they would change. But the problem was, the last time he felt the *Shift*, he had not willed it to happen.

He had not *shifted* fate himself. It was like fate had protected him.

He knew he was personifying something he had no concrete knowledge or idea about, but he couldn't get the nagging feeling out of his mind, nor the thoughts behind it.

He felt overwhelmed, like he didn't deserve to be alive anymore.

Kreo got up off the couch, the lightning crashing outside his broad, open windows lighting up his way, and walked in a fog to his stereo system.

He turned on the power button of the system, hearing the humming in the powerful speakers, and pressed 'Play' on the CD player. The first notes of one of his favorite albums started playing.

*Cross of Changes*, by Enigma.

And by the time song number three, "Return to Innocence," was playing, Kreo was on his knees, tears streaming down his face in the outward showing of the flood of guilt and shame, while his insides were breaking, even as his mind tried to heal.

He stayed that way for longer than he thought he would and wound up falling asleep on the carpet in front of the stereo. But the next morning, he felt better, and had the motivation to go on a run.

A stronger motivation than he thought he would, actually.

And so, he changed into jogging clothes and tied on his new Nike running shoes. He stretched out his legs and arms on the front grass of his apartment complex, and when he felt ready, took off running down the sidewalk of the neighborhood in which he lived, but which he had not had much time to get to know.

It was a Saturday morning, the summer sun was shining bright, the air was warm and slightly humid, and he felt great, all of a sudden.

So, he decided to put the past behind him, forgive himself like the therapists always told him he should, and to stop taking credit and blame for the shitty things that had happened in his life.

He decided that day to start living. And he would start by using this weekend to wash up, get his shit together, call Mya, and find some little joy in any way he could.

And that's just what he did.

Until Monday morning, when he walked into Headquarters at Cherry Point, and he was told directly to pack his bags and get battle ready.

He and his unit were shipping out again, not even three months since the last deployment, and he wouldn't be told where they were going until he had his troops on the cargo plane, heading back over the pond.

His mood instantly went to shit, right there amog the bright linoleum floor and flag-decked, fake-wood-paneled walls of the office of his CO.

*For fuck's sake*, he thought, marching back to his car.

*Why the hell did life have to be this fucking way?* he wondered, driving away.

Rage started building behind his eyes, giving him a headache. *Here we go again*, he said to himself.

Rage, indeed.

A violet hued, and deeply purple-winged ArchAngel stood next to his Father, looking down on a man who was ready.

They both knew it, and they also knew that the man below did not.

But seeing the future of the world below, and the haziness of that future, the Father knew that something was coming, and He hoped that they were all ready for it.

The future was usually clear to the Father of All.

He was proud of his Child, and He was proud of the man below. The pain and suffering he had experienced, and the strength he had earned from it, made a formidable Fate Maker, indeed.

A hazy future was worrisome, but manageable.

Jeremiel, however, saw the future a little differently than his Father.

The ArchAngel knew the man below intimately, and instead of having hope of the future, the ArchAngel Jeremiel was nervous.

*No*, he thought, his mind hidden from his Father temporarily. *He wasn't nervous*.

He was terrified.

# Chapter 23

Once again, light brown, almost white, dry, dusty gravel crunched under Kreo's desert-colored, summer-weight, military issued boots.

Sweat poured from under his Kevlar helmet, almost obscuring his sight, if not for the bandana he wore under it. And his nerves were on edge. More than they ever had been before, being in-country.

He kept his head on a swivel, being a good example for his troops. And as he looked around, he saw all fresh faces. Some straight from boot camp, others that had a little salt on them, but they were all new to him. He didn't like that, and he didn't like the anxiety he felt, shared on all those unfamiliar faces, either.

His unit was in the Kabul region of Afghanistan, awaiting word from the Northern Alliance to attack the capital city. It was winter, but Kreo still felt sweat streaking down his body. It wasn't the mild temperatures around him that made him sweat.

It was the pressure.

And not the pressure of command. He was okay with that. No, this pressure was in keeping his troops alive.

All of the officer training courses he had taken told him that he was going to fail in keeping all of his troops alive, however, it was impossible for him to believe that.

He had felt the ramifications of losing troops before. The pain, the guilt, the shame. And the absolute fear of it happening again.

And he couldn't go through that. Not ever again.

So, the pressure.

He was also feeling tons of fear. Trepidation. Angst. All the bad kinds of mindsets that he had been warned about, and which he had seen repeatedly cause failure on the battlefield.

Kreo was sure that as soon as the bullets started flying, he would be right as rain. He felt that as soon as he was put to the test, he would rise to the occasion as he always had.

He just needed to get through this waiting period.

Hurry up and wait, indeed.

So, he moved, and as he did so, he kept his head on a swivel as the late November sun beat down on him and his troops.

They were walking double file through a narrow pass in the mountains just to the east of the large city. It was a simple patrol, and the kind of mindless job that kept troops in shape, and busy, just before a major offensive.

Kreo couldn't hear anything except the constant chatter in the radio strapped to his belt, and in his earpiece, as well as the grinding sound of the gravel under the boots of his troops behind him.

He took several deep breaths, somewhat hampered by the Kevlar vest pressed tightly against this chest, and tried to calm his nerves. He thought he could feel the nervousness and fear from the younger troops around him as well, and that made the anxiety in his own mind and body intensify.

But he kept breathing, kept doing the things to take his mind off the fear, and kept moving forward, a good example for his troops, and for himself, frankly.

The radio squawked in his ear, almost too loudly. He wanted to smile at the jumpiness of his soldiers around him, and at himself. That was, until he heard the voice on the other end of the encrypted military channel in his ear.

"Contact, contact. Taliban spotted in sector 1-9, repeat, Taliban contact, sector 1-9, over!"

Kreo, and the twenty-eight troops behind him were on instant alert. They were dead center in sector nineteen, and the only troops supposed to be in this sector as well.

Kreo threw up his fist, stopping the troops behind him in their tracks, and alerting them to seek shelter. He spun his single finger pointed at the sky, and saw, and heard, his troops seek shelter in any way they could.

Suddenly, it dawned on him, and that's when he opened his eyes fully, and saw where he and his troops were.

They were in a narrow pass through two tall, hilly mountains, and caught in what he had come to learn was a 'kill box.' Kreo's past came rushing back down, an avalanche of memories and sensations, all at once.

"Fuck," was all he said before the bullets started flying.

Bullets came from both sides and above him and his soldiers, and the only thing he was able to utter as the full brunt of the situation came crashing into his consciousness, making his fight or flight sympathetic nervous system kick in, and adrenaline course throughout his body, was a soft warning to his troops.

It wasn't enough, however. They didn't hear him.

Because as his mind was suddenly, and cripplingly, caught in the fear, the anxiety, and the horror of what was happening, once again, it caused Kreo to do the one thing that he had been most afraid of.

In the midst of battle, his troops getting fired on from all sides, and death and pain raining down around him, Kreo froze up, and his entire world imploded brilliantly.

# Chapter 24

"Good God," the ArchAngel Jeremiel uttered.

He was looking down on a scene he had hoped to never see again. And fear coursed through his divine body.

Kreo lay on a dirty, sweat-stained mattress, once again, drugs and bad decisions coursing through the boy's system.

*This wouldn't do*, the ArchAngel said to himself, and he blinked out of the Spiritual Plane, and winked into the Physical, to do something he told himself he wouldn't do again.

But he couldn't let Kreo fail to become all he was to become, and therefore, as he winked into existence, taking on the look of a Marine MP, he reached down into the very center of Kreo's body, Jeremiel's divine hand fading out, and his aura seeping into the boy.

Jeremiel pulled the heroin out of the boy suddenly, and probably painfully for the child, and watched as Kreo's eyes shot open, and looked back at him, accusation and rage making Jeremiel take a step back. Kreo's eyes shut again, but his breathing regulated, and became steadier. He moved in his semi-consciousness and tried to wake.

And before Kreo could come fully into consciousness, and before Jeremiel could utter a word from his human guise, the ArchAngel felt all of existence *shift* around him, and unnatural pain racked the Being.

He was suddenly forced from his human Guise, to be standing next to Kreo in all of his Heavenly Glory.

"What?" the ArchAngel muttered, not knowing how he was suddenly in Angelic form, without expressly willing it to be.

Kreo's eyes were starting to open again, and Jeremiel tried with all of his Heavenly might to change back into a human guise, so as not to startle the young man. But it was no use. The ArchAngel would have had an easier time wishing to be a donkey than reverting back to his human form.

And that was when all of Jeremiel's worst fears were realized. They really had no idea what they were doing making the first Fate Maker in all of existence, and they surely could not control the outcome now.

"Well, shit," was all that Kreo heard when he finally came fully awake to see a seven-and-a-half-foot floating ArchAngel in front of him, and feeling more anger than he ever had in his life.

He answered the ArchAngel's exclamation as his surroundings became clear.

"Well, shit… indeed."

# Chapter 25

Lying on the sweaty, dirty mattress, Kreo's mind, once again, went back over the last couple of days, and once again, over how he had ended up in a dirty building, not unlike the one that he had woken up in years earlier.

And as he watched the hovering ArchAngel, panic in the Being's eyes, he superimposed the image of Mya banging on the dilapidated building's windows with the scene around him.

The rage did not dissipate as his memories flew back to freezing on the battlefield, days prior, and how he had sunk down to the situation he currently found himself in.

Surprisingly, however, as his memories flew uncontrolled through his mind, they were not jumbled and fuzzy from the drugs he had injected.

Rather, his mind and body were clearer than they had been in quite some time.

He felt great, yet the rage burned bright and fierce within his very soul.


Fire rained down from on high, and he heard screams and yells from his troops around him, but he couldn't move. He couldn't think. He was not only caught up in quicksand, but he WAS quicksand.

Static and screams sounded in the earpiece driven into his ear hole, and heat and pain surrounded him.

But the battle and cacophony around him could not hold a candle's whisper to the absolute maelstrom within his mind.

His men were dying, and he couldn't control the storm within him.

For the first time in his life, Kreo was without control of himself. He was an unwilling passenger on a trip his mind took on its own, and all he could do was hold on, tuck his chin, and wait for the ride to end.

A stray thought pulled itself from the fiery hurricane of his consciousness. A whispered voice, almost.

And it was telling him to just give up and die. It sounded a lot like his own voice, but another stray, wispy thought pulled away from the mental orchestra in his head, and it told him to beware the voice.

It was not his own.

It was darkness come alive within, and he could do nothing to stop its incessant whisperings.

The voice of the stray thought grew. It grew, strengthened, and became the only thing of which he was aware.

And he wanted to succumb to its oily, charismatic demands to give in, give up, let it all come crashing down, and to lay down and wait for the end.

He nearly did just that, but an even louder sound came from without, and it broke the frozen quicksand of indecision and absolute terror within.

A buzzing sound came close to his ear, and before he knew it, as in slow motion, blood shot up in front of his eyes, bright and beautiful in the November sunlight glinting off the weapons of the enemy above and around him.

He was shot, a shoulder wound, non-fatal, but enough to move his feet, find his voice, and the pain of the wound brought his mind back into his own control.

The maelstrom of emotions, memories, and terror popped like a lava bubble, and with it, the oily, dark voice.

He turned his head from left to right, letting the pain of his wound clear his mind and his sight.

And he suddenly knew what to do. His training, natural gifts, and experience all kicked in, and he moved with the new plan in his mind, dancing amongst the death around him, his weapon a part of him, his sights on saving his men.

And as his troops watched him come alive, blood dripping down the front of his desert-khaki uniform, rage in his eyes, and death on his mind, they, too, moved with their lieutenant, until the day was won, the wounded and dead were extracted, and Kreo found himself a hero, once again.

But no one knew what had happened within his mind. The fiery, frozen mindset and the oily voice seemed to have whispered and blasted at him for hours, or days, but after hearing the battle stories from his troops, as they decompressed after the simple firefight, he knew it was only a few seconds.

They didn't know he was a fraud, a coward, and a liability now. They didn't know that he would never lead them into battle again.

And as he found the heroin so readily available after taking the capital city of Kabul, and a deserted desert hovel to lose himself in the drugs, his troops didn't know that he had hung up his boots and weapon, to never lead troops again.

As the deep, thick morose and depression swam before his eyes, and the even thicker darkness settled in from shooting up the dark liquid, he was finally ready to die.

The peace that settled over him as darkness closed in was comforting. He found himself back within his mother's dark womb, ready to never exist again.

Until the light penetrated the womb of a mother he could not remember, and he was reborn, to come fully into his power, and to change the Fate around him, the way that he saw fit.

He found himself fully, after the internal and the external battles, and after giving up his life to peacefully drift away, he was reborn, and finding his full power, he fully came alive finally.


The ArchAngel Jeremiel, caught in a horrible inability to Will himself to anywhere else in the entire Existence, on either Plane, watched as the dawning of understanding and comprehension came into the Fate Maker's eyes, the determination and rage coming fully alive, and the world breaking open for it.

And for the first time in all of existence, an ArchAngel almost pissed himself from what he witnessed before him.

The Fate Maker was finally and fully born.

And the Divine had no control over him at all.

# Part 5
# Setting the Stage

# Chapter 26

"With this ring, I thee wed," Kreo said, smiling.

Mya smiled back at Kreo, looking up at him, shining in the sunlight entering in the church from a multi-colored stained-glass window behind the priest.

The glass divided the light shining in, breaking it up into a colorful display of rainbow-hued happiness, and Kreo's eyes shone in the light reflected from the pure white wedding dress Mya wore.

Kreo's smile grew.

"And with this ring, I thee wed," Mya smiled back up at Kreo, finishing the oaths to each other.

"With the power vested in me by our great Creator, and by the State of California, I now pronounce you husband and wife," Father Johnson intoned.

"Kreo," he whispered at the tall man standing before him. A man he had known since the man's boyhood. Kreo turned toward the elderly priest, his eyes wide and nervous.

"Kiss your wife."

Smiling brighter than he ever had in his life, Kreo turned to her, bent down, pulling the love of his life to him, and kissed her squarely on her soft lips.

The beating of his heart, and the stress that had been coursing through his body all that day went away with the kiss, and everything seemed right in the world.

They pulled apart, turned to the five guests sitting together in the first row of the chapel, and walked together down the aisle as clapping and hooting from their friends followed them.

Kreo led his new wife, love of his life, and his best friend in the entire world, who now would be known forever as Mya Fairchild-Green, out to their car to embark on their next adventure.

He loved the sound of that thought as he walked out into the late spring sunshine.

The grass was turning greener in the warm sunshine of Northern California. Trees were blooming, flowers were growing, and Kreo felt fantastic.

And after being halfway around the world for most of the last five years, Kreo was overjoyed to be home.

He was even more excited for his and Mya's honeymoon road trip across the country. It had been Mya's idea.

Father Johnson watched the young couple leave the old chapel with its peeling paint and decades of use and sighed deep in his soul. How he had prayed for the young man at one point in his life, and how, now, Father Johnson prayed even harder.

He knew the burden the man was under.

Father Johnson had seem it in the boy's future since Kreo was a small boy and had watched Kreo overcome extreme odds and survive where many of the children the elderly priest had helped raise perished.

Father Johnson was overcome with emotion watching the man walk out of the chapel with his bride, and whispering a quick blessing under his breath, he walked back to his office to remove his robe, and stole of duty, and find a nice cup of red wine with which to relax in memories.

Kreo turned to look back at the old chapel, remembering days as a child, spent praying and kneeling in the white stucco building, and wishing for the happiness he now felt.

Shadows crept in from the sides, but he kept them at bay.

This was a day of celebration, even if everyone at the wedding, and those wishing him and Mya a safe journey, did not know that he was a fraud and a coward.

And Mya's heart was full.

Joy filled her in knowing that she finally had everything she had ever dreamed of, and the boy of those dreams now would share her life in every way, moving forward, and living forward even more.

She glanced at her new husband's eyes as he tried unsuccessfully to unlock their car door several times. All of their close friends laughed as he grew frustrated at the lock.

He kept turning the key the wrong way, she knew. But she also didn't say anything, seeing the shadows enter his eyes, and leave again, just as suddenly.

The situation was turning funny, but she knew that Kreo was feeling the pressure, so she put her hand over his, calming him instantly, and turned the key the proper way.

Mya knew her husband, and she accepted him fully. *After all,* she thought to herself as she climbed into their now-shared SUV, she had saved not only his life years prior, but hers as well.

He just didn't know that fact.

*And he never would,* she promised herself, as she muttered a quick prayer of gratitude under her own breath and prepared herself to set off on a new and exciting journey with the man she had always loved.

*Maine coastline*, here they came, she thought, as her husband and her future drove forward, gas pedal pressed firmly to the floor.

# Chapter 27

For the week leading up to the wedding, Mya and Kreo had been staying at a wonderful little bed and breakfast right in the heart of Sonoma. It was called Seven Branches, and Mya had instantly fallen in love with it.

And after driving back to their room after the small, intimate wedding, they found themselves in each other's arms, awaiting the next morning, where they would set out for their honeymoon.

But in the meantime, they had a late lunch to attend, with the five guests that they had delicately selected to attend, and which they both looked forward to seeing and visiting, with relish.

Kissing his wife deeply and thinking ahead to where their lives would take them, Kreo found himself excited, half scared, but curious more than anything.

Mya found herself making plans within plans for her new restaurant, children, the whole fantasy.

And they both knew that if they couldn't keep their hands off each other, they would be late, and their friends and family would be half drunk before they got to the meal.

Walking back downstairs to the formal dining area of the bed and breakfast and venue, Kreo and Mya couldn't take their eyes or hands off each other. Happiness swelled in both hearts this day, and they both looked forward to many more days and years of the same.

The richly appointed dining area was empty except for their friends and family. The newly married couple smiled at everyone, and sat at the table, both facing the rest of the group, champagne glasses in hand.

Kreo watched his new wife as each new selection of hand-held food was brought forward from the professional kitchen somewhere in the back.

She judged each according to her own professional eye and pallet. Finding everything to her liking, the luncheon kicked off with a toast and happy, joyful stories swirling around the table.

Tony Lee, Mya's close sub-chef, was the first to offer congratulations to the new marriage.

Kreo liked the man intensely and looked forward to Tony moving with them out to the East Coast to help begin Mya's new restaurant venture.

Kreo knew nothing of the world in which Mya had worked so hard to rise so far, but he was as supportive for her career as she was of him finding his own calling and purpose.

He had spent the last six months trying to figure out what he was going to do with that very life. He was still at a crossroads but knew it would be something fantastic.

Just as his mind was ruminating on that very thing, his old war buddy, Ramirez, spoke up from the other end of the table and asked that question.

"So, LT, what're you gonna do now?" he asked Kreo.

Kreo smiled back at the young man. Memories came flooding into his mind, and he was almost washed away in them.

But Mya squeezed his hand on top of the pure white tablecloth, and he answered in the only way he could.

With humor.

"Don't know, buddy. Probably run for president or something," he joked.

Everyone laughed, even Mya. But Kreo was keenly aware that he really had no idea. He'd had a taste for music early on, and was then a soldier.

He really had no other experience.

He wondered, briefly, how to put those two things together.

But then he was brought back to the meal, and the task at hand. It was a day of celebration and joy. Not a day to get lost in the melancholy of his indecision and unease of the future.

And so, he enjoyed his and Mya's friends. And then he enjoyed a long walk in the grounds of Seven Branches, and most of downtown Sonoma.

Memories of a childhood in this place were pleasant for once.

The trees were bright, birds were chirping, flowers were growing, and the love of his life was on his arm.

He was happy and fulfilled this day. But worry for the future still nagged at his mind, not letting him forget that he didn't have a job, nor a drive to find what he was made for.

He shrugged it off later that evening, once again alone with the love of his life. He would figure it out. He was sure of it.

As he lay down with his wife, her warm body cuddled closely into his, the heavy blanket covering them both, and a stillness permeating the air, his mind grew foggy with sleep rolling in, and a dream like no other he had ever had.

*He was back at the side of his late father's gravestone. Kreo looked down at his body, and saw himself in his Marine desert uniform, weapons bristling at his waist and strapped to his back.*

*He could feel the heaviness of several magazines for his automatic rifle, and the flak vest pulled at his shoulders.*

*"That armor won't help you at all, where we are going," a voice said above him. Kreo started from the sound and looked up. What he beheld caught his breath.*

*It was the ArchAngel again. The same one from the all-too-real dream of his childhood, but unlike that time, the ArchAngel was now resplendent in gleaming purple armor, his violet wings spread out behind him like a cloud.*

*The armor caught Kreo's attention, and he knew he was taking too long staring at it.*

*But the ArchAngel seemed not to mind, so he took more time looking at it. And then at the double-bladed weapon, with mist leaking off of it, floating at the ArchAngel's side.*

*Kreo couldn't believe that the weapon seemed to be floating in thin air, just within arm's reach of the Being. But Kreo's focus went instantly back to the armor.*

*At first look, it seemed to be a suit of armor made during the medieval era, but in what Kreo could only describe as a steampunk form.*

*But what caught Kreo's attention more than anything was that the armor seemed to be writhing and moving like an older piece of machinery, or the innards of a sophisticated watch.*

*Kreo watched as the ArchAngel Jeremiel's armor reformed, and clicked around, protecting various parts of the Being's body. When the ArchAngel moved, his armor moved to protect and enforce whatever part was closest or most open to enemy attack.*

How peculiar, *Kreo thought to himself.*

*The ArchAngel smiled, as if he could read Kreo's mind.* Maybe he could, *Kreo thought again.*

*Soon, the ArchAngel cleared his throat, and motioned for Kreo to do something. Kreo was suddenly confused.*

*The ArchAngel rolled his eyes, barely perceptible in the shadows covering his handsome face. The shadows were made by the hair that cascaded in purple rivers down the ArchAngel's head.*

*But Kreo could tell he was supposed to know something critical.*

*Finally the ArchAngel spoke again.*

*"You ARE the Fate Maker, are you not?" he asked.*

*Kreo was silent. But at the same time, a nagging pull came to him from his very center.*

His very soul, *he thought.*

*"As the Fate Maker, you can easily bend this place to your will," the tall Being said. "And as I said before - that armor won't help you at all, where we are going."*

Kreo looked back down at this Marine uniform, perfect for warfare in the Middle East, but he suddenly realized that they wouldn't be going to the Middle East.

And so, Kreo made the dream world around him shift, and he was wearing the same form of armor as the ArchAngel, but smaller, and still camouflage-colored.

He could feel the armor wiggle and move around his body, and he felt like he was wearing almost nothing at all.

He kept his automatic rifle, sidearm, and ammo, however. That made the tall ArchAngel smile brightly.

"So be it," the Being said.

And then the two of them were in a different place altogether.


Kreo found himself suddenly standing next to the ArchAngel on a large stone outcropping, over a chasm which he could only describe as the pits of Hell.

There were flashes and flurries, steel ringing against steel, and loud bursts of light all about him. He was overcome with the sights and sounds of a battle the likes of which he had never seen and could never fathom in his wildest dreams.

The scene around him made the worst battle in his own life seem like a playground scuffle.

He could see several other equally fantastically arrayed ArchAngels fighting what seemed like darkness itself.

*And as if reading Kreo's mind, the ArchAngel next to him spoke for the first time in this dark place.*

*"These are my brothers and sisters. Both Ilks, and all of the Heavenly Hosts of Angels fighting amongst them," Jeremiel said.*

*"For this, Fate Maker, you were born, and for this, you were given Favor." The ArchAngel looked down on Kreo.*

*Kreo swallowed loudly.*

*"And it is for this very War you must hone your powers, and make something of your very life," he said, his voice getting louder in the abyss of space around Kreo.*

*And as Kreo processed the ArchAngel's words again, and looked up at the growing battles around him, a piece of the darkness separated from the ruckus below and approached the rock outcropping where Kreo and the ArchAngel stood.*

*Kreo suddenly saw a flurry of dark armor and evil metal moving toward him, looking for all the world as the exact opposite of the tall Being standing beside him.*

*He fired his automatic weapon at the encroaching Darkness and grinding metal, but only created sparks as the impacted bullets bounced off the being bearing down on him.*

*And as that darkness grew closer, the voice of the ArchAngel grew louder in his ears.*

*Kreo stumbled back in horror of the coming Death, but the ArchAngel Jeremiel simply took hold of the double-bladed halberd hovering still at his side, and swung the mighty weapon in a great, colorful arc.*

*The sound of nightmares and horror was like a clanging bell, as the Diamond-Steel weapon found purchase in the melee of metal before him.*

*"You must join us!" The ArchAngel's pained voice sounded loudly in Kreo's ears as the young man forced himself, and the splendid armor he had created, back to the world of the living, and felt all of creation* shift *around him, once more.*

Kreo Fairchild, the Fate Maker, awoke in a cold sweat, his hands still knotted around the handle of a gun that did not exist, and the screams of the ArchAngels doing battle loud in his mind.

He knew he wouldn't find any more sleep this night.

But then his logical brain took over, and he willed himself back into a light snooze, lying easy next to his new wife, and forced his mind to dream again of the simple future he wanted before him.

A much different future than the one the ArchAngel had shown him this night.

Two Beings looked down on the sleeping Fate Maker and had hope that the man growing to become something in the Material World he knew would become something even more in the Spiritual Plane he had just been given a glimpse of.

The hope of both Beings would be tested in more ways to come, despite their absolute best efforts.

The gleaming, armor-clad ArchAngel Jeremiel looked down on Kreo and had more doubt than his Father, the Creator of All, standing beside him.

And the Creator looked down on his Favored child, and still felt at peace. *After all*, the Creator of all the Universe, and both Planes of existence, thought to Himself, *there were many more things they would have to do before the Celestial Cataclysm fully took place.*

His unbounded mind went to plans within plans within plans.

Only He knew what was to come, and how it may very well be stopped before it ever even happened at all.

The Creator, the Father, the God of all, looked down on his child, and smiled.

# Chapter 28

The very next morning, Kreo and his new wife, Mya Fairchild-Green, started out on their honeymoon road trip, with tall cups of coffee and a music playlist Mya assured her husband would not repeat the same song twice, all the way to the East Coast.

They pulled up their brand-new SUV in front of the coffee and bookstore in the sleepy village, deep in the Napa Valley wine country.

It was a quaint little clapboard building, resplendent in summer décor, and already a little line of early risers waiting for their turn to make a coffee selection or browse through shelves of eclectic book covers had formed.

As was their custom, Mya stood in line to get their coffees while Kreo went into the building to find some small gift for his new wife, or even something for himself to while away the miles when it was Mya's turn to drive on the road trip before them.

Perusing the aisles of books, he thought about both his dream the night before, and his impending future and lack of prospects. He couldn't help it.

Catching his attention, and making him pause in his shopping, was a book on angels. It looked scholarly, and at the same time, had a cover resembling a fictional fantasy book.

He wanted it and didn't understand the compulsion. It wasn't one of his normal types of books.

And then he walked near books in a section covering current events and autobiographies.

Pictures of famous celebrities and politicians on the covers caught his attention as well. One stood out more than any other because he knew the man on the cover. Or at least, had heard of him.

Admiral James Scott's book on motivation and leading, bought by thirty years in the top echelons of the military war machine, was titled *No Excuses*.

Kreo thought the title was apt to his own situation as he picked up the book and added it with the one on angels, both now held tightly in his hands.

He finished his small purchases with a curio of an angel made in the visage of a small, kneeling, child. He had seen others like it in Mya's old apartment.

He looked at the name label on the underside of the kneeling angelic child. "Precious Moments," it was called.

He assumed his wife collected the adorable figurines. He hoped she did not already own the kneeling angel child.

He met Mya back at the car, exchanging bought items. She exclaimed loudly over the child figurine, and Kreo filed away the fact that she both loved it and collected the figures.

That was why he loved Mya. She loved simple things, and beautiful things, and like him, things that may just need fixed.

He got behind the wheel and headed out of town as Mya looked over the books he had purchased. She understood the military biography but could not place the book about angels.

So, she asked Kreo about it. He dodged the subject by just mumbling, "It looked interesting."

She knew there was more to the story but dropped it as Kreo pulled out onto the highway, heading east, and to their future.

Within several minutes, Kreo pulled the new SUV, richly appointed and, at least for this first morning of the road trip, smelling of thick coffee, out onto I-80 north and east, and headed toward Salt Lake City.

The surrounding greenery and wonderfully rolling hills would turn into deep desert and even more scenic views as the new couple drove through some of the most beautiful, descriptive, landscapes, that  highly characterized the United States.

As he drove, Kreo grew more into his love of his country and his marriage. He had been lucky meeting Mya, and even luckier that despite everything, she seemed to love him.

As for Mya, she settled into her seat, often glancing over at her husband. Memories overlay themselves in her mind as she saw Kreo at various times of his life, and how she had loved him through each phase.

She was excited for what lay ahead, and the easy silence opened between them as usual. They listened to Mya's road trip playlist on the stereo and smiled easily at each other as the miles fell away behind them.

Soon that afternoon, the mountains arose ahead of them, and Mya offered to drive. Kreo happily turned over the wheel, trusting in his wife as he always had.

He had never looked at Mya as a weaker person because she was a woman. He wanted to protect her, of course, but he knew that she was stronger and more able then he would ever be.

And as his wife took over the wheel, he pulled out the books that he had purchased that morning.

The military autobiography was as he assumed it would be. He had heard the same advice the admiral gave, for years.

But the book on angels, especially ArchAngels, grabbed his attention, and he was soon lost in the history and appearances of the ArchAngels to people all through history.

As the couple approached Lake Tahoe to the south of I-80, and Reno straight ahead, Mya would get Kreo's attention to look at the mountains and scenery outside the windows. He would glance up from his new book, but not for long.

The book was just that interesting.

Finally, Mya stopped interrupting her husband's attention, and instead found her own serenity in the beautiful scenery moving by outside her car.

Kreo could not believe the information which he was reading. And it had started with the fact that there were fifteen ArchAngels mentioned in different religious texts throughout history.

But instead of taking other people's accounts of what and how they had appeared to heart, he remembered dreams in his life where he was very much aware of the fifteen ArchAngels.

Because he had seen them firsthand. Every single one of them.

Kreo read about the earliest writings concerning ArchAngels. He read about the deuterocanonical Book of Tobit, and how it described the nine levels of angels, with ArchAngels being the top.

He read about early Jewish literature, like the Book of Enoch, which mentioned even more ArchAngels.

It spoke of two humans who had been transformed into ArchAngels by God, for their faithful work during their lives as prophets.

Kreo went on to read canonical descriptions of the first seven ArchAngels. They were older than the other eight mentioned in teachings like Zoroastrianism.

Zoroastrianism mentioned beings called *Amesha Spenta*, or "Holy Immortals," and especially detailed the exploits of one named Ahura Mazda.

In Zoroastrianism, the beings were said to inhabit immortal bodies that were able to operate in both planes of existence.

They were sent to Earth to protect, guide, and inspire humanity and the spirit world. In one text, called the Avesta, it explained the origin and nature of these ArchAngels.

Kreo went on to read about the very nature of these Beings in the Hebrew Bible. In Hebrew, they were called the *malakhi Elohim*, or Angels of God.

The word for angel in this text was *malakh*, meaning 'messenger.' So, literally, they were sent on Missions from on High.

That made sense to Kreo's soldier sense. He had often been sent on missions from command.

He spent the rest of the afternoon reading about ancient literature like the Kabbalah, which mentioned twelve ArchAngels in two distinct groupings.

The Talmud mentioned three of the top ArchAngels, and in both Merkavah and Kabbalist mysticism, again, it spoke about how humans were made into ArchAngels.

And in Medieval Jewish philosophy, a full and complete angelic hierarchy was described.

There were fifteen ArchAngels, in two different groupings, or Ilk's, and they were all mentioned by name.

In alphabetical order, they were named, and their names were:

Ariel

Azrael

Chamuel

Gabriel

Haniel

Jeremiel

Jophiel

Metatron
Michael
Raguel
Raphael
Raziel
Phanuel
Uriel
Zadkiel

And they were given symbols in ancient pictorial writings, including Sanskrit, Hebrew, Sumerian, Aramaic, and Hindi.

Among all of his reading he kept seeing these symbols, and as he turned a page, a huge rendering wheel of these symbols appeared.

The picture was one of those that felt like it had always been in his life, and it gave him a weird sense of déjà vu.

The book called it the Sigil, and it was both awesome and fearsome.

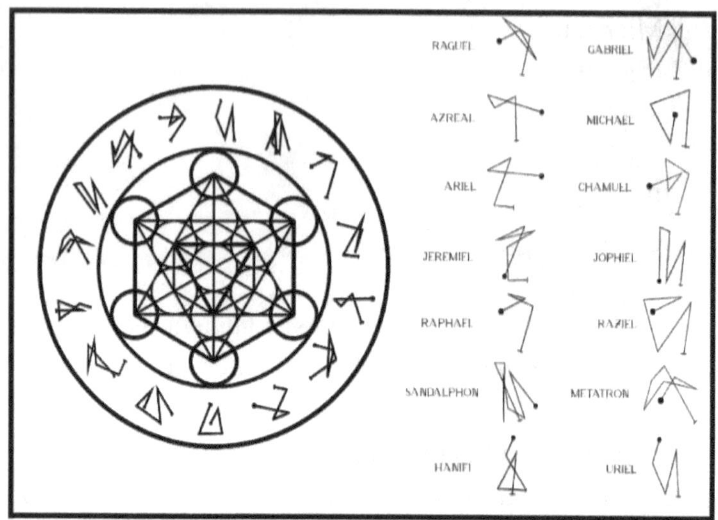


The Sigil burned in Kreo's heart, and it was enflamed in his mind for the rest of his life.

He kept reading.

In Kreo's own history and life, and being raised in the Catholic traditions, he only knew of three that were mentioned, however, as he read he learned that when the ArchAngel Raphael introduces himself in Tobit 12, he recognizes himself as the first of eight ArchAngels.

And then in Eastern Orthodox traditions, thousands of angels are mentioned, however only seven ArchAngels are venerated by name.

So, in all of human history, and religious teachings, Kreo could only actually produce a group of fourteen named

ArchAngels, and one that several religions believe was the top of the ArchAngel echelons.

The name gave him what he could only call heartburn.

That Being was named Metatron. Kreo looked back at the Sigil and saw that same name again.

"Sounds like a Transformer," Kreo said out loud. However, Mya didn't hear him over the music coming from the radio.

He needed more information. The mention of this singular Being was enticing, but hardly answered any of the hundreds of questions that Kreo had.

The first one was easy. Why did the name Metatron bring such abject feelings to his chest? He needed clarity and more information.

The book on ArchAngel history was comprehensive, but he needed to know more. And more than anything, he needed to know why and how these ArchAngels seemed to pop up into his life from time to time.

He had told no one about the dreams of the ArchAngels, nor his ability to sometimes change things. He had kept all of that to himself.

And as he read the concluding chapter of the book, a line toward the end grabbed his attention more than any other bit of information he had read.

It basically alluded to the fact that while the ArchAngels were messengers, and blessed with powers beyond his understanding, they seemed to be made for combat and war more than anything else.

And a single word grabbed him more than that. The mention of beings called 'Watchers,' and how the ArchAngels had warred with these Fallen Angels more than anything or anyone else in history.

When he read the word 'Watchers,' his ears started ringing loudly, and he felt a complete sense of déjà vu, as well as instant dizziness.

He looked over at his new wife, singing along to an Alanis Morissette song, and happily oblivious.

But Kreo wasn't happy or oblivious.

He was suddenly terrified of the future, and he knew that somehow he was smack dab in the middle of something that he had no understanding, nor inclination, of his part in.

The bubble of terror and fear grew in his belly, and he knew that bubble had always been there, and wasn't going anywhere, anytime soon.

He would very soon come to know and understand just exactly why he was terrified of the Watchers, and who and what they really were.

"Why me?" he asked himself.

He had no idea, but as much as he wanted to ignore his life, and what the future held, he felt that these ArchAngels, who he had spent the last six hours studying, would never let him forget.

*He was in this, for better or worse,* he thought, as he looked out the window at the growing duskiness of the sky, and the beauty of the world.

He took ahold of Mya's hand as she drove toward the east, and into the deepening gloom of Kreo's mind.

He held her tight, wishing that he had never heard of ArchAngels, Metatron, or this other group of beings, the ones called the Watchers.

What the hell were the Watchers, and why did that word, among so many others that had given him conniptions this afternoon, worry him so much?

He said the words again, feeling the taste of them in his mouth, and wanted to spit out the window.

He suddenly grew chilly in the heat of the spring evening. The Watchers were going to take up a lot of his time in the future, he knew.

He chewed on the words again and knew that his studying was nowhere near complete.

The Watchers.

*Not yet at least*, he thought at last, closing the book, and focusing back on the day at hand.

# Chapter 29

The happy newlyweds finally arrived at their first destination, right outside the sprawling valley metropolis of Salt Lake City. Here, they would start the first part of their celebrations.

But at the same time, Kreo had an ulterior motive. He wanted to find more books on these things happening to him and in his life.

As Mya and Kreo drove down into the Salt Lake valley, Kreo looked at maps on his cell phone to find their bed and breakfast. Mya turned on the FM radio to find local music but found a talk news report instead.

"As the Russian President, Vladimir Komarov, is sworn into office, his counterpart in the People's Republic of China is sworn in as well," the female news anchor intoned.

"Xi Gongping, who the world learned, early last year, is the leader of the new Communist Party in China. The government coup he led, which toppled the thousand-year reign of the last dynasty, killing some thirty-five thousand Chinese nationalists, took the reins of a country fast moving into global leadership in both economic and military strength," she went on.

Kreo had heard enough of world events to last a lifetime, and therefore, he reached over and shut off the news report.

"Let me find this hotel, love," he said to Mya. She simply nodded and drove under his guidance to their first honeymoon spot.

The couple drove up State Street and found the first stay of their honeymoon road trip.

The Inn on the Hill popped up in front of them on the left-hand side of the road, and the splendor of the hundred-year-old home astounded both of the newlyweds.

It was a dark evening, and the clouds were pressing in close overhead, threating rain, but the beauty and dark mystery of the hundred-years-plus homes of the neighborhood around Capitol Hill were breathtaking.

Right across from the bed-and-breakfast that they would be spending two nights was an equally historical home, build in the old revival gothic style.

The newlyweds smiled at each other in the bright, florescent lights coming from the street outside where they parked in the rear of the bed-and-breakfast.

This was their kind of neighborhood, and style of living.

They both excitedly walked into the century-old home, and the proprietor behind the desk in the inside hallway smiled at them with a knowing grin. He was an older man, his gray hair sprouting from the top of his head in disarray, but his clothes and manner were impeccably genteel.

"Welcome to the Great Salt Lake, lovies, I am Morris, and welcome to my home," he said with a midwestern accent and a soundless clap of his overlarge hands. He made the young couple feel right at ease.

While Mya chatted with Morris about the amenities of the bed-and-breakfast, Kreo found himself wandering through the lower level of the old gothic home, lovingly caressing the hand-carved wood of the bookcases and the staircase banister.

He loved the feel of old beeswax and the shine of careful upkeep and painstaking maintenance obvious in the condition of the furnishings.

He soon found himself in a wood-paneled room, resplendent in dark maroons and heavily shined mahogany. The darkly-finished wooden floor was covered with an ancient Chinese pattern rug, and pots near the windows were overhung with emerald-green ivy.

The room reminded him of old pictures of men's brandy rooms, heavy with cigar smoke and wisdom swirling through the air in discussions of politics, the weather, or the state of the world, spoken through the lips of gray-haired, venerable old men.

A red-felted pool table stood in the middle of the large room, and dark reddish-brown leather chairs dotted the remainder of the space. He felt right at home and looked forward to a game or two of billiards with his new bride.

A large bookcase made up the easternmost wall, and he wandered over to it, thinking instantly of the last several hours in the car, and his study of angelic matters.

He wanted to find more to read concerning this topic here in one of the most religious cities in the world, and as he perused the spines of several leather-bound books, he wanted very much for a title to jump out at him.

Alas, the bookcase was overheavy with several tomes of early American literature, and the required English works by Dickens, Keats, and Shakespeare.

Soon, Mya found him, sitting in one of the heavy leather chairs, staring off into the flames leaping brightly in the gas fireplace filling the opposite end of the room from the bookcase.

She walked up to her new husband and placed both of her hands on his strong shoulders, silently asking him to accompany him up to their room.

He picked up their bags – still sitting in front of Morris's front desk, and after bidding the elderly innkeeper a goodnight, made his way up the wide wooden stairs behind his wife, and followed her into the room at the end of the second-floor hallway.

As he entered the heavily decorated and sweet-smelling room, looking at his new wife in the glow of the amber-shaded lamps, he had a sudden inspirational thought.

He thought instantly back down to the room he had sat in, waiting for his wife to speak to the innkeeper, and he knew that was a snapshot. It was a bubble of time and memory that he would never get back again.

And in those bubbles – some in war, and some in peace, some in love and some lying on dirty mattresses in flop houses – those bubbles would never come again.

And more importantly, and in some ways regretfully, they didn't last forever.

It was the last thought he had before he succumbed to his new wife's amorous looks and got to know her deep into the night, in that age-old normal and most biblical way of newlyweds.

The very next day, the rain settled in for what looked like the week, which Morris, the sweet elderly innkeeper, told them was typical for that part of the season.

"It'll rain a monsoon, and the next day, the kiddos go and hike the mountain trails in the canyons. You'll see, you don't like the weather in the great state of Utah, stick around a day," he joked.

"It'll change the next," he finished the joke, laughing at this own wit.

That didn't quite make sense to Kreo, as hiking the trails in the canyon just to the south of the city was one of the things they had wanted to do, but he decided that he could find ways to pass the time in the steady rain in other, equally pleasurable pursuits.

Mya, on the other hand, after another quick tryst that very same morning, wanted to see the city, even in the rain, and wanted to do a bit of shopping, as well as trying local, religious-based foods.

Finding and sampling local cuisine was another of the reasons that Mya was so keen on this honeymoon road trip, rather than a destination vacation.

Being a world-renowned chef, as well as a restauranter, and a major foodie, Mya had quickly and permanently turned Kreo into quite a food snob.

However, he, unlike Mya, had sampled foods all over the world in his military travels, and hoped to one day take her to places he had been.

Like the amazing country, and food, of Asia Minor, better known as Turkey.

The food in that country was hands down the best he had ever had.

So, with gathered information from both Morris and Morris's lovely wife, Mildred, and umbrellas handy, the newlywed couple set off in their vehicle to find parking downtown, amongst shopping, restaurants, and, to Kreo's hope, bookstores.

The heavy, gray, wet clouds pressed in close, and the day dimmed with the diminished sunlight, but that did not dampen the spirits of either Kreo or Mya.

Streetlights were still burning due to the gloominess of the day, and the bright lights reflected off the numerous puddles dotting the hills and close roads surrounding downtown Salt Lake City.

The couple was in love, they were young, fit, and healthy, and with some money in the bank from both Kreo's military duties and Mya's successful restaurant in San Francisco, they set off on their leisurely day of bliss.

Finding parking on a rainy Monday afternoon was easily accomplished, and soon Kreo and Mya were holding hands, looking for coffee, a snack, and good shopping.

The sidewalks were deserted, the puddles from the heavy rain were fun to hop across, and wearing both boots and heavy sweaters packed for their fall trips in the New England area, the couple was as comfortable as could be.

That is, until Kreo was weighted down with bags of goods that Mya couldn't do without. She was in her version of heaven, being with the man of her dreams, shopping high-end stores, and loving the rainy, clean air of northern Utah.

Kreo could smell the salt in the air from the lake to their north, and while he, too, loved the rain, he was more on a mission than he let on to his wife.

Finding a small bakery that served gourmet coffee, Kreo sat his wife in a booth with her cell phone, a large cappuccino, and fresh chocolate croissant.

He looked around and saw that the shop was practically deserted, and upon asking the barista why that was, on such a gloomy weather day, he learned that the small shop catered to the protestant members of the city, and not the over-heavy population of LDS parishioners.

Apparently, he learned from the young girl, members of the Church of Jesus Christ of Latter-Day Saints did not partake of caffeine nor heavy sugar. Anything that could replace God, she told him, was frowned upon.

And the proprietors of the small shop were routinely threatened with being forced out of town.

*Just the kind of people he wanted to make friends with,* Kreo thought, as he headed back out into the rain.

He waved at his wife and blew her a kiss, as she smiled at him and took a sip from her large cup of coffee. He was in mission mode to drop all of the bags off at the car, and then find a particular bookstore.

He wanted to purchase something he had only that morning found on the internet that a bookstore nearby, which was another shop outside of the heavy control of the LDS church, claimed on its website to have.

Finally dropping off the numerous bags and packages he had been carrying for his wife at the SUV a block from the coffee shop, he turned up the street in the opposite direction, crossed over a busy intersection, and walked into a brightly painted storefront called Central Book Exchange.

The store was small, and stuck between two other equally small businesses, but the bright orange paint on the bricks of the building and the vast selection of books in the large front windows drew Kreo, and several other pedestrians in this part of town, into the warmth and nostalgically dusty paper smells of the interior.

Knowing exactly what he wanted, he immediately went to the information desk at the rear of the store and asked the young man standing behind the computer for it.

"Let's see," the teenager said.

He quickly clicked the keys on the ancient computer taking up most of the table he stood behind.

"*The Book of Enoch, Apocrypha Writings*," the boy said under his breath.

Kreo stood silently, nervous for some reason. He knew that there was a heavy population of religious zealots in this city, and he didn't want to stand out and possibly get run out of town by citizens carrying torches and pitchforks.

He knew his imagination was running wild, but he couldn't help himself.

He felt on the verge of an understanding that he had been searching for his entire life.

The book he was looking for was mentioned several times in the single angelic book that he had read on the trip to this city. But he still had no idea what it really was.

That's why he wanted it.

The teenager finished his typing and looked back up at Kreo. Kreo swallowed noticeably.

"Alright, looks like we do not have just that writing, but it is included in a book called *Missing Books of the Bible: Removed in the 19th Century*," the young man said.

He then told Kreo to follow him.

The two of them walked in single file between several rows of old books, new books, and magazines and newspapers.

The heavy dust smell of the old books made Kreo's nose tick, and he almost sneezed on two separate occasions.

But he refrained, as he did not want to offend anyone by not being completely in love with the smell, like so many others around the store.

He had overheard the topic come up more than once.

"Here we are, sir." The teen pulled up short at a tall bookcase in the middle of the large room. Kreo almost ran into the boy, as he had stopped so quickly.

The teenager reached up to the top shelf and pulled down a dark book with white squares on the front. There was writing inside the squares, but Kreo couldn't see it until the boy handed the book to him.

"Thank you," was all Kreo could say.

He was already engrossed in the book. He barely heard the boy answer with the usual, "Let me know if you need anything else." Kreo was already opening the cover.

The title page made his chest soar. At the top was the title of the book in a beautiful script-like font. And immediately under the title was a beautiful rendering of a gothic cross. A diamond was made from the filigree in the middle of the drawing of the cross.

The author of the book was simply called 'The Holy Prophets,' and it was published by Peachtree Press.

The publishing company's logo was at the bottom of the page, a large tree between two stacks of books. Perfect, Kreo said to himself.

And then he turned to the table of contents and his breath caught. There it was, halfway down the page. The

*Book of Enoch.* But above it were the page numbers for what was labeled as 'Apocrypha,' and a list of over fifteen other books.

Kreo knew that he had to have this book, and he knew that he would study every single word.

He was excited to read something outside of the age-old Bible he had grown up with, and he knew that answers would be found between the pages of the book he clutched to his chest as he walked back up to pay for it.

What he didn't know at that time was that reading this heavy book would kick off more than a decade of research and wisdom in the years to come.

His life changed once again in that bright, garishly-orange-painted bookstore.

And as Kreo walked back out into the rain, determined to gather up his wife and make his way back to the warm, mahogany-lined room at the bed-and-breakfast to read the rainy afternoon away, even the young man who had sold him the book had no idea how the simple transaction that day, amongst hundreds of others, would eventually change the whole of existence, forever.

# Chapter 30

Leaving Salt Lake was difficult for both members of the new Fairchild family, but they had to press on east. They had serious appointments to make on the eastern coast, and they couldn't miss them.

But they were already making bonds with places they had stayed on their trip, and it was getting more difficult to leave the beauty of the United States as they made their way through it.

The newly married couple drove south from Salt Lake on I-15, to meet up with I-70 E.

When they had made the itinerary for this trip, Kreo only had a few places he really wanted to see. One of them was a place he had been as a teenager, and one he wanted to share with his new bride.

Bishop Castle, right outside Pueblo, Colorado.

And so, they made their way into the Centennial State, and drove toward the western face of the great Rocky Mountains.

Kreo drove most of the way, as Mya had almost no experience in driving through mountains, and he also felt bad for making her drive most of the way from California to Utah while he studied the book about angels.

Thinking about that book made him yearn for the newest book of his collection on the angelic situation happening in his own life.

He wanted to go back to the warm, darkly-painted room at the bed-and-breakfast in Salt Lake and continue reading the books removed from the Bible.

He didn't understand a lot of it, but the *Book of Enoch* was the most interesting.

It mentioned in length the ArchAngels and the Watchers. He read over several passages many times to understand the old words.

He was beginning to get a better understanding of the heavenly Beings, but he was still so far away from where he wanted to be in the ancient knowledge.

Several hours into their trip to their next destination, Mya began to discuss the differences in types of Mexican foods, and her desire to try both the local 'green sauce' variety that southern Colorado was known for, and the more spicy 'red sauce' variety so popular in places like New Mexico, Arizona, and Texas.

And so, as they neared the Vail Pass on I-70, Kreo adjusted their route, and took the exit for 24 South, toward Leadville and Mounts Lincoln, Harvard, and Antero.

*They were really going to do some mountain driving now,* he thought.

That's how the couple found themselves, after nine hours of driving through an eventless, rainy day, pulling up in the evening gloom to a small town, smack dab in the middle of the state, called Westcliffe.

They began looking for a hotel or a motel to stay the night. Also, they were famished, and really wanted some decent food.

Driving into town from the west, they saw quaint little shops, a number of four-by-four pickups, and several midwestern wood-framed buildings full of outrigging shops, bakeries, and liquor stores.

One liquor store, in particular, stood out amongst the rest, due to its bright lights, its attachment to a small, two-story motel, and the tall, Christmas-tree-lights-adorned stature of a deer out front.

*It was an exceptionally large deer, so must be an elk,* Kreo thought as they drove closer and slowed.

"This looks like an adventure," Mya said as Kreo pulled into the parking lot facing the motel rooms on two floors.

"Indeed," was all Kreo could say, as he looked to the west and the three tall peaks of mountains still shining white on the tops, even this late into the year.

The view was breathtaking.

They got out of the car together, stepping into the crisp, late summer air. The clouds had followed them from Utah, and the sky was dark and gray.

It was cooler than they had figured, so Kreo reached into the backseat and retrieved their rain jackets. As Mya put her jacket on, she shivered in the absence of the sunlight she was more accustomed to.

They walked into the brightly lit liquor store to inquire about a room and a hot meal. Kreo assured Mya that they would get a bottle of something good before retiring for the night.

They were still in a celebratory mood; however, they were both pretty tired from the long car ride that day.

Standing behind the short counter and surrounded by colorful bottles and liquor labels was a muscular man with a short, dark beard, piercing eyes, and an easy smile.

He greeted them loudly as they walked through the showroom floor, and it was hard to not grin back at the large, boisterous man.

"Howdy folks, come right in!" the man boomed across the small space. Kreo looked around at the small shop, but saw that they were alone with the man, and he was obviously speaking to them.

Kreo walked up to the man and was at a height with him. *Big guy*, Kreo thought to himself, as he pulled his wallet out of his jeans, and inquired about a room for the night.

"Sure, sure, no worries," the man said. "I'll ring the missus and get you squared away."

No sooner had Kreo and Mya could turned and started looking at the neatly arranged bottles, than a woman came in, with an even more inviting smile, and scooped them up in a huge rush out another door, and back toward their vehicle and the motel rooms.

She pulled a key from a front pocket, exclaiming over Mya's beautiful dark hair, and wishing secretly that hers wasn't as blonde.

"Around here," she told the new bride, who walked into the small, cramped motel room behind the energetic woman, "dark hair is revered. Too much old Dutch blood, really," she said.

She smiled at the newlyweds knowingly and asked if they were just wed.

"We are!" Mya told the woman, and they shared a secret smile that Kreo could not decipher. He assumed it was just a woman's thing and went about looking at the small but adequate room.

"Well, you met my husband inside. His name is Brian, but everyone since he was born just calls him 'Moose,'" the friendly woman told the couple.

"Alrighty, check out is at ten, and if you need anything, just dial zero on the phone there," she said.

And with that, she was back out the door into the evening gloom and still heavily damp air.

"What just happened?" Kreo asked his bride as she sat down on the soft bed.

"No idea, but let's go find some food," Mya answered. "I'm so hungry, I can eat that moose outside."

"I think that's an elk, dear," Kreo replied.

He smiled, and she smiled in return.

*Man, he loved this woman*, he thought as he followed her back out into the wet, heavy air and darkening sky.

Walking down the somewhat busy main street of Westcliffe, they soon found themselves standing in the parking lot of a nice little restaurant and motel mix, a block off the main road.

*Seemed like every business in this small mountain town doubled as something else*, Kreo thought.

The sign above the door said it was the Silver Cliff Mountain Inn and Restaurant, but another sign directly below the main one said, "AKA Willie's."

That made them both laugh.

Soon, they were inside the warm, casual yet comfortable restaurant, being seated by a lovely rotund woman named Dot.

She took them to a rear booth near the wood pellet stove and gave them both menus. She suggested the sweet, iced tea, and the nightly special of Chicken Fried Chicken.

"What is chicken fried chicken?" Kreo asked his world-renowned chef of a wife.

She merely shrugged. "I assume just fried chicken," she said.

They soon both found out with overflowing plates of a huge serving of fried chicken, smashed flat and heavily breaded, served with mashed potatoes, white gravy, and sweet corn.

"So, it's basically chicken fried steak, but made with a tenderized chicken breast instead. Interesting," Mya said, digging in.

"Goodness," Kreo said to Mya. "No wonder we have an obesity issue in this country." Mya just grinned around a large mouthful of chicken and mashed potatoes, smiling back at her husband.

But both plates were soon wiped clean with the basket of rolls, glasses were empty of iced tea, and their stomachs were so full they knew they would need a long walk to sleep comfortably.

And they did just that.

Walking around the small town, looking into windows, and smelling the sweet mountain air was exhilarating. The mountains that surrounded the small valley that the town was nestled in were daunting, and still snowcapped.

Mya and Kreo both felt right at home in the small town.

"It's like something out of a Hallmark movie," Mya told her husband, her hand warmly ensconced in his, and both of them able to see their breath in front of them.

"I would love to see it at Christmas," she told him as they walked back to their room at the Antler Inn.

"We'll have to come back and visit then," he told her as they got ready for bed, and another drive the next day.

However, Kreo was excited to share Bishop Castle with his wife, and he knew it was only a thirty-minute drive from where they lay down their heads.

They would be there the next morning.

He fell asleep remembering the time that the boys' home had taken him and several of his fellow classmates to the handmade castle, snuggled deep in the Green Mountains.

The very mountain range that lay just to the east of Westcliffe, Colorado.

The next day dawned bright, clear, and dry. Kreo left the room early to get in a short walk and hopefully find cups of coffee to surprise his wife with.

He left her sleeping soundly and smiled as he lightly closed the door to the room.

Kreo walked out of the parking lot and headed back west. He could smell coffee and wanted to explore in the daylight the things he had seen the night before.

And as he looked up the road right outside the small motel, and faced to the west, the mountain range they had traveled near to get to Westcliffe loomed large. He just had to see it more clearly.

Kreo made his way past a couple of small coffee and bakery cafés – again chuckling to himself about the dual nature of most of the businesses in the small town – and a grocery store.

He filed away the businesses for later and walked to the westernmost end of the town.

A park at the end of the main street of the small mountain village came into view, and as he walked into it, the buildings and cars, traffic and people fell away behind him.

All that was between him, and the majestic mountain range a few miles away, were two people walking dogs, and a scattering of farms and ranches at the foot of the range.

It looked as if the mountain range was made up of four main mountains, all topping out in the clouds. He could barely make out the peaks, but the slopes up to the tops were scattered with trees, snow, and several swathes of what he assumed were ski resorts and runs.

He didn't know enough about mountain living to know for sure, but the sight before him was stunning, just the same.

He sat on a large rock, staring at the range of mountains that ran north to south, and pondered his life, his recent thoughts and studies, and the road ahead with Mya.

He dreamed of a future where he was in his element and knew what he was made to do.

The cascading splendor of the mountains in front of him helped him realize that he would be fine, and that life was short, the world was old, and he only had a small part to play in it.

That made him feel less heavy, and his breathing and his heart rate soon returned to normal.

He had been feeling the weight of responsibility ever since the all-too-real dream the ArchAngel had given him.

The ArchAngel that he now knew was also all too real. And all too focused on Kreo himself.

*Another problem for another day*, he thought as he got one last look at the majesty before him, turned, and found coffee and scones for him and his soon-to-be-awakened wife.

An hour and a half later, they found themselves walking up the stone steps on the southeast corner of the magical castle of Kreo's youth.

"When I came senior year, the Father couldn't get me out of the van. I was so nervous to be outside California, and I was feeling so damn scared of the future," Kreo told Mya as they climbed up into the hand-hewn castle.

"Father Johnson told me something that has always stayed with me," he told her as they walked into the cathedral of the castle.

The innermost room, bright with sunshine cascading through the multi-colored panels of the stained-glass wall. It was exactly as he remembered it from years prior.

He took Mya by the hand again and twirled her around in a dance in the very middle of the Cathedral, beneath the stained-glass windows and metal girders overhead. She giggled as he spun her around.

He could barely take his eyes off of his bride, but the steel girders, and the intricate scroll work of the metal around them was a bit of an obsession for him as well.

He continued telling her the story.

"He told me to pretend that the castle was mine. That I could live in a castle, if I could only pretend hard enough, and wish for it," he told her.

"And do you wish to live in a castle, my love?" she asked him, as he pulled her in close for the remainder of the dance, music playing in both of their minds that only they could hear.

"Oh, yes," he answered. "You and me, kid, with room service and a beautiful view!"

They moved out of the cathedral and walked the close quarters of the circling stairways up to the top rooms and the accesses to the steel girder bridges and platforms at the very crest of the tall castle.

Kreo had not gone up on the top when he was a kid, and he wanted to now.

Mya wasn't so sure about the safety and support of the steel girders, but he talked her into it with the promise of a beautiful view and even better Mexican food in the next city they would travel to.

The came out of the twisting stairwell to the very top of the highest tower of the castle. The whole of southern Colorado was open to them as they looked down through a mountain pass to the east.

Both of their breaths caught as the view spread out clearly for more miles than they could count.

Mya was grinning broadly as she looked down over the entire world, it seemed, and she turned to her husband and whispered to him.

"Is this what it feels like to be the Queen of All You Survey" she asked.

"Yes, my love. And one day, you will be," he answered back.

Mya wanted to spread her arms out like the actor had done in the movie *Titanic*, and scream that she was flying, but on this glorious day, she kept her overexuberance at bay.

But Kreo did not.

Spreading his own arms out wide, the gentle, warm wind tousling his hair, and his wife laughing behind him, he whooped loudly in the air, and heard the loud noise echo down into the valley, where it caught the warm jet stream of air, and, in his mind, made it all the way out to the oceans of the far side of the world.

Kreo Fairchild's heart soared, his soul was clear, and as he pulled in his new wife tightly against his body, he was at peace once again.

Finally.


Two hours later, they were in the midst of the deep valley they had spied from the top of the castle up in the mountains, in a small city called Pueblo, and seated at an old, scarred tabletop, about to indulge in green sauce enchiladas at a small place downtown called Papa Jose's.

Soon sated, the newlywed couple headed out of Colorado after the heavy but delicious lunch, and drove east.

The sun was shining, the music was blaring, and for a little while, at least, all was right in Kreo and Mya's world.

They were embarking on a new adventure, with a new spirit, and every leg of their road trip brought them closer to the joy they had only wished for up until now.


Two Beings looked down on an unfolding narrative and pondered how they could use the situation to further their own goals. Goals that the two people below, blissfully unaware, yet strangely still understanding, would not enjoy the fulfillment of.

The smaller of the two Beings, clad in all purple armor that wriggled like serpents, and with a bright violet aura about him, looked up to his Father and still felt trepidation.

He, more than the Father (and he did not want to pursue the route of those thoughts) knew that the man and woman below were moving toward normalcy and a routine life.

And while that would be new and exciting for them both, the lives of two humans weren't worth more than the whole of Creation.

Jeremiel did not like what he was seeing.

He had not worked decades in the Material Realm to create the Fate Maker, just for the man to live a normal life.

*No*, Jeremiel thought to himself ruefully, *the man below would need to be tested so much more to* Become.

"My thoughts exactly, my Son," the Creator said to the ArchAngel.

Jeremiel had not shielded his thoughts. Another thread of thinking he did not want to pursue.

It was as if all of Creation was coming unraveled.

"Don't fret Child. Kreo Fate Maker will not let us down, nor abandon our cause," the Creator's voice soothed the tall ArchAngel.

But still, as ArchAngel Jeremiel's weapon winked in and out of existence near his left hand, he was worried.

The display of the lack of control over his own Heavenly weapon showed the ArchAngel's angst and fear.

The Father laid a comforting hand on the Jeremiel's broad shoulder and instantly calmed the warrior's fears.

"He will have no other choice."

The voice of the Creator of All was precise and wise. Jeremiel simply vowed to wait and watch.

He still felt he could persuade Kreo to their side in the coming Cataclysm.

The Creator, however, knew what must be done. *They walked an exceptionally fine razor's edge with the man below,* the Creator thought to himself.

A fine, and extremely sharp razor's edge, indeed.

# Chapter 31

It was September, it was chilly, and the trees were starting to change into their more festive autumnal hues in the New England states.

Kreo stood alone on a rocky outcropping near a lighthouse. The lighthouse was on its own little island, across a tiny channel just large enough to need some sort of basket and pulley system to get over to it.

It was called Nubble Lighthouse, in York, Maine, and Kreo was once again in love with a place, and a people.

*The air was chillier than it should have been,* he thought, glad for the heavy peacoat and wool scarf Mya had purchased for him. She had purchased a lot for him the last month. And he felt incredibly emasculated over the fact.

He knew that he had to figure out what he was going to do, and he needed to figure it out quickly. He did not want to be a burden on his successful wife. She would never see him in that light, he knew, but he needed to pull his own weight.

He had the Montgomery GI Bill that he could use for school, which was a godsend, but he didn't know what he would study.

He had no direction, and he felt the earth under him figuratively give way. He needed solid ground.

That took his mind to finances. Mya was more successful than they had let on. Her single restaurant in the Bay Area was thriving, and even not being there, it had been doing a steady business built on her model, all summer.

She was practically wealthy at this point, but opening the new East Coast restaurant, he knew, would stretch her cash reserves.

But she wanted to do it solely on her own merit, and he knew the wisdom, and the potential return, of her shouldering the burden herself.

Looking at the crashing waves of the north Atlantic ocean against the Maine coast, he thought back over the last four weeks, and their drive, first east, and finally, straight north.

They had left Colorado on a very sunny day and drove south to Texas to catch I-40. Coming into the East Coast further south, in North Carolina, gave them the opportunity to see more of it, according to Mya's planning. And she had been so right. Driving north on I-95 along most of the Eastern Seaboard had been worth the entire trip.

But before that, they had stopped several times in states like Texas, where they sampled the other style of Mexican food in Amarillo, at a lovely place called Rosa's Café. The bright colors of the restaurant, and the delicious food had made it worth the entire trip.

Staying overnight in Amarillo, they were able to visit a tourist stop called The Big Texan, where Kreo ate the best steak he had ever had.

They had heard about the decade's long-standing tradition of someone trying to eat a 72-ounce steak and trimmings in an hour, and they had been lucky enough to witness just that feat being done by a local baseball player the evening they stopped in.

They had made it through Oklahoma, stopping at the Bombing Memorial for an hour of quiet contemplation and prayer in Oklahoma City.

Mya had especially been touched by the pillars for the victims, but none more so than the smaller pillars for the children killed in the 1996 blast.

Arkansas went by in a blink, and then they were in the beautifully green and mountainous state of Tennessee. They had spent almost a week visiting first Memphis and then Nashville.

It had been another struggle to leave, as they had fallen in love with the people, the culture, the music, and especially the food.

Kreo was fearful that he was gaining more weight than he could work off, but after a couple of days of the heavy southern fare, Mya and he had agreed to take morning runs together.

Running together had been something they had done for many years, and the habit came back in full force. Kreo felt truly thankful that he had made it through his military career without losing a limb or the ability to fully use his body.

And Mya was thankful that she took time away from her career to focus on her new marriage, her body, and plans for the future that she formulated while jogging next to her husband.

After they left Tennessee, they stayed on I-40 all the way to North Carolina, where the interstate had connected with the large north-to-south-running I-95, straight west of Wilmington.

They stopped briefly on the coast, as Mya had never seen the Atlantic ocean, and being just an hour's drive from it was too much pressure to turn north without seeing it.

They stopped overnight in a lovely small town called Hampstead, and were soon running wild, barefoot, on white sandy beaches, and catching the salt spray from the ocean in their hair.

The experience was exhilarating, and they stayed most of that night right on the beach, having met some local military families that were having bonfires next to the large expanse of the Atlantic Ocean.

Singing along with a guitar playing Marine, around a large fire made from driftwood and dreams, Kreo felt fully back home with the world that he had known for so many years.

Being able to tell war stories with some of his Marine brothers and their families made him feel almost whole again.

Mya saw the change in her husband, and saliently vowed that she would work her ass off to get Kreo to a place where he was helping and in that world again.

The next day, shaking the sand from their clothes and sandals, they headed back to I-95, and drove straight north.

Mya noticed the studious look on her husband's face after the joyful reminiscing on the beach and let him have time, while she drove through the rest of North Carolina, into Virginia, and approached their first really heavy stopping point in Washington DC, to figure himself out somewhat.

She knew the pressure he was under, and she did all she could to not make him feel worse than he already did.

She knew he would find his way. He always had, and it was one of the main reasons she had loved him for so awfully long.

When they finally arrived in DC, six and a half hours from where they started that day, they had driven straight to their hotel for the two weeks they would stay in the City.

Mya had work-related meetings the entire time they would be there, and Kreo had wanted to see the sights, but also to get out of the city and travel south into Maryland.

The Naval Academy was in Annapolis, and he was so excited to see the historic military university, as well as the Marine monuments and shrines in both DC and Annapolis.

They soon settled into a comfortable routine during their stay in DC. Mya would go with Kreo in the mornings to see the monuments and find out-of-the-way shops and eateries around the various neighborhoods of Washington.

In the afternoons, she rode off with a wave from the window of an Uber or a taxi, headed toward Alexandria, Virginia, and Old Town.

Her new restaurant, a Southern Food expansive eatery, was going to be located in a two-hundred-year-old building that had been frequented by George Washington himself. His home and his grave were located at Mount Vernon, only nine miles south of her restaurant.

Kreo would jump into their SUV, and every afternoon would drive south into Southern Maryland, toward the Chesapeake Bay and points unknown.

They would meet back up for dinner in the city, or in Alexandria, and talk about their days. It had been a quick, heavy two weeks, but they had both gotten so much done.

Mya, of course, had set the building, planning, and logistical schedule back on track for the restaurant that she had named after her mother, Dixie, and Kreo had finally figured some things out about himself, his future, and where he wanted to be.

As he stood on the granite outcropping overlooking the Maine coastline, feeling the salty sea spray hit his face like it had done in North Carolina, only this time much, much colder, he thought back to the day that he had found St. Mary's City, and the home he wanted to build his life in with Mya, and their future.

After a week of travelling to see military history sites and exhausting the brief list of things he had wanted to do, he finally got around to finding out about the Civil War monuments and battlefields around the DC area.

He spent two days between Gettysburg, a short three hour drive out of the city, and a place that had jumped out at him on his map.

It was called Point Lookout, Maryland, and the haunted POW camp from the end of the Civil War, Fort Lincoln, intrigued him to no end.

So, after waving goodbye to his beautiful and successful wife once again, he headed south into Charles County, and then into St. Mary's County, Maryland.

The drive south was breathtaking.

Lush and fertile pastures, surrounded by soaring trees and greenery brighter than any he had seen so far stretched out before him, and as he approached the Chesapeake Bay, he found his place on the planet.

He was driving through southern St. Mary's county, countryside on both sides of him, when he rounded a steep turn, and a bay to his right, and a beautiful college campus to his left, opened before him like a living painting.

A deep, colorful tapestry.

His breath nearly left his body as he felt a deep sense of déjà vu and a feeling that he was home.

He slowed down, trying to capture the entire area in his brain. He wished with all of his heart that Mya was with him to share his feelings.

A tear rolled down his face as he drove through the area and came to a historic park called St. Mary's City.

It was the location of the very first settlement of Englishmen in Maryland, and one of the first in the entire United States.

According to signs, brochures, and a guided tour that he took the very next day, the settlement had been being excavated for years, and they had dated some of the pottery and left-behind vessels found in the dirt back to the start of the 1600s.

Now he understood why the police vehicles in St. Mary's county stated that they were the "First Sheriff." A lot of firsts for this country happened right there in St. Mary's City.

He took the remainder of their time in the Mid-Atlantic region visiting all over St. Mary's county, and trying different restaurants, meeting new people, and even touring the Navy base located nearby.

The base was the largest employer of the area. Called Patuxent River Naval Air Station, it was the headquarters of NAVAIR, and being a former Marine officer, he was well acquainted with NAVAIR.

Mya's restaurant was a mere fifty-minute drive north, and as he drove down to a place on his GPS called Piney Point, he discovered St. George Island.

And that's when he found the home he was going to buy his new bride, and live their entire lives together in.

On the water, taking up two full acres, and quiet and private, the home would only be possible in his budget if a miracle happened.

He had been so overwhelmed by the discovery of the large, two-story home, and its grassy acreage, its proximity to St. Mary's College, and its own dock on the Potomac River, that he knew that it was time to put his mostly ignored power of controlling Fate to the test.

And now, standing on the shore of the Maine Coastline, his fantasy home to his south by ten hours of driving and two weeks in the past, and him pondering how to afford the home that he felt destined to own, he finally figured out how to achieve it.

The only problem was, how did he use his powers, his *Favor*, to his advantage?

He reached into his front pocket, feeling a small slip of paper there, slick in its receipt-like texture, and smiled.

He knew suddenly what he had to do. It was so easy, it was laughable.

Kreo Fate Maker tightened his hand around the slip of paper, closed his eyes and envisioned himself and Mya at the large colonial home on St. George's Island.

He focused his eyes on the outcome he wanted and pushed his Will out into the Universe.

He felt his entire world *shift* around him, and he smiled. He didn't even need to worry.

What he had envisioned, and what he had just done, would safely and securely take hold of that evening's outcome, and he would be able to afford anything that he wanted.

He had just won the Powerball lottery, and it hadn't even been drawn yet.

He spent the rest of the day eating a lovely lobster roll lunch with his bride, and awaiting the drawing that night, and his victory, bought with his powers and the ticket still in his front pocket.

He had purchased it on a whim as they had stopped for gas in New Hampshire.

His life had only just begun, and he had finally used his powers for his own purposes, and his own gain.

The world would be his for the taking.

The smile didn't leave his face for weeks to come.

# Inter-Mission 2

The large, accessible area surrounding the Heavenly Throne buzzed with excitement. Finally, they felt, they were all going to find the underlying cause of what had been happening for such a short length of time, but at the same time, for almost all of this Creation.

The All Father, Creator of All, sat upon His Throne, made of His own countenance and Aura, and looked down at His children. Level on level of angelic forms flew around Him, singing praises, beating their wings in time with the Glory of all Heaven.

It made the Creator exhausted to see the constant movement, the constant adoration. The Noise of Praise.

He held up one hand, a hand that had created all the heavens and the earths, and silence fell around Him. *Thank God*, he thought. A small chuckle escaped him.

And His Glory brightened around Him.

The Creator looked down on His Host of ArchAngels and gave them the answers they had wished for, all this time.

"My Children," the Creator said, His volume gentle, and His words light.

"My Children, we know now that which has encroached onto this Plane of Creation."

The entire heavenly host of angels, the ArchAngels milling around on the golden floor in front of the Throne amongst the first to go silent, all looked at their Creator and not a sound was made.

"We have been under attack by what I call *Antithesis*."

No one moved. No one said a word. Not a sound was made in all of Creation, on the Spiritual Plane, or the Material. All were waiting on the Creator's next words.

"And I have no idea how this came to be," the Creator said.

And there it was.

All of Creation's fears realized. Even the Creator of All, the All Father, the Alpha and the Omega, had no knowledge of, nor understanding of, what was happening. And from where *Antithesis* had come.

If God had not created the other Existence, who did?

*And the worst part of it all* – thoughts bounded around in the minds of all the creatures in the Spiritual Plane – *the worst part was, this* Antithesis *seemed hell bent on not only destroying this Creation.*

*Antithesis* was hell bent on killing the All Father.

The opposite of all of this Creation… was trying to kill God.

The Creator held up his hand again, and the din quieted down once more. *They had all figured it out,* God thought to Himself.

"My Children, do not fret. Let he who has ears to hear, hear," He said.

"Do not fret. I have set in motion that which will win this War for Creation. I have set in store, through all of the Missions set before you over the last millennia, that which will prevail. All will be well, my Children," God intoned.

"Do not fear, my angels, my love, my Creation."

"For your Father has devised a Plan."

# Part 6
# Fate Becomes Him

# Chapter 32

Sitting on his long, wooden dock, stretching deep into the Potomac River, Kreo pulled the lightweight rope toward himself.

He loved the feel of the water on the white strands of the rope and loved even more when the crab trap came clear of the water, a few feet below him, and he saw the rapid movements of all the crabs he had caught.

*Tonight was going to be a wonderful crab boil*, he thought. Mya would love it.

Maryland blue crabs had become a favorite delicacy in their home, and pulling them from the water at the rear of their home themselves made the dish even better.

He set about checking the sizes of the crabs in the crab pot and threw back the females and the smaller males. He kept the number ones, and some of the number twos, and put them into a used and dirty five-gallon bucket half full of river water next to him.

He set in another frozen chicken neck in the pot and lowered it back into the water.

Repeating the process with his other crab pot placed on the other end and further out on the dock, he gathered up a good bushel of crab, perfect for a long and leisurely crab boil for that night.

When Mya got home from the restaurant, he would surprise her with a full boil, with all the fixings, on their oversized, pergola-covered rear deck. He was looking forward to it, and he knew she would love it.

Kreo and his wife had lived in their new home on St. George's Island in deep St. Mary's County, Maryland, for almost two years.

They had decorated the home in things they each loved, and they had both found purpose and joy in the everyday routines of work, play, and spending as many waking moments together as they could.

Since winning the lottery, and working with an entire team of financial advisors, lawyers, and business wizards, Kreo and Mya were now worth a comfortable hundred million dollars.

The money was stored in several investment vehicles, real estate, Mya's restaurant chain, which was up to three locations now, and the home they shared on the Island.

Kreo was in his second year of poli-sci classes at St. Mary's College, and he routinely took his new boat up the St. Mary's River, which branched off of the Potomac, and tied up at the school's own dock, taking his books from the boat and walking to class.

He was the envy of his entire class, but since he was at least a decade older than all of them, they were all used to his lifestyle, and had all visited his home, and the parties he threw, a couple times each semester.

Mya and Kreo were both involved in local matters and politics.

Being a wealthy couple, her owning several successful restaurants, and him running a successful online business helping exiting veterans finding employment opportunities in the defense sector, it was no surprise that they were asked to be on a new board almost every month, and having an 'in,' as it was called, with the more affluent circles around Washington D.C.

And while it seemed like everything was going absolutely perfectly, there were still nights of no rest, and a deep sense of uncomfortableness within Kreo.

He felt like he was still not where he was supposed to be, and not doing what he was supposed to be doing.

He always felt like time was slipping away from him.

But he sure couldn't complain about the life that he and his wife led.

He went about setting up the crab boil needs on the outdoor kitchen at the southern end of the large deck. He looked up at the growing trumpet vine, slowly covering the sides and tops of the large pergola overhead.

The vine was mostly green at the moment but would be growing dormant as the fall months they were currently in turned to the colder, holiday months.

That thought made him smile. He looked forward to the Christmas season now with more relish than at any other point in his life.

He was ready for the rounds of parties in DC, having his fellow students over for dinners and traditional gatherings while they were all away from their own homes, and the décor that Mya relished in, here in their large home.

They could both do without the deep cold of a Chesapeake Bay winter, but the new traditions they had established over the last two years would cover up the uncomfortably cold season.

He looked down over his catch of large blue crabs. It was the final week of September, and the crabs were finally running big.

He could catch them through December, but he had learned the previous year that the best times to catch the delicious blues was this week through Thanksgiving.

It was Saturday, and he had the house to himself, with zero places to be.

Mya only made cursory drives into Alexandria, to her restaurant, Dixie's, on Saturdays, to give input to the weekend menus, and to make sure they were staffed through the busy fall weekend.

Old Town would be lighting Christmas lights across the centuries-old streets soon, and the flower baskets on light poles, overflowing with color and beauty through the summer, would soon be dormant as well.

Mya had fallen in love with the historic district, and Kreo and fallen in love with the rivers, the Bay, and the people of the Mid-Atlantic and the Chesapeake Watershed.

He went into his double garage on the side of the large home, and took out a package of kielbasa sausages from the deep freezer.

Taking the heavy meat links into the kitchen inside the home, he pulled cobs of corn from the refrigerator, two frozen bags of deshelled and deveined shrimp from the freezer, and put everything into the large plantation sink in the kitchen's island.

Walking over to the spice cabinet and doing his best to not disturb any of Mya's carefully organized spices and victuals, he pulled out a large canister of Old Bay.

The yellow, blue, and red canister was halfway empty, as it had become a staple to not only their own cooking, but the expectations of food in deep southern Maryland.

Kreo opened the red lid of the can and inhaled the deep aroma of the legendary seafood spice. He still loved the smell.

He pulled out a bag of red potatoes from the pantry, and set them to boiling on the stove, in the large, stainless-steel pot he would use for the eventual whole of the boil.

The chores of preparing dinner for his love kept his mind occupied as the sun set outside the overlarge windows facing back out onto the Potomac River, and soon, he saw the Edison lights decorating the underside of the entire pergola come on with the timer he set.

He took a dark beer from the refrigerator and turned on his streaming music list on the artificial intelligence home system. Soon, his favorite music blared from speakers all over the large home.

The lights eventually came on in the home, and the deep, delicious smell of the Old Bay added to the boiling water on the gas stove overtook every other sense in Kreo's mind. He whistled along to a favorite song by Pink as he prepared the rest of the crab boil.

When the rest of the food was ready, and he needed to cook the crab, he carried the heavy pot, using large oven mittens, out to the outdoor kitchen, and placed it on the large burner made just for this occasion.

He reached under the stone-worked grill and turned on the propane valve. Soon, a deep blue flame appeared under the overlarge pot, and he was ready to begin cooking his afternoon catch.

He checked his cellphone and saw that Mya had texted him forty-five minutes earlier that she had left the restaurant. *Good,* he thought, *right on time.*

And then he slowly placed the still moving crabs into the boiling water. Contrary to widely held belief, the crabs did not scream as they perished in the boil.

Kreo took a deep, heavy breath of the cool Maryland air, looked out over the river to the fading and colorful sunset, and felt at peace.

The crab boil and fixins' smelled delicious, his favorite music was playing, the Edison lights overhead cast a festive air, the waves of the river lapped against his granite rock bunting leading up to his green lawn.

And then he heard Mya's car tires crunch on the driveway to the side of the house. All was well in his world.

He heard the heavy gates closing at the head of their property, and her car door shut in the garage. As she walked around the side of the house, having seen the lights on the deck lit up, she exclaimed in glee at the smell and sight of the crab boil.

He soon had her comfortably ensconced at the large picnic table on the middle of the deck, the lights bright overhead, and the butcher paper laid out in front of her.

Handing her a glass of white wine, he flourished the boil out onto the paper covering the table.

"Good God, Kreo, this is enough food to feed an army!" she exclaimed.

But her eyes lit up at the heavily spiced shrimp, potatoes, sausages, and perfectly cooked Maryland blue crab.

"Just my thoughts exactly," he said with a wink as his plans unfolded in his mind, and he shared them out loud to his wife, deep into the night.


They were soon stuffed full of crab and the fixings and laughing gently at the next phase of their lives, the phase that Kreo explained to her, that night, and how exactly they would enact the plan.

Mya's eyes glinted in the light of the deck, her hands were dirty with crab juices and Old Bay, and she was overjoyed deep in her heart as her husband explained how it was time to have a child.

All of her easy, light, and daily manipulations to lead Kreo to that very fact was an inside joke she would always keep to herself.

But, oh, how she loved the excitement in her husband as he rattled off names and plans for the nursery next to their master bedroom on the second floor.

What he didn't know, and she would also keep to herself, was that she had stopped using her birth control a full three months previously.

Kreo would get his way, she knew, and they would be pregnant before Christmas of this year. She knew in her heart that they were both ready.

Really ready, finally.

# Chapter 33

"Honey, honey, what's the matter?" The tone in Kreo's voice was not helping the situation, and he knew it. But his wife was nine months pregnant, and he was almost fifty miles away.

"It's okay, Kreo. I'm okay. Just my water broke," Mya answered him. She could hear shuffling and heavy breathing on the other end. And she smiled through the pain in her lower abdomen and back.

Their daughter was coming, and it seemed she wanted to come today.

"I'm on my way. Can you get across the bridge and over to Georgetown?"

There was a panic in his voice. Mya just smiled and tried to calm him down.

She certainly didn't need him to wreck the car on the hour-long drive to the hospital. And it being a Wednesday afternoon, he would certainly hit traffic.

"I can make it. Jan is going to drive me over. We're about to leave now," she told him.

He was distracted. She knew he was getting everything prepared and put into the car. "Yeah, yeah, good, good." His voice faded.

"Kreo," she said. "Kreo." Her tone firmed up so he would hear her.

Finally, he stopped in his tracks and listened. She could hear his breath smooth out over the phone receiver, and his heart rate slow for a few moments.

"Our daughter is coming today, Kreo. Remember that and just get to me safely," she told him. She could almost hear his smile through the phone.

"Yes, she is. Okay, my love. I'll see you soon. Getting into the car now," he said. And then they disconnected, and she allowed her restaurant manager, Jan, a remarkably close and personal friend, to drive her across the Key Bridge, and to Georgetown Medical.

She gave a silent prayer in the car as her contractions started, and pain enveloped her mid-section.

Just a little prayer for their family, and for Kreo to arrive safely, and in time to see their daughter come into the world.

As he drove north as fast as he could, listening to talk radio, his mind fixed firmly on getting to the hospital on time to make sure that Mya was okay and taken care of, Kreo was fighting the urge to sink down into a hole again.

The color on the trees outside his windows didn't even register to the man. The beauty of the landscape flying by his vehicle didn't register. His mind was in the past. And it was making him feel like he didn't deserve the good things happening in his life now.

This had been quite a common thread in his mindset lately. As his life got more complicated, and so many good things stacked up in it, he was afraid of losing everything.

And he felt that way because of things in the past, and how much he had lost, that had been completely out of his control.

As a boy, he had lost both of his parents early. That wasn't his fault. He had been bullied and picked on by the boys in the home he had been placed into. That had not been his fault.

The first love he had ever felt for someone else had destroyed his fragile mind and heart, and no matter what he had done for her, that had not been his fault either.

He chose to join the military because his life had become an endless spiral of destruction, and they had sent him all over the world, fighting wars that he had not chosen.

And while volunteering for the work had been his doing, losing friends in battles and wars that had only served the interest of politicians and rich people had not been.

Ever since he took his own life into his hands, fixing the wrongs in it, and finally getting to a place where he was happy, fulfilled somewhat, and was growing their family, he once again felt like life was out of his hands, and something would happen that was once again not his fault.

Nothing was wrong, and nothing had gone wrong, but he couldn't help feeling like he was about to be punished for taking over his own life.

And that made his mind turn to the obsession he'd had for over a year. The research he had done toward the ArchAngels, and their hold over his life, taking him down into rabbit holes of information that he still didn't completely accept, made him feel like the angels had more lessons for him to learn.

They wanted something from him, and he was afraid, deathly afraid, that their way of making him comply, or to be strong enough for their needs, necessitated him losing everything that he had.

If he continued to lose loved ones, a life he now cherished, and was thrust where he didn't want to go, he would only have one thing to blame it all on.

The ArchAngels.

His mind went back to his wife, who he thought was completely alone and hurting right at that moment, and he pushed the accelerator on his powerful Mercedes sedan.

"Today, the President of Russia, Vladimir Komarov made final retaliatory remarks at the UN Council meeting in New York. His plans to re-annex the Crimea Region of the former USSR, as well as a threat to the NATO-recognized state of Ukraine have the rest of the world wondering if the next World War is on the horizon," the voice intoned over the radio in Kreo's car.

He was driving as fast as he could up I-295 into Washington DC, trying as he could to get to Georgetown. The interstate was almost bumper to bumper, and he banged his hands on his stirring wheel in frustration. He checked his phone again.

Nothing.

He didn't even know if his daughter had been born yet, or if his wife was okay. His frustration grew in commiseration with his fear.

Terror, really.

His ears barely picked up the news report on Talk Radio as he maneuvered his uselessly powerful car in and out of traffic. He picked up on a few words the newscasters were saying and knew that it would come up when he joined his classes again the following year.

For now, he had taken the semester off as Mya's pregnancy entered into the final stages.

Just as he thought he would burst in fear and rage, a single lane opened up in order for him to join the 395/695 turn-off toward Georgetown.

He could see the buildings across the river in Alexandria and Crystal City, and as he swung back north on the western side of the City, he could see the great gothic buildings of Georgetown University.

Within those powerfully old streets, deep in history and tall trees, lay the hospital where his wife was currently delivering a baby.

His palms were sweating, his heart was beating loudly in his chest, and it seemed like he could only hear the pounding in his temples as he drove the last few miles through colorful trees, deep within the season's changings, and grew more frustrated with every stop sign he had to obey.

Finally, he pulled up to long term parking at the hospital and chose not to carry all of the bags and belongings with him. He simply needed to check on his wife.

He grabbed his wallet, took the keys with him, and left everything else.

Practically running into the information booth on the bottom floor of the hospital, he blurted out his name and his wife's name to the petrified teenager behind the desk.

"I'm sorry, I'm sorry," he gasped, almost out of breath.

"My wife is delivering. Her name is Mya Fairchild-Green," he told the girl.

She nodded her understanding and started clacking keys on her computer.

"Third floor, Maternity. She is currently in room 3108," she told him with a smile.

He barely heard the room number as he ran for an elevator.

Luckily, he wasn't held up by anyone else, or anything else, as he ran to the double doors leading into the maternity wing. The doors were locked, and he frantically hit the blue and gray OPEN button.

A sound buzzed above his head somewhere, and a voice came on the speaker next to the door.

"Can we help you?" the voice asked, sounding bored.

"Yes, yes," Kreo practically yelled into the speaker. "Mya Fairchild-Green, please."

"Come through the double doors, take an immediate right, and come up to the nurse's desk, please," the voice said.

Another buzzer sounded, and the double doors opened on their own in front of Kreo. He was running as soon as they were wide enough for him to fit through.

He approached the nurse's desk to see three nurses in various pastel-colored scrubs looking at him with what he could only call sympathy. His heart sank into his shoes.

"Is my wife….? Is she okay…? My daughter…?" He couldn't form a coherent sentence.

"It's okay, sir," a blonde nurse spoke up first. "Mya is fine. Her blood pressure is not what we want it to be, but she hasn't delivered yet," she told him.

She smiled as his breath left his body.

"She is just in there, room 3108," the nurse said.

She pointed at a room directly across from where they were sitting, and he approached the large glass windows slowly. He didn't want to spook Mya.

The glass doors in the middle of the hallway ..opened as he approached them, and he moved aside the heavy curtain that had blocked him from seeing into the room from the outside.

He walked into a dimly lit room and was dumbfounded at what he found.

Mya Fairchild-Green, the love of his life, his most precious thing in all the world, was lying in a large hospital bed, sheets pulled up to her chin, as she chewed on ice from a Styrofoam cup she held in one hand.

Her other hand was connected to a tall IV stand, and various machines with wires and plastic things secured to fingers with medical tape. Light glows from the pieces taped to her told him they were monitoring all of his wife's vitals', which was a relief to him.

She smiled the warmest, brightest smile he had ever seen on her face as he ran into the room.

All the panic, fear, and trepidation from the long drive from the coast vanished as Kreo crossed the space between them and reached down to hug her.

He tried to do it gently, but she grabbed onto him harder than he had ever felt from her little body and didn't let go for several seconds.

"You made it," she whispered into his ear. He smiled.

"Well, I had a movie to finish, and I wanted to check the crab pots one more time before I left," he joked.

She gave him a chiding look as he stood up and backed away.

"I'm kidding. I thought you were laying up here, alone and in pain, holding our daughter," he said. "It was a hell of a frustrating drive."

"Nope, Jan just left, and I have been given the loveliest drugs through an epidural. I'm just peachy," she told him, and kept chomping loudly on the ice from the small cup.

He looked at what she was doing quizzically, and she just rolled her eyes.

"Supposed to calm my nerves and make me less hungry," she told him. "But me and this little lady are starving!"

She enveloped her large belly with both arms, and almost dropped the cup of ice.

He simply nodded as a small grin formed for the first time on his face. He hadn't smiled all day, he knew, and it was a tremendous relief to see his fears were unfounded.

As he stood there looking like a goof, watching the miracle of labor and eventual delivery, the door swooshed open behind him, and a small, petite nurse entered, already putting on gloves.

He quickly moved out of the way of the quick-moving nurse and sat in the chair on the other side of the small room.

"You must be Dad," the nurse said to him.

He nodded. "Kreo Fairchild," was all he could say.

She smiled at him and looked down at Mya.

"Alright, Momma, let's lay the bed back. I need to check how dilated you are," she told the soon-to-be mother.

Mya complied and put the cup of ice down on the small table next to the bed. Kreo tried to take it from her, but his body and hands just wouldn't respond as fast as normal. Mya smiled again at him as the top of the large bed moved slowly downward.

The nurse had pushed a button on the floor with her foot and the head of the bed lowered down until Mya was comfortable with her legs bent under the hospital gown that Kreo was just noticing.

The nurse smiled at the looks on the young couple's faces and reached under the gown and pushed her hand up into Mya.

Mya's face grimaced at the invasion and the pain of the movement. Whatever the nurse was doing was soon over, but Mya's face kept the same look of pain.

Kreo was concerned but knew he was completely out of his element.

"Alright, about nine centimeters, Momma. You're gonna have a baby soon," the nurse said.

She pulled her hand out from under the gown and tried to keep her gloved hand close to her so that Kreo and Mya couldn't see the blood covering it.

But Kreo saw it.

"Alright y'all, I'm gonna step out and call the doctor. We have a baby about to be born," she told them.

Kreo heard fear in her voice. That made his stomach clench. Hard.

She exited the room as quickly as she had entered, and Kreo scooted the chair closer to the bed to take his wife's hand.

She looked like she was in pain, but Kreo guessed that it was mostly fear.

And that's when an alarm sounded loudly in the room and echoed deep within Kreo's mind and soul. Mya's hand went limp in his.

He looked at his wife's now unconscious face as medical professionals ran into the room, coming from everywhere, scattering the tranquility of the room that had seemed so normal only a few seconds earlier.

All Kreo could do as they pulled him bodily from the room was yell his wife's name, over and over and over again.

# Chapter 34

Alone in a small waiting room, the door closed, blinds drawn, and deep depression settling in, Kreo felt like he was in the darkest place in his entire life. And that was really saying something.

The nurses and orderlies had ushered him into this small room with vague promises that all would be well, and they just needed him out of the way while they saved Mya and the baby.

He was sitting in a lonely chair against the windows on the far side of the room, his head in his hands, with prayers and petitions screaming in his mind to the Almighty, the ArchAngels, hell, even to unknown dark presences, promising his life to spare hers, when he felt a presence in the room with him.

Without looking up, he felt a great gust of wind against him, a brightness lighting up his eyelids through his hands, and almost blinding him, even with his eyes closed.

He knew instinctively who and what was in the room with him, and he felt a sudden panic.

Not at the Being's proximity to him in the real world, but in what he would have to give in exchange for his wife's and daughter's lives, and what the ArchAngel would ask for in return.

"Fate Maker," was all the ArchAngel said. Kreo still didn't open his eyes, nor take his head out of his hand. He knew the Being would hear him.

"What the hell do you want in exchange?" was all he asked.

"Same as always. Since you were born, and we came into your life. We require your help," the silky-smooth voice said on the other side of his closed eyes.

Kreo had known what the Being would say, but it still seemed like an out-of-body experience to know that he had been made for so much more than even what he had achieved so far in his early life.

Kreo took a deep breath, steadied himself, and finally looked up into the countenance of the ArchAngel of Dreams and Visions.

He was once again shocked at the sight of a heavenly Being directly before him. But after all of his obsessive studying, and his earlier experiences with this Being, he knew them to be very real, and a very real threat to everything he wanted in his own life.

The ArchAngel Jeremiel was in a human form, the bright light, extended wings, and deep aura gone for the moment.

He looked simply like a beach bum Ken doll, dressed in loose white pants and a flowing white silk button-down. Kreo wished that he looked half as good as the man/angel standing before him.

Jeremiel was even standing before Kreo barefooted, the Being's skin a deep, dark tan color.

"And what does that look like, Angel?" Kreo asked. He kept himself from looking around for the surfboard that surely was close by.

There was a twinkle in the Being's eyes, like he had won a great victory. Kreo wanted to punch the look out of the ArchAngel's face. But the ArchAngel did not answer Kreo's question.

Kreo asked one more, final question, hoping that the ArchAngel could not lie.

"Is her or the baby's life even in danger, Angel?"

The answer was not one that Kreo expected.

"There are no guarantees in this Plane, Kreo. I can tell you that whether or not her or your daughter's lives are in danger, we still need your help."

The ArchAngel paused suddenly, as if hearing directions from someone or something that Kreo could not see nor hear.

"And we will give you all assurances that we will do everything we can do, which is quite substantial, here in this Plane, for your family," the ArchAngel said, smiling at the man.

"How do I know if I even need your help? It's not like you've helped in any other way in my life," Kreo told the Being.

"We have done what was needed for you to Become," was all the Being told him.

He didn't want to argue with the ArchAngel. He would be too much out of his depth, disagreeing with a Being that was much older than Creation itself.

And he certainly did not want to belie the point that this ArchAngel had caused more pain in Kreo's life than any one man could handle.

He didn't want to remind this ArchAngel that he had already told the Being to pack sand, in so many words.

And with all of that marching through his mind, Kreo felt like this was the biggest decision of his life.

On the one hand, everything he loved was hanging in the balance, and on the other, a promise to help the very Entities that had caused so much pain and destruction in his own life.

He had no idea if this ArchAngel, or that which he worked for, would not continue taking from Kreo, even with their promise to save Mya's and the baby's lives.

His mind, and something in his soul made the decision for him, and his words shocked even himself, as they came spewing out of him, with little control over them, or even himself in that moment.

"Go fuck yourself, Angel. I'll take my chances," he said to the Being.

He looked one more time defiantly at the tall human form and didn't wait to allow the ArchAngel to awe him in full Angelic transformation and repose, if Jeremiel chose to switch forms in front of Kreo again.

He put his head back in his hands, and wished for a miracle, from whatever Other Beings heard him in the cosmos.

The ArchAngel was gone the next time Kreo opened his eyes and picked up his head.

He had heard a quiet noise from the direction of the only door leading into this small hellhole of a room.

It was the ward's doctor, young for his profession, but in the typical green scrubs and white lab coat.

Kreo almost fell out of his chair with shock when the doctor told him the news he had been waiting over an hour to hear.

"Mr. Fairchild?" the doctor asked him. He simply nodded to the young man.

The doctor then smiled, easing all of Kreo's fears even before more words came out.

"Your wife and your daughter are fine, Mr. Fairchild. If you'll follow me, I'll take you to your family."

Tears fell from Kreo's face at the words, and he quickly jumped up and followed the man down the hall, and to the most happiness he had ever felt in his life.

A nagging thought kept him from feeling the complete ecstasy that he should have been feeling, however.

He didn't know the repercussions of denying the ArchAngel's pleas for help, once again.

He had no idea what he had just unleashed, and what the fallout would eventually be.

But in the meantime, he meant to enjoy his family, and their health and happiness, as much as humanly possible, for as long as he could.

# Chapter 35

Kreo carefully carried his baby daughter into the house, trying hard not to wake her as she lay asleep in her car carrier.

He placed the small cradle down on the floor just inside the kitchen and was suddenly at a loss at what to do. He had to go back out into the garage to help his wife into their home, but he would have to leave the baby alone in the kitchen.

His mind and body suddenly froze, and he had no idea what to do. Panic arose in his chest and then into his foggy brain.

And then, like an alarm through a foggy, storm-tossed night, the car horn sounded loudly behind him, and he was brought out of his reverie to run back out into the garage.

"I told you I had to pee, Kreo," his wife told him as he approached her side of the car in the cavernous garage.

Sound rebounded off the tall white shelving all around the room, and he bent to hear her correctly.

"Sorry, honey. I didn't know if I could leave the baby alone in the kitchen," was his way of explaining.

She smiled at him, but still motioned him to help her out of the car. She was in a lot of pain after giving birth to their daughter.

As he helped her into the downstairs bathroom off the kitchen, and she settled into the relief of relieving herself, he went back to his new daughter, and removed her slowly from her car seat.

Both of his girls were exhausted, battle-worn, and needed as much rest as he could give them.

That's what he did. He took care of his girls, and made sure that they were both soon warm, comfortable, and drifting off to sleep.

There was a heating pad on Mya's back, a body pillow in her arms and along her body as she lay on her side, the end of it clutched between her knees. She was covered in her mother's childhood quilt, lovingly handmade by *her* own mother, and breathing heavily in sleep almost immediately.

Emma Dell Fairchild was also asleep, nestled in the ornate, beautifully handcrafted bassinet next to their bed. She was loudly sucking on a pacifier, and was wrapped in a soft, pink, hand woven baby blanket that they had received in the mail a week before Emma was born.

Mya's grandmother, the same woman who had made the quilt his wife was wrapped in, had also made her new great-granddaughter the blanket within which she was swaddled.

Kreo stood in the doorway of his bedroom, listening to the sweet sounds his girls were making, and was overcome with the emotion of the moment. He sank to his knees in gratitude for where he was, what he had, and who he was with.

He knew he didn't deserve the tranquil scene in front of him.

He had messed up too many times and made too many mistakes to deserve the love in that room. He had hurt too many people, made a mess of himself too many times to think that God would grant him the gifts he was now responsible to protect.

As he looked down at his sleeping girls, both with dark hair spilling out around their cherubic faces, he prayed as hard as he had in that lonely hospital room, or on the battlefield, or as a boy in the orphanage. He prayed to be worthy of the people in that room, who would look to him for protection and leadership.

He didn't know why his mind fixated on the word. Leadership.

Other than the military, he had not really thought about what that word meant.

But he knew it now. As a leader, it was his solemn duty to protect these precious girls given to him when he didn't deserve them at all.

He would protect, nurture, and serve his little family with everything that he had. He knew that now. Looking down at the little girl who had been named for both his and Mya's mothers, he knew what he had been made to do.

And as tears fell from his eyes for the gratitude he suddenly felt, and gratitude for the responsibility he now cherished and relished, on his knees he figured out his purpose, why he had been given Favor, and why he was on this earth.

He would lead and protect his beautiful little family, and then his wonderful community, and then the people of his country.

As he had done in the military, and with the direction he had chosen with his studies, he knew he was given everything that he was given to simply protect others.

He dried his eyes, went downstairs to answer calls and emails, and never, from that day onward, lost sight of the fact that while he was a born leader who had learned wisdom through mistake after mistake, and he was also made to protect.

Smiling as he heard Mya's mother and father on the other end of the phone asking after the girls and planning their flight out from California the following week, he knew who he was, what he was meant to do, and for whom he was meant to do it.

He had once again figured out who he now was, and with the new additions to his life and his responsibilities, he felt new strength enter him for unlocking the next level of his life, and his purpose.

Kreo Fairchild, new father, and newfound protector, savior – hell, even leader – would need all of that strength and more for what was to come.

He knew that with every fiber of his being. Of his very soul.

# Chapter 36

The new, and extremely tired, parents sat in the back of the large, warm room, trying to keep Emma quiet.

The precocious newborn was the delight of all of the elderly women gathered together in the stuffy auditorium, but there were more important matters to discuss, and the community educator's group didn't need the distraction of the most beautiful and perfect baby in the entirety of the world – at least according to her parents.

And those were the thoughts going through the new father's mind as he listened to the dire news coming from the front of the room.

Mya reached down and adjusted the pacifier in the baby girl's mouth again, trying against all hope to quiet the fussy infant. And while Kreo listened to the discussion in the room, he was constantly distracted by his new baby.

His mind was torn between their time in the hospital, which he was sure he had PTSD from, and back to the work at hand.

Momma and baby had been fine at the hospital. Mya's unconscious spell had come from her blood pressure dropping drastically.

And while that was a very scary situation since she had been so close to giving birth, the doctor and nursing staff were able to revive Mya long enough to deliver Emma.

Kreo was not incredibly happy about being rushed from the room when Mya had passed out and the alarms from the blood pressure machine started sounding, but after the doctor had explained that until they had known just what had set off the alarm bells, it was the hospital's policy to remove the family as quickly as possible.

Emma Dell Fairchild was born a beautiful and perfect eight pounds and six ounces, measuring twenty-one inches long.

Kreo had never seen a more perfect baby, and Mya had never been more beautiful to him as she was then, sweat soaked, and red faced, being sewed back up by medical students, and holding their precious new baby.

He had been led back into the room by the young doctor to laughter, grins, and a very jovial atmosphere now that the emergency situation had been fixed, and all had been well.

The nurses had helped him hold his daughter for the first time, and he had even been able to give her a bath.

Emma did not enjoy the frigid air hitting her skin and wailed loudly until the warm water was washed over her. She quieted down and enjoyed her father's ministrations to clean her off.

Two months later, and many restless nights of dirty diapers, crying fits, and rocking the small girl in Kreo's new rocking chair, they took her on her first outing, to a local meeting of the Maryland Community Educators group.

There was currently a very heated debate happening over zoning and erosion efforts on the Chesapeake coastlines.

Kreo and Mya had been invited because they were large supporters, both financially and with their time, of most of the local committees.

Kreo's attention was diverted from his noisy baby girl for a few minutes as several issues were finally presented for discussion and solutions. Loud, boisterous voices competed with each other to be heard.

No one seemed to have any solutions on the issues, but everyone seemed to have a lot of problems. And that's when Kreo had an idea.

He stood up suddenly and shouted above the rising voices and heated discussions. All eyes turned to him, and all the voices died down as they saw who had spoken.

After all of his challenging work over the last couple of years, everyone knew who he was, and that he was an important member of the local community.

"It seems to me, with everyone having a different issue, as well as no solutions forthcoming, that this committee is in need of leadership," he said.

"When I was in the Middle East, and things went belly up, we looked to leadership to show us the way out."

"Therefore, I volunteer to take all issues and problems to a list, and by the next meeting, and after discussing each issue with other elders gathered here, we will address each issue, and give solutions, or at the very least, what work needs done, to answer everyone's needs."

He heard a bit of grumbling, especially coming from the members of the local crabbing conglomerate. But most of the people in the room knew Kreo's past, and his accolades. They had all, as well, benefitted from his and Mya's generous donations to the various non-profit groups scattered around the large auditorium.

And as Kreo sat back down, having volunteered to lead this rabble to successful resolutions to many local issues, he had no idea that he had just kicked off what would take up most of the rest of his life, and his foray into local, and then national, politics, finally building up to international and global leadership.

But it had all started right there, in a warm, stuffy auditorium, amidst local blue-collar workers, crabbers, farmers, and educators, and would eventually grow to the largest global stages known to humankind.

Once again, places that Kreo had never thought possible, but which he had a strong suspicion other Entities had known all along and had orchestrated the entire thing into one of their damn tests, all over again.

A Being looked down from the Spiritual Plane, a plane abuzz with anxiety and stress, which he had never seen before, and saw that what he had wrought was coming to fruition nicely.

Jeremiel, the ArchAngel of Dreams and Visions, looked down on the man he had helped create and answered Kreo's wonderings aloud.

The ArchAngel spoke to the affirmative of Kreo's suspicions but said it aloud in a place were no living creature would hear.

No living creature could hear, of course, what the ArchAngel verified, but many unliving creatures of *antithesis* heard, loud and clear indeed.

# Chapter 37

"John, listen to me, we cannot do both the renovation AND the campaign. We just do not have the funds," Kreo said into the phone.

"And you know they track these things. Campaign financing has been a hot button topic since the late eighties, thanks to unscrupulous financiers," he finished.

He was trying not to get heated. He was developing a reputation as a hotheaded and trigger-happy politician.

That reputation could be used for his benefit, but it did not sit well with certain demographics.

It worked wonders with others, however, and there lay the crux of politics. Trying to make everyone and no one happy at the very same time.

He heard the affirmative nod coming from his campaign manager on the other end of the phone, and hung up, trusting the man to do what needed to be done. Renovating his campaign offices in Washington D.C. was a needed cost, but one which they could not afford.

Not this close to the election.

Knowing no other calls would be coming in today, a day that he had scheduled off to spend time with his family, Kreo looked around his office, settled comfortably and deep within his and Mya's home on St. George Island.

He had not been home as much as he wanted to lately, and he felt deep sorrow for that. His daughter was growing right before his eyes, but his increasingly busy schedule was getting out of control, and he felt like his small family paid the price for that.

He sat back in his comfortable leather chair behind his overflowing desk, crammed with statistical reports one staffer or another had given him, or current events, or hell – he sighed deeply – dirt on his opponents.

He had a precious afternoon free of the pressures of work, and he didn't want to spend it thinking about the campaign, the coming tour, nor the duties that would take him, once more, away from home.

Glancing down at the red folders scattered all across his desk, and knowing the secrets and dirt they held within, he briefly wondered if he had it in him to use the information at the debates coming at the end of the summer.

Those files and papers he kept hiding amongst the clutter. He didn't need anyone to see what he had paid several private investigators to find out about the men and women running against him for the state Senate seat for District 7.

Sighing, he thought back over the last four years, and the cost his choices to run for office had inflicted on his family.

A whirlwind of activity had forced Kreo into a leadership role that he had asked for but had not been ready for. It seemed everyone needed something from him, and as the days and weeks turned into months and months of meetings, problem fixing, and harder work than any other Kreo had known, he found himself flourishing.

He discovered that he had a real knack for leadership, and had surprised himself and Mya on his fresh and mostly original ideas for changes that could and should be made, locally, and as time went by, at a county or state level.

But it hadn't even been his idea for him to run for the county commissioner's seat.

But when he had acquiesced, he had been elected in a surprising landslide.

The first year in that position, the county of St. Mary's had passed a balanced budget, infrastructure had improved 78%, and he was celebrated anywhere he went.

Other politicians promised change, but none usually provided it.

Kreo supplied real change in droves. He couldn't help it. It was his nature, and his gift.

He found himself fully, and found real joy in the public appearances at the fairs, markets, ribbon cuttings, and monthly commissioner meetings.

His county was one of the first in the entire state of Maryland to hit a zero emissions rate of a small pandemic that had sprung up, and he was applauded in Annapolis as he had received commendation from the governor.

The headlines in several papers and online news sites showed the pictures taken of him standing tall and strong next to the aging governor, and in every case, bold words stated that new blood was coming, and he was the future for the state.

After that, more whirlwind activity caught him up, and he found himself cast into the limelight at the state level in the capital.

He did not want to run for the governor seat when it came up the next year, but he had his eyes on the incumbent seat of the state House of Delegates.

But once again, he had no control over matters.

Instead of running for, and winning, one of the 141 seats of the state legislature, he was cast once more into the rarer, and higher-level position of state senator.

He had won, again, in a landslide. No one had ever seen anything like it.

Now, one of only forty-seven state senators, he had made it only two years into his four-year term before he was once again lifted up by his peers, his constituents, and even the state executive branch, and made the Majority Leader of the House.

And four years after first running for a state seat, he was once again faced with a world seemingly at odds with his own wishes, and thrust into another leadership role, that being a run for the federal Senate seat in Washington D.C. for the state of Maryland.

He was barely forty years old, and he was running for the Senate.

He wasn't the youngest man to do that, not by a long shot, but looking at the current body of senators, he knew he was woefully inexperienced, once again.

And as he thought about the road ahead, with zero doubt that he would win the seat, he once again felt like he had as a new Boot in the desert, not knowing his ass from a hole in the ground and feeling like everything he did would be a mistake.

He was starting over new, once again, in a new world, on new terrain, but this time, he was entering it with experience, and not just hurt and pain.

He looked back up at his desk, remembering all the work that lay ahead. He was financing the campaign with both money from donations and fundraisers. But he was also kicking in more than three million dollars of his own money.

This was the big time, and he really needed to do everything he could to assure victory. And so, his eyes went back to the red folders, and once again he wondered how he would handle using the information.

He was pondering his own personal integrity when he heard the back door open and running footsteps approaching his office. He smiled as he heard laughter, and could envision his baby girl, pigtails bouncing behind her, running pell-mell toward her father.

He stood up from behind his desk and moved around to greet both his baby girl, Emma, and his beautiful and understanding wife as well.

Emma squealed even louder when she saw her father, and jumped into his waiting arms with a smile that lit up his whole life. He closed his eyes and whispered a remarkably familiar prayer of thanksgiving for the love he had in his life.

He didn't know what he would do without his girls.

He kissed his gregarious baby all over her face until she pushed him away with laughter and yells to stop.

He smiled even broader and looked up to see Mya approaching the office. She was smiling as well.

He put his daughter down to run and find a snack, and reached for Mya like she was a life preserver, and he was adrift on an emotional and lonely sea.

She didn't say a word as she folded into the arms of the man she loved more than anything on the planet, and just let him sigh longingly over her head.

She felt his body, tight and rigid when she had walked in, start to relax, and she knew how much strain he was under.

She told herself that she wouldn't add to his stress that night.

But there would be something they must talk about soon, she knew. She smiled into his chest as she felt phantom movement in her abdomen. It was a pained smile, and only she knew the issues and fears to come.

Oh yes, she knew.

They had lots to talk about the next day. But for now, she was here to help him strategize his next moves, to go over gossip she had been privy to in her restaurants, and news about how intelligent Emma was, and how everyone in the entire world just doted over the small girl.

Today, she knew, as she broke away from her husband and the love of her life, today would be for the here and now, and tomorrow could be for the future.

She needed to give Kreo that much, on this day, with the worry she saw barely masked within his eyes.

She would do what she had always done for her man today, and support him in being the best he could be. Tomorrow would be for other concerns.

# Chapter 38

A few years later, Kreo found himself staring out at the world. Not the whole world, he knew, but into camaras and bright eyes that would remember the day forever, and tell many others they had been there.

"In a world of madmen and tyrants, we must do all we can to meet the issues and problems on the same battlefield that these men use." Kreo was almost yelling into the microphone.

"You fight fire with fire and meet madness with dogged resolve and madness of your very own," he said.

Kreo paused for dramatic effect. He knew his next line would light up the world.

"And when it comes to fighting the bloody battles that need fought, I know with all certainty…"

He paused again.

"I am the man for the job!" he yelled.

The crowd went crazy. His political and campaign slogan had followed him everywhere, and people all over the country, and even the world, had used the slogan for almost everything.

T-shirts, coffee mugs, red, white, and blue ballcaps. All of it had the same short slogan, blaring at him everywhere that Kreo went.

"I am the man for the job!"

And as he left the podium amidst all of the adoration, cheering, and waving of flags, he knew deep in his heart, finally, that he really was the man for the job.

The world was going to hell, and this country needed a soldier. It needed a leader. It needed someone who had seen some shit and come out the other side.

And he knew that better than anyone.

Kreo stepped amongst other men and women in suits and dresses. Smiles lit up the Botox-injected faces, and eyes that had seen riches and the better sides of life twinkled as he walked by. None of the sycophants had known, nor experienced, a history like his, and they loved him for it.

His story had been told, over and over again. The whole country knew that he had been an orphan.

The whole country knew that he had been wounded in battle as a Marine.

The whole country even knew that he had lied to get into the military, had been hooked on bad drugs, had even been homeless.

And they loved him for it. Against all odds, everything that he had ever messed up, fought against, hell, even royally destroyed, made him even more relatable to the masses who sung his praises.

He was becoming the hero of the little guy, the shining example of someone who came from nothing and achieved everything.

And the rich people who shook his hand so vigorously at the moment loved him for those very skeletons that had come out of the closet earlier in the campaign.

He was real.

And he was the man for the job.

He knew deep in his heart the truth of things. He knew that, almost daily in his meteoric rise through the political levels, he had shifted fate. He knew that he had used his gifts and powers to get where he was, and where his family was, but he was okay with it.

Because he also knew that he was the man for the job.

Crowds of admirers, cheers from fans, screams of his name and his slogan from thousands of mouths was the headiest feeling that he had ever experienced.

And it made him realize just how unique and rare he was. It made him believe with all of his heart that he really was the man for the job.

He was led back through the crowded backstage of the auditorium by the Secret Service.

After four more years of being a Senator from the state of Maryland, after all of the parties, the lunches with lobbyists, letters from constituents, his name on almost every groundbreaking piece of legislature over that time and being in the limelight of the country's highest stages, he was used to the security detail around him, Mya and Emma almost every day.

But now that he was running for the very highest office in the land, it was an entirely new and unique experience every single day.

He had zero freedom anymore.

He couldn't go anywhere without being recognized, but it was a sacrifice he and Mya were okay accepting for the changes needed in this world, that he felt only he could make.

And that's why, at the end of the day, he knew he was exactly the right man for the job.

The current tensions all over the globe, and the atrocities and human rights violations in other countries showed that the United States needed a man just like him.

That fact alone scared the hell out of Kreo Fairchild, but it also created a rage in his belly that he had only ever felt in wartime.

He thought he knew what was going to happen in the world, and he used the war-mongering platform that other presidential candidates had used; it was serving him well. The world was on the brink of implosion, and the country needed the kind of leadership that only he could supply.

He was the man for the job.

It was a mantra that he said to himself daily now. And as the days turned to weeks, and the weeks turned toward the months leading up to November, he was slowly starting to *become* the man for the job, and he was grateful for it.

Another thing he was more than grateful for were the two people he was led to in a back room behind the stage that was still being bombarded with praise and cheers.

His girls greeted him with smiles and open hugs, telling him how great he had done, and how loud the cheers were. He smiled down at them, and only vaguely held an image in his mind that his family wasn't all present. But that was a matter for another time.

For now, he was going to enjoy his girls, and a surprise he had for them later.

He looked down at his diminutive wife, enjoying the smile on her face. A smile that had been absent for quite a while. She was slowly coming back to herself, and he was more grateful for that than anything else.

Mya had put her restaurant career on a backburner ever since he had become one of the youngest senators in history.

And after their son had been born.

The son that no one talked about.

Kreo looked down on her once more and smiled. Oh, how he still loved his wife. Even more now, after everything she had been through.

Mya was his best and highest-level advisor, and she knew that security for her family, and even their extended family and friends, was more important than keeping the restaurants running smoothly.

Truly, she missed her work, and missed the free use of her gift of cooking and running a kitchen. Being a chef had been her entire foundation of aspirations before Kreo came along and changed all of her carefully laid plans and dreams.

She was slightly bitter to that fact, but was pragmatic first and foremost, and so knew that Kreo's campaign, and the help he would give the world was paramount.

She knew that Kreo needed her, and she was fine with now helping build his career as a politician, even as he had done early in their marriage for building her own career.

She wasn't completely worried about her restaurants, however bitter her thoughts turned, as she had the best managers and friends who helped keep the doors open, and the tables full.

She checked in with everyone once in a while and knew that she would one day get back to work.

But in the meantime, she needed to support Kreo, to watch him and help him become everything she knew he would one day become.

Emma, one of the smartest and most successful third graders at the prestigious private school in Washington D.C. adored both of her parents, but her father was her true hero. She adored the tall man, and secretly wanted everything for him like her mother.

They often talked about the men in their lives, and Emma felt so blessed to have such wonderful parents, and a strong family, even with the challenges with her brother.

And she knew, even her own father had grown up with so much less. Gratitude had been hammered into her from an incredibly early age, and she had never fought against it, being a naturally good-hearted little girl.

*Daddy was the luckiest man alive,* she thought, as he held his girls.

Knowing about his own early life, she loved the way she found herself and her mother looking up at him, and how the many people, friends, advisors, confidants, and staff around the room saw in her Daddy the answer to many prayers, dreams, and plans.

Kreo was thinking along the same lines as his little girl.

He was so extremely lucky, and he knew that he could never drop the ball like he had done at the end of his military career, or when he was a young man.

Or when their son had been born early and with so many complications.

He had not been at his best, leaving the struggles to Mya and Emma, as he had concentrated so hard on his career and his climb to the place he was currently enjoying.

But he knew that he had turned that corner for good, and he was once again the man that he should have been.

It had been a short but heavily emotional time for everyone, and he was grateful that it was mostly behind them, and they could enjoy the current adventures around them.

He was so glad that his small family had risen to the occasion, and he was so awfully glad that his wife was smiling again. It was too hard without that in his life.

So, he knew that he could never drop that particular ball again.

There was entirely too much at stake.

"Shall we go home, girls?" he asked his small family.

Both his wife and his daughter nodded and smiled up at him. He wanted to make them happy.

So happy.

When they were escorted to the black SUVs with the mirror-dark tinting on the windows, and with a small police escort, at least through the streets of D.C., Kreo smiled back at the girls and told the driver the thing that both of them had wanted to hear for months.

"Sam, drive us down to the island, please," he told the darkly-suited man behind the steering wheel. The man who had protected and stood watch over his family for four years now.

"Yes, sir," Sam said in reply.

He turned the darkly-tinted SUV toward the highway and radioed back to the escort.

Kreo turned and watched the two men on motorcycles, lights pulsing in the chilly evening, turn away from the SUV, and he settled back into the comfortable leather seats of the armored vehicle for the long drive down to the Chesapeake.

He looked over at the girls, seeing the excitement on their faces for going back home. They often talked about missing the home that they had been absent from for most of the last four years.

He knew that they got away with more than other politicians in the past by every now and again being able to steal away to their remote home, to feel like, and be, a normal family for the short times that schedules allowed. But the girls missed the house, and the water.

And it made his heart sing that the girls in his life were happy. He did everything he could to see the looks presently on both faces.

"So, honey, tell me about this math quiz you aced today," he said to Emma as they all got comfortable.

"I will, Daddy, but first, can I ask for something?" Emma asked both of her parents in the warm enclosure of the beautifully appointed SUV.

Kreo nodded at his daughter, who was turning into a smaller version of Mya more every day.

He couldn't deny his girls a thing.

"Can we have crabs, please?" Emma asked hopefully.

Kreo smiled even brighter. Oh, how he loved his little Emma. And how he looked forward to the mundane weekend of crabbing, cooking, and enjoying his entire family.

He ruefully looked down at the carpet of the car for a moment but then gathered his feelings quickly, the politician within him coming to the surface once again.

He smiled at Emma, who smiled in return, hope filling her eyes. He nodded and spoke to his baby girl at the same time.

"Of course, honey. As soon as we pick up your brother."

Emma smiled in return, even as Mya's face dropped dramatically.

Mya had no desire to see her son.

# Chapter 39

Charles Elliot Fairchild, Charlie to his family, and Chuck to his sister, lay in his hospital bed, surrounded by stuffed animals, pictures of his family, and an around-the-clock nursing battalion who saw to his every need.

Not that he had a lot of needs or had seen any of the things that Kreo assured he was surrounded by in the sterile room.

Charlie had been born four and a half years earlier, and he had been born with almost every conceivable thing against him.

He was a preemie, he had been born starved of oxygen as his umbilical cord had wrapped around his throat twice, and he had been in a vegetative state ever since.

Naming their son after the very girl that had brought Mya and he together in the first place had seemed ironic, but they had done it with love and hope.

That hope was soon dashed, however.

The small boy, who looked so much like his mother, but with his father's coloring, had never had a first word, first steps, nor would he ever see the beauty of the world around him.

That thought usually set both Kreo and Mya into a deep, dark place when they allowed their minds to focus on the unfairness of it all.

The doctors had told Kreo and Mya that Charlie would never have a life. He would probably not make it to his tenth birthday.

All Charlie seemed to have control over were his eyelids, and small, guttural groans and moans that escaped his small lips every time he was moved for bathing or changing his diaper.

Mya had gone into a deep depression after little Charlie was born. She took the blame for everything that had happened to the small boy, no matter what anyone told her. Only her daughter, and the unfailing love of her husband, could bring her back from the brink she had suffered.

Kreo instantly felt like all of his sins had come back to punish him. But as the days turned into weeks, and months turned into years, he saw the miracle of Charlie, finally, and what his small son brought to him as a gift.

The gift of humbleness.

And the gift of never forgetting that life could be turned around for the worst in a heartbeat. Seeing his son struggling to breath every day had reminded Kreo of where he had come from, and the huge blessings they all shared now.

So now, as the young boy was turning five years old soon, Kreo had arranged for his care at a long-term medical facility in deep southern Maryland.

Whenever the family was home, Kreo would arrange an ambulance to follow the family, bringing their youngest back to his home, his room, and another cadre of nurses to see to his needs, while he spent time with the rest of the family.

And that's exactly what Kreo called ahead to arrange as the family rode in the bulletproof and armored SUV, all the way down to St. George's Island. The ambulance would meet them at their waterfront home, ready for a small reunion, as the family had been away for a couple of months this time.

The campaign had kept them all extremely busy.

Pulling up to the tall colonial house on the banks of the Potomac River made the entire Fairchild family finally feel like they were home. This home had been their escape from the world for all of Emma's life, and, it seemed, Kreo's and Mya's married life as well.

The lights were on already, and the house was lit up against the dark night closing in.

Sam pulled the dark SUV up to the side garages, the tires crunching on the white stone and broken shell driveway, and Emma squealed when she saw Mrs. Harris wave from the kitchen window. Kreo and Mya both smiled big grins at their daughter's happiness again.

"Let's get inside and cleaned up for dinner before Charlie gets here," Kreo told his daughter.

Mya and Emma smiled up at him. *Oh, it was good to be home,* he thought.

The small family rushed inside while Sam parked the SUV in one of the external garages on the property. He lived nearby in the small community of Piney Point and was eager to be home as well. Other security would see to the family for the rest of the night.

Emma was the first through the back sliding doors and into the kitchen, bounding into the arms of the older Mrs. Harris. She and her husband, Bud Harris, lived in the large home adjoining the Fairchilds' property.

Kreo and Mya had hired them years earlier, and the retired couple had happily moved to the island, taking over the estate responsibilities of the home, and the family, when Kreo's career had really started to skyrocket.

Mya had to warn Emma to be easy with Mrs. Harris, who, in all of her eighty-five years, seemed just as spry and healthy as anyone, and had an incredibly special love for the young girl who was currently trying to break her back with hugs and kisses.

Bud Harris came walking into the kitchen as Mya and Kreo removed their jackets. He wiped his hands on an old red shop rag, and Kreo nodded and smiled at the older man.

Bud had become like a father to Kreo, and Kreo loved the man dearly. He had special plans for when the Harrises were too old and feeble to look after the small family, though Kreo hoped that time was long in the future.

He sometimes felt torn in his heart for keeping the couple working, but the Harrises often reminded him and Mya both that they felt alive again for the first time in decades.

Looking after the Fairchild family's affairs, their home in southern Maryland, and looking forward to the family's infrequent visits, the older couple were given new purpose and joy, so late in life.

No, Kreo knew, looking at the older man, who was explaining how the propane tanks needed proper filling before the weekend ended, and that a fan in one of the upstairs rooms needed balancing, these beautiful people were family now, and he was blessed to have them in his employ.

He would take care of them through the end of their lives in recompence for their care of his own family.

Kreo's heart swelled with love and happiness as he took in the tranquil and familiar scene in the kitchen of the large home. Oh, how he loved his life.

"Mr. Fairchild, is Charlie expected this evening?" Mrs. Harris asked the patriarch and politician of the family.

She loved the young boy as her own, just as she did the rest of the family. She, more than anyone else, knew the despair that Charlie's presence often brought Mya, and had spent countless nights comforting her.

"Yes, ma'am. He should be here shortly. They left from the center about the time we hit Leonardtown," he told the woman.

The Center for Life Enrichment was the medical facility where Charlie stayed while the family lived in D.C. or were on the road. It was a God-blessed place that the Fairchild family supported completely. A large endowment from Kreo saw to its needs, and he assured that it was staffed with the best and brightest.

A constant security team watched over Charlie, while doctors and nurses saw to his daily care. It was the best that Kreo could do for his son, while also seeing to his responsibilities to the other people around him.

He still felt like shit leaving his son there, every time the busy family had to drive back to D.C., and being only an hour or so away was still not recompense for the guilt Kreo felt. He had no other choice, he knew, but that didn't stop the feelings.

"Then I'll get dinner started as the rest of you go and unwind. Everything is where it always is," Mrs. Harris told them all.

Being an epitome of efficiency and care, Mrs. Harris turned to the kitchen that was practically hers, and started preparing what looked like a pasta dish. Soon, delicious smells filled the noses of the rest of the family, as they went off to their separate spaces to get re-acquainted with their home away from home.

As Kreo left the elderly couple to their tasks, he was reminded by his daughter that he had promised crabs over the weekend. He pulled Bud Harris aside.

"Are the crab pots in good condition, Bud?" he asked the older man.

"Yes sir, shiny and fit, just like the blues like 'em," he answered back in his rough, southern accent.

"Emma wants crabs, and I could use the quiet of some fishing and crabbing tomorrow. Can you make sure everything is set up?" he asked. Bud nodded.

Kreo had zero doubt that everything was in even better shape than he would or could have kept it himself, but duties away from home made him have to leave that work to others. He was getting better at not feeling out of place, or useless, as time went by and his responsibilities grew.

The lifestyle he had wished for had come with unfamiliar feelings of guilt over the fact that he never had enough time to get everything he was responsible for done, but it was slowly getting easier to rely on others for what he didn't have time for.

But it was still a terribly slow process.

His internal feelings, that he had trained himself to not show outwardly, were still a jumbled mess sometimes, and he often felt like a fraud.

He didn't want to focus on that as he climbed the stairs to the bedrooms. He needed to remember the day, the success of the speeches, how well the campaign was going, and to be a bastion of positivity for his family as their youngest arrived in a few short minutes.

As he walked into the master suite that he shared with his beautiful wife, he glanced over at the flat screen TV mounted high above their sitting area.

The TV was set to CNN, and he saw himself, smiling behind the bright lights and red, white, and blue backdrop at his speech a few hours earlier. He couldn't hear the news report, but he was fairly sure he knew what they were saying.

This was becoming old hat, and he knew he was getting used to it all.

As he walked toward the bathroom where he could hear Mya making noise, he looked back at the TV as the picture moved from him giving his best speech to pictures of both Vladimir Komarov and Xi Gongping.

He instantly stopped walking and looked for the remote to hear what the news reporter was saying.

"...he would enter his presidency during one of the most trying international environments seen by any sitting president since World War Two," someone was intoning as he turned up the volume.

"The world political stage is poised for war, and if Kreo Fairchild becomes president, and is, in fact, the man for the job, he will have one of the toughest, and most explosive international policies to handle.

"The world stage is ready to implode, and it will take a strong president, and an even stronger man, to see this country through the current landmine of the world," the voice finished.

Talking heads all had their own opinions, Kreo knew, but this one was almost dead-on.

He didn't want to think about the two countries who, for years, had been competing for world domination while weak and diplomatic leadership had set the United States in a solid third place, in almost every way that counted in the world.

*The two dictators would be a worry for another day,* he thought ruefully, as he again set the TV to mute, and walked into the large master bathroom to see his beautiful wife undressing from the day and getting ready to put on more comfortable clothing.

Kreo caught her from behind before she could put on her comfortable clothes, and pulled her to him. She was wearing only underwear, and he saw not a blemish or aging on her perfect body. If she had either, the love he had for her blinded him to anything negative about his wife.

Oh, how he loved this woman, and was still turned on mightily by the sight of her, almost nude.

She giggled as he pulled her against his fully clothed frame. He also kept himself in shape, and she was still extremely excited by him.

"Honey, we don't have time," she laughed as he pushed his crotch into her from behind. She tried to wiggle out of his strong arms.

"We'll make time," he shushed her as he maneuvered her over to the sturdy marble sinks and raised her up onto them.

She sat facing him, her legs open and inviting to him. He eagerly undressed, and consummated their union right there, hot skin pressed against cold marble, ending up on the heavy shag rug below the sinks.

And they did have time. Because they were the masters of their fate and destiny and controlled the environment around them.

The rest of the people in the house were just as happy to allow the couple the time they needed for each other.

Several knowing smiles were hidden as the couple took a full half hour to come down for dinner, finally joining their entire family, faces flushed, smiles bright, and happiness extending around the table as they all ate.

The tranquility was deserved, and the happiness pervaded, but it, like most things, wouldn't last much longer. The family didn't know this at that time, but still they relished it as long as they could.

Far more sinister and painful nights would come.

But for this weekend, before the campaign finished, and the rest of the world beat a path to their door, the family enjoyed themselves as much as they could, thinking it would all last forever.

# Chapter 40

The confetti fell, the music played, Kreo was elated, Mya was nervous, and the world went round and round as the fiftieth President of the United States was elected in the largest landslide since FDR's second term.

The newly elected leader of the free world stood on stage at the famed ballroom of the Walter E. Washington Convention Center.

He was flanked by two large American flags, which stood slightly in front of all fifty of the US state flags. It had been a deliberate and time-consuming effort to display all of the flags, but Kreo had been insistent. He wanted to start his term as a man for all the people, not just the states who had voted him into office.

Dressed in a simple yet expensive dark blue suit and red power tie, Kreo stood next to his beautiful wife, Mya Fairchild, now First lady, who was adorned in a jet-black Dior gown, resplendent with a double loop of white pearls, showing her ever growing elegance and poise.

Mya Fairchild-Green had already been likened to Jackie Kennedy more than a few times in the media, and on stage next to her tall and dark-skinned husband, she proved the comparison with dignity and grace.

Kreo smiled brightly at the cheering crowd, directly into the cameras stationed all around the room, and showed the world that he really was a man of the people, for the people, and with the people.

That was the very reason he had won in such a decisive victory. The American public loved him like they had not loved a politician for generations.

And deep in his heart, as Kreo was congratulated over and over, slapped on the back, and shook more hands than he could count, he knew he'd had no small part in that victory.

Using his inherent power over Fate had assured victory, but he also knew that bigger things were at play in the world. He was uniquely qualified, and needed, for the coming world stage issues that would change the course of humanity. But he knew he didn't pull all of the strings of current events in his own life.

He wasn't that powerful.

He knew that fact both instinctually, as well as by his intensive study and research.

Standing between her parents, perfectly dolled up and coiffed, stood little Emma Fairchild, dressed in a beautiful white dress, her deep, dark hair done in pigtails and ribbons.

She was the epitome of a smaller poise, as she emulated her mother, and looked up lovingly at her wonderful father. The pride for her family shone on her face, and she knew just how lucky they all were.

The First family was the shining example of the American people, and they loved them even more knowing the tragedy of their pasts, the present with the son who was missing from the celebrations, and even more for having all come from almost nothing.

Already, several books had been written about Kreo's early childhood and climb through the ranks of the military, and just how much he had sacrificed for his country.

The country loved him even more knowing that he had taken a bullet for his country. Not since Roosevelt had a stronger, more military-disciplined leader taken up residence in the White House. And the country was ready for this man, this leader, this epitome of the American Spirit, to lead the country into world leadership once again.

The family was led into the crowd of upper crust well-wishers and financiers by the Secret Service. They were old hats with the intensive security now, and they all effortlessly moved through the throngs, giving each person a feeling of unique attention.

They left no one out, and stayed well through the night basking in the adulation and praise from constituents, lobbyists, and even other politicians who had hung their hats on the Kreo Fairchild hook. Or better yet, what would become his coattails.

The Fairchilds would not be moving into the White House until the next year, a few short months away, but the following days and months would be busier and fuller than any other time they had known in the spotlight.

What was known as the presidential transition, the time through the holidays after a general election, leading up to the presidential inauguration, was one of planning, maneuverings, and getting the old regime out of office while the new took over.

Kreo would be busy filling his Cabinet, and he had a wonderful plan that he had learned from reading how Abraham Lincoln had accomplished it.

Old Hickory, as he had been known, had maneuvered his way into the Oval Office in one of the most brilliant and tactical strategies ever seen in American politics.

But even more brilliantly, Abraham Lincoln had then filled his office, his Cabinet, and his closest advisory committee with the very men he had run against and had debated during the intensely heated campaign.

Abe knew that he had been the most unqualified man amongst the august group of conservatives at that time, and so therefore had made friends, colleagues, and partners with the men, rather than mortal enemies.

Kreo planned to do the very same thing.

And the media had caught on to the ploy early, and Kreo was so much more celebrated for that fact than almost any other move he made during the campaign.

When even the mainstream media loved you, Kreo and his advisors knew, you could do anything with the Executive branch of the Federal government. Kreo planned to do just that and more in the coming four years.

The evening of the election wore on till the early morning hours, and picking up his sleeping daughter from two chairs pushed together after the formal dinner, Kreo and Mya made their way to the running SUVs in the underground garages of the center.

They would be heading back to St. George Island for their last holiday season all together in the large home on the Potomac River.

They just had no idea that it wouldn't be because they would be in the White House the next year.

They had no idea during the transition period that the First family's time was quickly winding down, and that this Christmas really would be the very last the entire family spent together.

The Powers that Be, two very tall Beings in the Spiritual Plane, wondered as they watched events unfolding in the world below, if Kreo and Mya would have made the same decisions had they known what they were to face in only a few short months.

The ArchAngel Jeremiel wondered quietly to himself if Kreo would have done anything the same if he were aware ahead of time of what he was soon to face, and of the people and things that he loved so very much that he was about to lose forever.

*Surely not,* Jeremiel thought to himself, ruefully admitting to loving the man below. Jeremiel had been the catalyst for so much pain the man had witnessed and suffered.

Oh, how Kreo would hate the Heavenly Host if only he knew what was to come.

Jeremiel's worry and fear over that fact overrode his satisfaction of Kreo finally coming into his own and now being the most powerful man in the entire world below, but even more than that, the man who would go on to become not only the leader of the United States and the West, but of the entire world itself.

Jeremiel still believed that had Kreo known the cost of that power ahead of time, he would never have spoken up at the small community meeting, years earlier.

# Chapter 41

And finally it was Inauguration Day.

A cold, blustery winter day in Washington D.C. dawned bright. The sun rose late that morning, as if still in winter slumber, but as it crested the horizon to the east, Kreo awoke with a determination that felt like a pit in his belly.

He knew that he had a whole lifetime of work ahead in the next four years, and he was excited to get started.

He and Mya and Emma were at their large home in Montgomery County, Maryland. It was nestled in the beautiful town of Potomac, like many other politicians and

Capitol Hill personalities. Here, he had not stood out as a senator, nor even as a presidential candidate.

But once he had won the election, everything in their entire world changed. They had spent most of the holiday season at their home in deep southern Maryland, if for no other reason than to be all together, and to be as secure and safe as possible.

The world had beat a path to their very door, indeed.

Kreo arose before the sun was all the way above the horizon but could still see the brilliant reds and pinks it cast outside their bedroom bay windows.

He looked down at Mya sleeping peacefully. He was so overjoyed that she had broken through the depression that had set in after Charlie's birth. She was angelic in the light of the early morning, and Kreo gave silent thanks to the Heavens for his most precious and beautiful gift.

Mya had changed his life more than any other person or thing, and he didn't know what he had done to deserve her. And now, as their lives would take an even more awesome change, she had faced the future with stoic courage and determination, even more so than Kreo himself.

He watched her breathe for a few more moments, marveling in the beauty of her, and in their long years together. He was reminded suddenly of when they had met, and the very first conversation in that coffee shop in Berkeley, so many years earlier. He knew he had loved her then, even if he had been smitten with her best friend, the namesake of their son.

Kreo could almost smell the roasted coffee beans from that bustling college coffeeshop, and he could remember vividly the green steaks in Mya's dark hair, the wit in the twinkling of her eyes, and the amount of determination in such a small body for great and wonderful things.

And as Kreo looked down on her, sunlight starting to creep across the large bed, almost to her eyes, he realized that not only had Mya achieved all of her own goals and aspirations, but she had also helped him achieve his own.

He knew he didn't deserve her, and he vowed once again, standing a little too long looking down at her, that he would work his entire life to repay her for all she had brought to his life.

Kreo turned and walked down the hallway to their kitchen. The Secret Service staff had already brewed an army's worth of coffee in the large, industrial appliances that Mya always insisted upon. He was alone for the moment, reveling in the quiet. He knew that wouldn't last long.

Not on this auspicious day.

As he poured himself a large cup of the aromatic brew, adding in a few drops of caramel almond creamer, he went over the agenda in his mind for the day. They would be departing for the Capitol soon, and he would swear his due promises to the country, the world, and to his own family and close circle of Cabinet members.

He smiled as he took the first sip of coffee, remembering that he had asked for, and had been granted, the rights to use the same small Bible to swear his oaths on that Abraham Lincoln himself had used.

*How very fitting,* he thought to himself as he sat at the breakfast table, newspapers spread out in front of him.

The Bible was a part of the most secure periodicals of the Library of Congress. It was only brought out for the most special of events, a presidential inauguration being one of the lower hanging reasons. That thought made Kreo smile again.

He relished the quiet of the early winter morning. He didn't know why it was so quiet, when the entire house, and the capital itself should be buzzing like an angry hornets' nest, but he was thankful for it.

And that alone gave him pause. *Why*, he asked himself, coffee and newspapers momentarily forgotten, *was it so quiet?* He should have already been surrounded by family and staff.

Kreo looked down at the kitchen floor, the dark gray tile that Mya had loved so much they had installed the same in their home on St. George Island. The tile was disappearing in a covering of dense fog.

*What the hell?* he thought, alarm starting to course through his body. He jumped up, looking for the source of the fire or something burning, causing the fog. *But fires don't cause fog,* he thought.

He retraced his steps back upstairs, to his bedroom, following the increasing heaviness of the fog, and the rapid movements it made as his shuffling feet stirred it. He was at an almost complete panic. *Why was no one around?* he kept wondering.

And as he burst through the double doors into his bedroom, the rising sun still casting long rays of bright light across it, the bed resplendent in a myriad of colors from the light, he stopped dead in his tracks.

He saw his wife, still beautifully asleep in the dawn light, and a large figure standing next to her, looking down.

This was the first time that the ArchAngel Jeremiel had approached him in his waking life. And Kreo did not like how that made him feel.

The ArchAngel was clad in his moving armor once again, purple aura and bright metal bringing its own light into the room's shadows.

His large wings were folded back against the back of his Heavenly armor, and for that, Kreo was thankful. He remembered how big the Being was when fully displayed.

Later, Kreo would not forget the panic and fear that seeing the Being gave him, and what the ArchAngel being here in the Material World meant, especially on this particular day.

But on this day, he was about to become the President of the United States, and one does not achieve that status in life without poise and control.

So, he just stood there, heavy blue and gray fog swirling around all of them, waiting for the ArchAngel to tell Kreo why he was here.

It didn't take long for the tall being to turn to him and answer that very question.

"Well met, FateMaker. Congratulations on your rise in this world," the too-tall Being told him.

Kreo didn't respond. He just waited for more unwelcome news from the presence in his life who had caused so much pain and strife.

"What do you want, Angel?" Kreo heard himself answer finally. The phrase sounded vaguely familiar.

"Just a warning, Kreo," Jeremiel told the man.

Compassion and love radiated suddenly from the ArchAngel's eyes, and Kreo was taken aback. He had never seen such a look from the Being.

Kreo couldn't respond. Too many crashing emotions and thoughts fought for supremacy within him, and he was suddenly and overwhelmingly caught in a panic again. His very chest buzzed with the emotions, and he instantly became lightheaded.

*What now?* was all he could think.

"Simply this, FateMaker. You are still needed, and you are still not ready," the large ArchAngel said.

Kreo's sudden panic turned instantly to rage.

"What the hell does that mean, Angel?" he almost shouted.

It was becoming increasingly difficult to remain calm outwardly. Inwardly, he was a maelstrom of emotions. None took precedence in his mind, so the storm continued to rage inside him.

"You're almost to your Full Glory, FateMaker. It will merely take one last push," the Being told the shaking man. Jeremiel almost smiled as he felt the man tense and plan to attack the large ArchAngel.

Almost.

He had too much compassion and love for the man standing below him to smile at the emotions and actions that he, the ArchAngel Jeremiel himself, had created and enacted within the man.

Before Kreo could launch himself, kamikaze style, at the seven-and-a-half-foot ArchAngel, Jeremiel disappeared without a trace.

All at once, like rising from the bottom of a deep water, ears popping, and almost losing his balance, the sound of the world around him, people bustling and talking all at once, swept back in, and Kreo's momentary rage and emotional storms ceded.

It was once again the most dizzying and uncomfortable feeling. But it paled in comparison to the absolute terror now coursing through Kreo's system. *What the hell had that meant?* he kept asking himself, even as the rest of the day unfolded in front of them all.

Speeches given, vows sworn, and the cold pressing in so frigidly, it would be commented upon, even with the rest of the day's activities, on newscasts and in reports, for years to come.

Even with what the day portended; it was usually what would start the stories told of that *fateful* day.

How frightenly cold it had been.

# Chapter 42

The single sniper shot rang out over the din of millions of people lining the streets of downtown Washington D.C., clamoring to see the new president and first lady, with almost no recognition of what it had been.

For the better part of three hours after the assassination attempt, most people, even those standing right in line with the first family, didn't know what had happened.

No one there on that day could say they saw a thing.

It was a surprise to those witnessing the family walking down the middle of Constitution Avenue, as they later watched the local news that evening, that anything had even happened.

No one could see the world *shift* around the first family. No one could hear the scream erupt from the president as his power over the concept of *Fate* once again saved his life, and moved the trajectory of a single hollow point rifle round away from his body, and toward the one walking next to him.

No one had the eyes, nor the power, to understand that *Fate* itself had just been thwarted.

Not a single soul in all of Washington D.C., except the man with the power, could say that they even felt things change around the cacophony of the moment.

But more than a few eyes saw the first lady fall to the ground, a blossoming red stain slowly growing against the pure white of her expensive and elegant winter jacket.

And only one set of eyes saw the president scream in a state of panic and guilt while being ushered into the bulletproof and armored car driving slowly behind the first family down the packed avenue.

He had tried to reach for his wife, his screams going unanswered, but the security detail around him had done their jobs too well.

But that single set of eyes belonged to young Emma Dell Fairchild-Green, whose small, gloved hand had been in her mother's when the single sniper shot disrupted a perfectly brilliant and frigidly chilly day.

And changed Emma's life, and her family's lives, forever.

# Part 7
# In All his Glory

# Chapter 43

Kreo Gabriel Fairchild, the fiftieth President of the United States of America, sat behind an antique desk in the south end of the Oval office, the most prestigious office in the entirety of the world, and didn't notice a thing about him.

People in suits, with radios in their ears, came and went, as did several staffers, advisors, and military officials, but he didn't see any of it.

He had his head in his hands, sounds suppressed by the roaring in his mind and his ears, as he only had a mind for one thing, and a single image burned within.

Mya Fairchild-Green, the love of his life, and one of his only reasons to live, lying dead on the concrete street, blood blossoming from her chest, staining the pure white material of her dress, and he, unable to reach her.

How his mind, body, and soul burned.

He felt a hand on his shoulder and tried to shrug it off at first. But the hand insisted.

Kreo looked up into the face of his father, back from the grave, ready to dispense revenge for all Kreo had changed with the power that he saw now was a curse.

But it was only his closest advisor, John Simone.

A close friend for several years, John had advised Kreo from his first campaign, running for a county commissioner seat. It seemed a thousand years earlier, and all he could think of now was how supportive Mya had been.

"Sir. Kreo, sir." John had almost no words.

But work needed doing, and Kreo could see the resolve in John's eyes.

"We have to make a ton of decisions, Mr. President," John finally decided on a title.

Kreo didn't want to correct his friend. At a moment like this, people needed a leader. A symbol. And the presidency had always been at least that much.

Kreo cleared his throat. He didn't notice the tear that had escaped and had run a channel down his left cheek.

"Yes, yes. Get everyone in here. Let's have a chat," he told his advisor. John nodded and left to gather as many people who mattered as he could.

It had only been three days, Kreo knew, somewhere deep in his thoughts.

He didn't even know where Emma was, or his son, for that matter. He couldn't quite seem to focus.

But he had to.

Kreo looked down at the rarest desk in the world, in the most secure office in the world, and wondered just what the hell he was doing there.

He had a job to do, he knew. But his first task was to find out who had tried to kill him and had killed his wife instead.

*What the hell did you do in a situation like this?* he asked himself. *Where the hell do you start?*

But a deep black rage began to glow in his heart and in his soul, and he knew it would be an inferno before the day – or hell, even the hour – was through.

He would find who had the audacity to change the future of his family, his whole country, for that matter, and he would exact retribution like the world had never seen before.

And as the leader of the free world, and one of the strongest militaries in the world, a military that he still held rank in, and memories of battles big and small, that was not a small thing.

Someone would pay with their lives and the lives of their own soldiers as soon as he found out who had done what no one had been able to accomplish since JFK from the grassy knoll.

This was not Dallas, however, Kreo knew. And succeeding with an assassination attempt in the heart of the very capital was ludicrous.

But it had happened.

And it had succeeded. He almost lost the calm he had gained only a few short moments before.

Luckily, people started gathering in front of him, along the rear wall, and sitting on the twin couches in the middle of the large office.

He had work to do.

They were all brought to a sudden standstill, all sound in the room sucked into the vacuum created as a senior military liaison ran into the Oval Office, almost shouting the information he brought to the president.

It was General Greer, who had been the full-bird colonel who had promoted Kreo years earlier. Kreo loved the man like the father he had mistaken John for moments earlier.

And General Greer didn't stand on tradition, that was for sure. Kreo's ears rang with the words, like everyone else in the room.

"It was China and Russia, BOTH," he screamed into the bustle of the Oval Office.

And that's when the world reverberated with the clash of emotions within the people in that room specifically, as well as in every household on the planet.

What came next, well, Kreo would assure his wife's death would only be the very beginning of.

The scary thing – historians would later say – of that first of many meetings in the Oval Office, the truly scary thing was, when General Greer uttered those world-ending words, the President of the United States only smiled.

# Chapter 44

In the late twentieth century, the political, economic, and communication climates of the world were in extreme flux.

The Gulf War, as well as the war in Afghanistan, had dwindled the United States Military might, as well as put an extreme strain on the country's economic future.

After three straight liberal administrations in the White House, and the purposeful drawing down of the military, in which Kreo himself had gotten caught up, other world super-powers had come to the forefront of the global race.

The two biggest movers following the decline of the US were Russia and China, followed closely by India, the

European Union, and, surprisingly, the decades-old 'Axis of Evil' countries, like North Korea, Cuba, and several Middle Eastern countries.

Both China and Russia had their entire governments shaken up in coups and takeovers. Both had gained international prominence with advanced military technology, especially the introduction of hyper-sonic-speed weaponry.

Both countries had joined forces, secretly, to dismantle the West even more than the West had done to themselves.

Trade agreements had the US playing catch-up, and in almost every single international meeting of government leadership, the US was begrudgingly invited, but not placed in the spot of prominence like days of old.

And that was the foreign political climate that President Kreo Fairchild found himself in, a week after his wife had been assassinated, and the rest of the world seemed not to care a bit.


As he stood at the gravesite of his beloved wife, and the woman whom he had planned to spend the rest of his life with, the rage of the situation boiled in his belly, fire burning behind his dry eyes.

Emma held his hand, and Charlie was in a laid-back wheelchair nearby.

It seemed everyone around him was in tears. Sniffles, and outright pain and mourning, filled the air surrounding Kreo Fairchild, the FateMaker, but he himself could not shed a tear.

He wondered, suddenly, if Job of the Bible himself had shed tears when hit after hit had taken everything from him, all because of a Higher Power who wanted something from Job.

*If only Job of the Bible had known the truth*, Kreo thought.

Job would have burned it all down, and damn the Creator who had taken it all from him. And Kreo felt that exact same way.

The only difference was, Kreo knew the truth. And the truth, in this matter, did not, in fact, set him free. Instead, it cast him in a deep and dark pool of rage and despair.

And he had only a sole source to take it out upon. The entirety of the rest of the world.

He squeezed Emma's hand a little too tightly as he thought about exacting revenge, and she let out a squeak that added to the tears already streaming down her little face.

He apologized profusely to his baby girl, bending down and picking up her small frame.

He could feel the sobs and shaking in her little body, and that infuriated him even more toward the Higher Power who had taken everything from him for Its own purposes.

Hugging his daughter to himself tightly, he looked at the beautiful, dark gray coffin being lowered into the ground in Northern California, where Mya had set in her Will to be buried, and let the rage overtake his better judgement and mind.

Later that day, after thousands gave him condolences, and food was eaten, drinks were drunk, and mourners went back to their normal lives, Kreo called an impromptu meeting of the Cabinet, along with most of the military leadership who had traveled for the funeral services.

They met in an upper room in the largest hotel in San Francisco. *Back home once again,* Kreo thought to himself as his advisors gathered.

The Bay Area, where it had all started out for him, so many years earlier.

He looked out the tall hotel windows at the Bay and could make out the Bay Bridge a few miles away, spanning across the water toward the Albany Hills.

The Albany Hills where his own parents were both buried.

The rage did not go away that day, or any day after.

But it was temporarily forgotten with the planning of withdrawing the United States military from around the world, and bringing all of their resources and people back home.

They would need every single American troop for what lay ahead.

Every. Single. One.

On the other side of the planet, deep within an armored and reinforced room at Vosdvizhenka str., 1, Moscow, 121019, Russia, the president answered a red telephone.

An interpreter was always needed as an interceptor on that particular phone, and he heard the voice of his favorite, Sergei Pamporovo.

The State Chairman of the People's Republic of China was telephoning, and President Vladimir Komarov was delighted to hear the other man's voice.

President Komarov waved at one of the beautiful and blonde secretaries to turn down the state sanctioned newscast on the large screen television mounted on one wall, and the president took his eyes off the moving video of the American president at the gravesite of his late wife, holding his little daughter like a frightened bear cub holding its own mother.

"Ah, Chairman Gongping," President Komarov said into the red telephone handset. He could hear his interpreter relaying the message in Cantonese.

"We have succeeded, yes?" he asked.

The answer came back in two parts. The first was in a language he couldn't understand, to his own chagrin, and the other in the soft, gentle voice of Sergei.

"Like the Japanese after World War Two, I'm afraid we have awakened a sleeping giant," the chairman said cautiously.

"That was generations in the past, Comrade," the Russian president said, smiling.

"The American government, and its people, are not the same giant, anymore."

"Then I suggest we finish the job, and completely annex the entire Americas immediately," the answer came back.

President Vladimir Komarov could hear the fear, as well as the resolve, in the Chinese leader's voice. It made him smile even more.

Even this man, who could be the largest of Russia's foes, was a weak and scared little man. He controlled the vastest and richest military on the planet, and he was still frightened of his own shadow.

*Men were made differently in Mother Russia,* President Komarov thought to himself as he agreed with the Chinese state chairman.

"Preparations have already been made, Comrade Gongping. Have no fear. Russia will do its part," he said.

He was talking through clenched teeth; other men's fears infuriated him.

"My only concern is that we did not kill the Bear Cub. Merely took away his wife," Vladimir said into the phone.

He heard the chairman sigh loudly.

"Yes, I still have no idea how Shang Chin failed in his mission. But he played our hand, and now, we must finish what we started."

"Even if we did not sever the head, only removing his right arm," the chairman finished.

After Sergei interpreted the Cantonese, President Komarov smiled more broadly.

"My dear Comrade, this is even better. Angry men become stupid men. Trust the plan. We will be splitting the spoils of the conquest of the Americas very soon," he said in way of dismissal.

He hung up the red phone.


President Vladimir Komarov, former head of the Federal Security Service Red Taskforce, and murderer of thousands of men, women, and children smiled at the room around him.

His smile grew as he saw the American people mourning the loss of a single, stupid woman on the large television screen.

The crying Americans, deep in their grief, surrounded the young President of the United States.

The American president's eyes shone with fear and despair.

President Komarov decided to celebrate that evening, a little earlier than he had planned. A young, nubile woman was waiting for him, handcuffed to the foot of his bed, naked and afraid.

He could never control himself when he knew that his victims were full of terror.

It made the victory oh, so much sweeter.

As he walked out of the armored and secure bunker, he missed the television picture as the cameras panned closer to President Fairchild's face.

And he missed the look in the man's eyes that he would have mistaken for fear and terror.

He missed the fact that that look actually spelled out doom and ruin for his precious Motherland.

And as he walked up the long halls of the Kremlin, back to his apartments where his victim lay whimpering in her tears and fears, he missed the fact that it had been his own doing, and that doing spelled out his own Fate.

And the Fate of millions of Russians who did not know what awaited them all, from the simple planning session taking place at that very moment, halfway around the world, in the city by the Bay, where Kreo Fairchild had been made the FateMaker, so many years prior.

It would be a Fate different than anyone, or anything, could have foreseen, on that historic day, when a wife and mother was buried, and where two world leaders made the mistake of believing another leader was anything other than what he had seemed, all of his very incredible life.

# Chapter 45

"I don't give a good fuck how much time it will take to abandon all of the foreign bases, or the impact it will take to the host country!" President Fairchild screamed at the military brass meeting in the Ready Room of the White House basement.

"You bring all those troops home, and station them at the bases here. They will need to be ready to deploy and support the National Guard units at the borders. Gentlemen, I cannot stress enough the danger we are all in," the president reiterated.

Admiral Johnson-Myers, Head of the Joint Chiefs, simply nodded. The rest of the officers in the room looked at the admiral and gave up the arguments.

"Furthermore, I want to know how we are faring with the civilian contractors pulling out of their contracts with our allies. I gave six months. It's been seven," Kreo said.

"Mr. President, sir, ummm," another aide started. Kreo simply looked at the colonel.

"Umm, yes. It is quite a process, sir. It takes time, and the companies are all complaining about the profit losses, as well as the penalties they are taking on not completing contracts all around the world," he finished.

"Again, I don't give a good goddamn! This is a war of maneuver, gentlemen. There won't BE any contracts or work around the world if we don't survive," Kreo practically shouted.

His military bearing took over, and he calmed his voice considerably.

"Just bring everyone home. We have to shut down the borders and enact the travel bans before that Chinese fleet gets to the West Coast and the Russians find out what we are doing," he said.

He had a plan, but it was risky and dangerous for the entire country.

The public had zero idea just how much danger they were in. And that's what worried Kreo the most. They couldn't go public with what they knew. The media had to stay in the dark, and the public had to act like it would be business as usual.

They just wouldn't be able to keep the withdrawal of US troops from foreign lands quiet.

But Kreo had a plan for that as well. If all went well, every American soldier and foreign worker would be home for Christmas.

Just in time for the invasion, north and south of the United States. Mexico and Canada were in for a world of hurt, and the kickoff of that campaign would turn the world into 'every man for himself.'

That was exactly what Kreo needed to happen to save his country, and maybe the rest of the planet as well.

Kreo finished the meeting with a final statement.

"Gentlemen, we have to lose to win. Remember that. The trap cannot be set, nor the ambush successful, if the other world leaders think we have fight left in us," he told the room.

"Bring them all home!" He reiterated his words with his fist lightly pounding the dark mahogany tabletop in front of him.

The greatest military minds around the table simply nodded. The plan was sound. But they all knew that all plans and strategies fell apart as soon as the bullets started flying.

*Only this time, it wouldn't be bullets flying,* more than one mind around that table thought. It would be missiles flying through the atmosphere of the planet faster than any bullet ever could.

The hypersonic missile programs were progressing nicely, and some sudden breakthroughs in the last month looked quite promising indeed.

The anti-missile defense systems being developed in shared labs around the country had shown even more success than the missiles themselves.

A maneuver war, indeed.

Later that day, walking in the rose garden, Kreo came across his daughter talking to herself, the knees of her white tights stained green from the deep, dark grass under her.

"Hello, honey. Whatcha doing?" he asked her.

She looked up at him, the sun in her eyes. She shielded her eyes and smiled.

"I'm talking to Mommy," she said.

His heart hurt suddenly. Like all the air rushed out of him. He had no idea what to say to his daughter. How to comfort her, or how to assuage her grief and fears.

But as he looked at her smiling, familiar face, he realized that she was probably adjusting better than he was.

It was sometimes hard to look at her, as she looked so like her mother it killed him. His chest hurt, the emotions buzzing within him mixing with the fear of what was to come in the world.

He didn't know what to do, so he just stood there in the sun, staring down at his eight-year-old daughter, wondering how he had been so lucky to have such a beautiful baby like her.

"Daddy," she said suddenly.

"Yes, honey?" he answered.

She squinted back up at him, and he could see that she was pulling the petals off a dandelion. His heart felt like bursting, and for the first time in an exceptionally long time, he felt tears well in his eyes.

"Mommy told me to tell you that you shouldn't kill all those people," she said.

He was shocked. How did she know?

She kept talking past his shock.

"And Mommy said to tell you that it isn't going to make any difference. This world has to just go the way it has to go," she said.

He could hear Mya's words coming from Emma's lips. He didn't know how to respond.

He was the most powerful man in the Western World, and he couldn't find the words to speak to his daughter, who went, smiling and laughing, back to playing after saying two sentences that shocked his soul.

"Honey," he finally said. "Honey, tell your mom that it has to be done. It can't be stopped now."

She just nodded, still playing with flowering weeds in the thick grass.

And under his breath, as he turned and walked back toward the Oval Office, nodding to the Secret Service agents protecting his daughter, he whispered, "And tell her that I miss her like crazy and I don't know how I can go on."

He was too far away to hear Emma reply. She smiled at the small yellow flower in her hand.

"She knows, Daddy. She said you're going to be simply fine," she smiled.

She could feel her mother's hands on her shoulders, and the soft kiss her mother placed on her left cheek.

Emma giggled an eight-year-old girl's laugh and heard the answering giggle in the soft breeze of the warm, sunny day.

# Chapter 46

Sergei Pamporovo relished in his human form, taking every second of time in the Material world for granted. This existence was one which he knew would suit him well, for millennia, if allowed to continue.

*The problem was*, the Watcher thought to himself as he gorged on the meat of a large herd animal, set before him at a splendid, ornate ball, *this existence would soon be extinguished, if the Mother had anything to say about it.*

He did not want to think of the Mother. To do so brought instant pain to his angelic synapsis.

He'd had to anchor to this human form, giving up the freedom of his powers. But he still relished the pleasures of the guise.

The demonic Watcher, within the human sack of skin, bone, sinew, and blood, could not get over the feelings of tactile contact. Even picking up the metal fork next to the ceramic dinner plate was ecstasy. His first few days as a mortal were an overwhelming cacophony of sights and sounds, but most importantly, touch. He could not stop touching things with his human hands, and as he learned deeper pleasures with other parts of the human guise, his lust for touch and pleasure overrode this mortal mind.

But he was also sent with a job to do. This time, it wouldn't be to simply Watch.

This time, he was to be a catalyst for war.

He reveled in the thought of a new fight, with human opponents, but still as brutal and savage as a Celestial Fight with the damned ArchAngels.

Just thinking of the Beings made him look around sharply, as if they could see him consuming the elk steak before him, or notice the pressure of the woman's hand on his human thigh, under the white-tablecloth-covered table.

He felt certain appendages of this human body respond to the woman's touch, and he reveled more in the pleasures to come that very evening.

As a Watcher, he had been created with a more feminine countenance. His name had been Asael. But that was a lifetime ago.

Being in the human male body certainly had its advantages, and he felt an awakening of his wisdom and knowledge. What a strange and amazing assignment, indeed.

He drew the woman's hand off of his thigh, hearing her sigh next to him, and he turned his attention to the head of the tables lined up in military precision. The president was addressing the gathered crowd of Russian dignitaries.

Sergei needed to listen, so he could report back to the Mother.

"…and we are Russians! War in winter is nothing new, and the Western army's blood is too thin to defeat Russians in the snowy wastes!" President Komarov was practically shouting.

Sergei knew the short, balding president was deep in his vodka.

"We will conquer through the northern of the Americas, and we will set a wall of Russian artillery at the northern borders of the United States and bombard their gutless country until they are on their knees! And then Russia will be the most powerful country in the world!" he slurred.

"To the Motherland!" he screamed.

Raising his glass of vodka, he threw it back like water. Many Russian leaders around him did the same.

And over the loudspeakers scattered around the large, ornate, and heavily gilded room, the Russian Anthem, "Patrioticheskaya Pesnya," began playing.

Its eerie music caused everyone in the room to stand, turn as one in a militaristic display, and raise hands to the bold red flags lining the western walls of the ballroom. The deep, Russian lyrics were sung with a mixture of pride, patriotism, and fear.

Sergei could see it in their eyes as they sang along with the inebriated president, who sung the anthem louder than anyone in the large, cavernous room.

Fear. Over-encompassing terror. Oh, how he marveled in it, in both his human form, and her Watcher countenance.

After the anthem was sung, and more toasts were given to the victory of the Russian people, Sergei approached the head table, and was waved through the security around the president with a nod of the balding man's head. Sergei approached the leader and bent down to speak in his ear.

"Comrade President," he addressed the man, speaking in Russian. "A call came in earlier, while you were engaged in your apartments, with, ummm, your secretary," he said with a smile. Both men were aware of each other's proclivities.

"Who was it?" the president slurred back to the interpreter.

"The chairman from the People's Republic of China, sir," Sergei said. He could see the president's neck begin to turn red. Thel of the Communist Party in Russia was not a pleasant man when angry and deep in his drink.

Sergei could care less if the president grew angry. He had a message to relay to the leader, and he meant to have a little fun with the man.

"The message I am to relay to you, Comrade President, is that the Chinese fleet is in position, and you should begin your raid of the country of Canada," Sergei said. No such message had come through diplomatic, nor secret, channels but this idiot wouldn't know that.

The president sprang to his feet, spilling his vodka and seafood dinner all over the pristine white tablecloth. Sergei sprang back with dexterity uncommon in humans and listened as the pompous ass of a leader declared to the assembly that "I've just been informed that the battle for the world… has begun!"

Fists struck tabletops, people stood and started shouting, and some idiot in the sound room began to play the Mother-forsaken anthem again.

Sergei hated these people but put up with them for the Assignment the Mother had sent him on.

He would do his job here, infiltrating the Russians, getting in close to the president, all to make sure that they failed when the decisive battle was on the line.

*No one*, Sergei thought to himself as he exited the room, the demure woman catching up to him to help with his own evening entertainments, *no one would expect what was to come.*

And that was the real fun of the Assignment the Mother had given Her favorite Daughter.

The rest of it was simply the cherry on the top of the cake. A cake that the Host of ArchAngels would soon come to choke on, Mother willing.

Sergei Pamporovo, also known as the Watcher Asael, the Arrogant One, nodded to another man standing guard over the assembly of Russian leadership, who happened to be one of the other Watchers within the Kremlin, another of many.

Asael laughed hysterically, all the way to her bedchambers and the gruesome, bloody fun found within.

# Chapter 47

Kreo stood at the bow of the US Navy's largest destroyer, the USS Zumwalt.

He knew that they had deceived the enemy by making them think he was on the flagship of the Pacific Fleet, the USS Ronald Regan aircraft carrier.

But he was three ships off middle, so as to be a smaller target for the aerial maneuvering of the enemy aircraft.

He was staring up at the ship's motto written in white paint on the bow gunwales, "*Pax Propter Vim.*"

Peace Through Power.

He laughed silently to himself at the thought of the world still being a peaceful place, no matter how powerful he had made his country. And his goal in the Pacific over the next several days was to show their main enemies anything BUT power. *No,* he thought chuckling to himself. *Peace through power would come later.*

Much later.

He was in the Pacific Ocean, with the men and women of the Pacific Fleet, the most powerful navy in the world, to do one thing.

Lose.

It was a classic chess strategy, but not one popularly picked up by modern day militaries. He was sacrificing his queen in order for his knight to take their king. To the military minds, the losses were not worth the outcome.

The president's mind was focused on the fact that the losses would be heavy but would have to be justified by the safety and security of the many.

President Kreo Fairchild just hoped that his soul could handle the strain. But after seeing his wife, the epitome of his own peace, killed in cold blood, he believed that he could handle the loss.

He secretly looked forward to this. His rage needed dampening. His anger needed settling.

And his overwhelming despair needed a blanket of calm, calculated strategy, and for the loudest cacophony of fighting, blood, and battle, to be soothed.

Ex-Marine Lieutenant, battle-hardened, and broken, bloody, and wounded veteran widower, President Kreo

Fairchild needed someone to kill in return for the murder of his precious Mya.

And he may not get the chance to get his actual hands dirty, but he was about to be responsible for thousands of deaths on both sides of the coming engagement. He just hoped it slaked his need for blood.

As his knuckles turned white holding the top of the gunwales, he thought back to the strategy, the plans, the simplicity of it, and what he had enacted back home, only days earlier.

The first news reports of the US pandemic hit the airwaves four days prior.

That same day, President Fairchild had enacted Martial Law for the first time since 1963.

But never before in the entirety of US history, had both the president and the Congress enacted it together in a sweeping bi-partisan move to 'protect the public, while maintaining control over escalation of illness to every part of the globe.'

What the world did not know, and what only a few people really had the entire scope of, was that for weeks leading up to the national declaration of Martial Law, President Fairchild's entire administration had worked around the clock, and achieved unanimous acceptance and support for the ever-increasing threat of global warfare.

As soon as Russian ground troops had been spotted in both Mexico and Canada, it had been apparent to everyone in the Federal government what the end goal was. China and Russia wanted the United States and its natural resources, as well as its position as an international trade and military leader.

They were tired of playing second and third on the world's stage.

So, through exhaustive and thorough Cabinet meetings, strategy and brainstorming sessions, and back-room deals struck with members of both the Senate and the House, President Fairchild, being the Commander-In-Chief of the entirety of the US military complex, was given total and unequivocal control of the entire United States.

Even the meetings of the governors had given support to the Executive branch of the Federal government, and President Fairchild was using that extreme power to enact his own plans for not only saving the American public, but to exact revenge and control over the world governments who had the gall to attack both the US and his own family.

On the evening of December 7th, 2025, an inauspicious day in US history, President Fairchild used his newly formed control over everything in the US and held a formal conversation with every citizen of the country, his familiar face taking over every single screen in every home in the United States.

Even that much control was an unprecedented event for the country with the most freedom in the world.

"My fellow Americans," he began.

Sitting behind the antique oak desk in the Oval Office, surrounded by twin American flags, and wearing another, smaller pin of the same red, white and blue on the lapel of his expensive Brooks Brother suit, he maintained a sense of calm, dignity, and leadership.

Polls would later tell him that he had the attention of not only the majority of the American people, but the world itself.

"I won't mince words. I won't coddle to the masses. And I will be as straightforward and honest as I am currently able to do," he said into the single television camera standing tall before the presidential desk.

"The Centers for Disease Control in Atlanta has informed this administration that a new strain of the COVID virus, a virus that we thought we had control of several years ago, has flared back with a mutation that makes it extremely volatile, extremely contagious, and particularly deadly," he said with a straight face and a somber tone in his voice.

"Tonight, this administration, along with bi-partisan support from Congress, have enacted Martial Law for the entirety of the United States, and all of its provincial territories. We have enacted an extreme travel ban, and procured, opened, and liquidated all state of emergency coffers and stockpiles," he said.

He knew that would strike panic in the US.

But better for the panic to be condensed into a social terror strategy, than to tell the public what the real reason was for the takeover of all of their precious freedoms.

"There will, of course, be regional and state mandates for keeping this pandemic under control, and every single thing that this administration, this government, and the thousands of front-line workers can do, we will. We need to work together as one people to assure that we do not lose potential millions to this airborne disease," he said.

He could almost hear a proverbial ball dropping as the American public took in all of this information.

And two minutes after his historic address to the people of the United States, government workers, law enforcement, national guardsmen, US military personnel, even park police and rangers, shut down almost every public meeting place, restaurant, store, library, church, school, even most medical offices. The public outcry was swift and loud, and just as quickly squelched.

After all, the US had just gone through the exact same four years previous, and the practices of isolation and staying at home were almost ingrained with the public.

Nightly update addresses and controlled media practices over the next few nights assured the US public that this State of Emergency would be over quickly.

Just enough time for Kreo to enact stage two of the Plan, and start killing the enemy at their own games, but also his own troops, sacrificed for the greater good, to assure the rest of the world that the United States of America was not only on its knees, but also extremely vulnerable, its belly showing for all the world to see.

He was creating a worldwide ambush.

And not one of his enemies would see it coming.

And now, deep within the north Pacific Ocean, at a navigational point that would go down in history as the worst US Navy defeat, President Fairchild watched from the forward gunwales of the most advanced destroyer in the world as several squadrons of fighter jets screamed overhead, and a barrage of artillery was launched from the two carrier groups of US ships toward the combined navies of several enemy countries.

The US Navy was woefully outmanned and outnumbered, but like the tales of old, of the American Wild West, the US navy went into the battle with full guns blazing, hoping against all hope that a surprise attack would throw off the enemy ships, and create space for an American victory.

The enemy, as usual, was nonperturbed, and answered back, like a thundering cloud of death and destruction on the US fleet.

A fleet that had no idea what was happening, or who was actually orchestrating their very own deaths.

# Chapter 48

Modern naval battles were fought on three fronts, even though the combatants were engaged solely, surrounded by thousands of miles of bare ocean, with no land in sight, even on radar cross sections.

The Battle for the Pacific Rim, as it would later be known, was fought on the surface of the waves, below the water, and in the skies above.

Men screamed and died, blood rained down all around, and fire floated on top of the waves like bright orange and red foam, and all around the president, the cacophony of war was a familiar lullaby.

He didn't know if that was a good thing or not, but it made him feel more complete than he had since his Mya had been taken from him.

The enemy had surprised the US fleet with a flanking maneuver from the south, and ships held back in reserve had quietly slipped into the melee toward the middle of the bloody day.

The US Navy, of course, had known of the enemy's maneuverings, and orders from the Commander in Chief, thwarting those of the Vice Admiral in Charge, had assured that the US fleet would lose the day.

There wasn't a military officer alive who would purposefully lose a battle, killing thousands of US troops. *Luckily*, Kreo thought to himself as he relieved the admiral of his command via radio conference from the mess hall of the Zumwalt, *he was no longer a Marine Officer.*

And so, fighter jet squadrons screamed overhead, dogfights too numerous to count and explosions rocked the large ships below. The ships themselves sent salvo after salvo of hot lead and missiles toward other ships flying full red flags, who sent the same back at the ships flying Old Glory.

And under the waves, unseen by those above, but the shudders and explosions still felt deep within the steel coffins of Navy ships, submarines fought each other silently, in the depths, and all that was left of those brave seamen was wreckage that floated up to join in the burning metal on the surface.

Under cover of darkness, and after a full day of battle and death, only three USN ships limped back toward Pearl Harbor, in Hawaii.

None of the ships that had survived were larger than the destroyer class ship the president currently resided within.

They had left another ship, a frigate, behind to sweep up survivors in the water. Hundreds if not thousands of orange ink puddles dotted a piece of the ocean miles wide, showing the frigate where survivors' life vests had released their telltale marker.

It had been a swift and decisive victory for the enemy fleets, the first naval loss for the United States since WWII. As the remaining ships limped back to Pearl, joyous laughter and celebrations could be heard from the three aircraft strike groups of the enemy that remained.

The enemy was too caught up in the surprise victory to realize that only two out of eleven carrier strike groups from the US Navy had entered into the battle.

Kreo knew that the enemy was convinced that the sweeping pandemic, which had been so diligently handled by the US government, had brought the military to its knees, without the combined force of the Russians and the Chinese having to lift a single hand.

And that's exactly what Kreo and his closest advisors had planned and enacted, and it was hugely successful. Never before had such a global hoodwink been theorized, let alone successfully played out.

Kreo was actually impressed with his administration, as well as the American public, in their work in assuring his plan worked.

But he also knew deep within his soul that he had been using his powers over Fate more times during the previous six months than at any other time in his life.

He felt exhausted deep in his soul every single time, and he didn't know if he could go on.

Only the memory of his wife, bloody chest opened up in the street, could keep him on his feet as he figure-headed the biggest scam in the history of humanity.

And as the remaining pieces and parts of the two aircraft carrier strike groups puttered into Pearl Harbor late the next morning, being let free by the enemy fleet, Kreo knew it was time to set off the second phase of the Plan.

He had to make sure that the enemy countries took the bait and attacked the United States mainland from the north and the south, and with everything the combined coalition of enemy countries had to throw at them.

Stage two would be the hardest, and most sophisticated part of the plan.

And he would, once again, have to dupe his own people. Only this time, it wouldn't be the public, or even the military he needed to dupe.

It was much more complicated than that.

He would have to dupe his own administration, Cabinet, government, and those who thought they were in on the real plan.

He would have to double cross those he had used to double cross the public and the military itself.

President Fairchild now knew, as he boarded Air Force One, bound for his home on St. George's Island, that the next phase of the Plan would be his, and his alone, to enact, and see to its conclusion.

He was suddenly and overwhelmingly terrified as the large Boeing 747-200B flew back to the mainland of the US, and the terror did not go away until it was all said and done, and the world's power and leadership was shifted to a level unknown, unseen, and unheard of in all of human history.

# Chapter 49

During the short but deadly War of 1812, British Naval forces, at that time the strongest in the world, harassed the US East Coast, and laid waste to defensive and strategic areas like the Maine coastline, Baltimore, where Fort McHenry would change the tide of battle, and of course, the sacking and burning of Washington D.C.

The British warships were not harassed at all as they entered the Chesapeake Bay and made their way up the wide and gentle Potomac River, all the way to the very center of Washington D.C. and the tidal basin.

After the war of 1812, Congress and the presidency saw fit to assure that Washington D.C. would not remain defenseless any longer.

Several forts were constructed along the ninety-six nautical miles from the mouth of the great river, all the way into the deep and wide tidal basin within the confines of D.C. proper.

Fort Washington, Fort Necessity, and sixty-six others were constructed to protect the nation's capital. The forts were heavily in use during the US Civil War, as the famous river was the demarcation border between the North and the South.

On the Maryland side of the river, banks of cannons pointed at the waterway, and on the Virginia side, dug in forts and troop barracks housed the Union's forces, even giving of the most famous Union Army, under General Lee, the moniker "the Army of the Potomac."

The Potomac River, even at its large, miles-wide mouth, was the most strategic area to the protection of Washington D.C., by way of a naval attack on the capital.

In the deep winter of 2026, President Kreo Fairchild stood on his own long, wooden dock, which extended forty-five feet into the Potomac, only a half-mile from the mouth of the great river to his south.

On St. George's Island, he was, for all intents and purposes, standing at the mouth of the only artery by ship into the great capital city, and the government within.

The wind was biting, and the spray off the three-foot waves on the river stung the president's face. But he faced into the heavy wind with determination and grit.

He was, after all, the most powerful man in the world, even if his enemies undervalued and underestimated him at every turn.

Over the last two months, Russian forces had invaded the snowy wastes of Canada to the United States' north, and Chinese Nationals had had a tough time gaining ground in Mexico to the South.

But they had gained that ground, and now both countries' ground forces threatened the United States in a pinching formation at both borders.

At the same time, the mixed Chinese and Russian navies had transitioned the Panama Canal, having used extensive force against the government in that impoverished country to allow passage, and swung up the eastern coast of the United States, laying anchor directly off the Mid-Atlantic Coast, in international waters.

And every single missile silo and underwater nuclear-powered submarine in both countries' arsenal was pointed at the United States' western coast.

California had been practically evacuated to medical evac sites deep in the Midwest. In fact, most of the US population had been taken into the very center of the country, in the largest human evacuation and human encampments ever seen.

Kreo Fairchild and his Federal government had done everything they could to convince the outside world that the United States had lost a third of its population to the sweeping and unstoppable Pandemic that seemed only to impact the US, and that its military might was bowed under the weight of facing warfare on four fronts.

And that's exactly what President Fairchild had envisioned. It was a simple plan, but had a million moving parts, all orchestrated in a global dance the likes of which had never been seen before in human history.

His mind tried to scatter, thinking over such a large operation, and he silently thanked the gods that he had had such sweeping approval from the US population, and that certain things had transpired in the last decade to get that same population ready for such a time as this.

*It was quite fortunate,* the president thought to himself as he watched the headwaters of the wide Potomac River, covered in a thickening fog, and heavy with moisture in the wicked winter winds, *that for once, the American people seemed willing to work together to save their own necks.*

*Now*, the president thought, *it was time to finish this trivial matter, and the secrets that he had held close to his chest through the entire ordeal were ready to be launched, literally, as the combined Naval forces steamed into the Chesapeake Bay, and made for the supposed deserted Washington D.C. tidal basin.*

President Kreo Fairchild put his hands deep into the pockets of his jeans and fiddled with the small electronic contraption held within the lefthand-side one.

He just needed to time everything right, and the last two years would all be worth something. He still wilted under the pain of losing Mya, but today, on the second anniversary of his wife's death, he was ready to enact his final vengeance on the rest of the world.

And the small electronic button in his pocket would be the very catalyst of that revenge.

His mind still on what was to happen that day, he barely heard the footsteps coming up behind him, quiet in small white winter boots.

"Daddy," Emma said quietly.

President Fairchild turned in the harsh wind of the winter day and looked down at his growing daughter. She was ten years old, but still looked every bit of a baby in his eyes.

"Yes, baby," he said down to her.

"Daddy, are you sure about today? Do you really think this will change things?" she said.

She looked up at her father with a wisdom that shocked and perplexed him. Over the last two years, his Emma Bear had shown a remarkable ability to learn secrets she shouldn't have known, and had a wise and decisive air about her, contrary to the youthful shine of her heart-shaped face.

*A heart-shaped face so like her mother's*, Kreo thought to himself.

He steeled himself from the thought, and the tears that the thought usually brought. Today was no day for tears, nor for weakness.

"I'm sure, baby. There's no other way," he told her.

He reached out his hand, and she took it. Smiling up at her wonderful father, Emma Fairchild hurt for the man he had become, so bent and determined in his revenge.

"OK, Daddy. I just had to ask one last time," she said into the winter wind.

"I know, baby. Why don't you go inside and get some hot cocoa with Mrs. Harris?" he told her.

She squeezed her father's hand, and with a final, beautiful smile, beamed up at him.

*Her smile and trust in him made everything he was about to do worth it,* he thought, glancing back to the north.

And as he thought that simple thought, he saw the thundering bow of the flagship of the combined Russian and Chinese Navy, now breeching the sovereign lands and waterways of the United States of America.

The first and only battle from an outside invader was about to begin on US soil, and President Kreo Fairchild had a surprise for the rest of the world that they wouldn't see coming.


At 8 a.m., Eastern Standard Time, on the morning of January 20th, every television, cellphone, laptop, computer screen, and any other electronic device that could connect to the world wide web went blank.

The president used a built-in system for emergency situations that took over every web-enabled device in the United States.

What was about to transpire would not go out on the airwaves to give the rest of the world time to prepare.

As the vast combined Navy made its way up the Potomac, some fifty-five vessels of enemy force stretched out along thirty miles of river bottom leading into the capital.

After all of the ships crossed under the newly built 301 Bridge connecting southern Maryland with the northern neck of Virginia, and the lead ship came even with George Washington's ancestral home at Mount Vernon, an event that had never happened in the entirety of human history took place, all within the span of ten minutes.

And President Fairchild, standing at the end of his own wooden dock, at the mouth of the Potomac River, pushed the red button in his pocket, as he watched the last frigate flying a Chinese flag make its way past his own home on St. George's Island.

With the pressing of the red button in the president's pocket, several things happened, all at once, and only known fully to the man who pressed it.

Even his own government and closest advisors had no idea what was going to happen with the proverbial pressing of a single button.

With the pressing of the red button, President Kreo Gabriel Fairchild killed a full third of the human race, with technology that was unstoppable, untraceable, and accomplished its goals within minutes.

Billions of people perished in nuclear cataclysm, and the world would never, ever, be the same again.

There was not a single country within the world that was not then affected by the pressing of the button, even the United States.

But the majority of the US population had survived, except for those fighting at the borders, and the victims of a single missile from a Russian destroyer that was not stopped before it hit the Mall of Washington D.C. and destroyed the White House, the Washington Monument, and cracked the base of the statue within the Lincoln Monument.

Outside of that single missile attack on the US, the most powerful country in the world was decided within a few precious moments, and from that day onward, the human race was changed, irreversibly.

Back on that wooden dock, stretching out into the Potomac River, the cold, winter wind on his face, and the spray from the frozen waves at his feet, Kreo dropped the electronic box with the single red button to his feet, now useless, having fulfilled its deadly purpose.

Kreo fell to his knees and wept frozen tears into the quiet, whispering wind that held no secrets for him that day, or any day after.

# Chapter 50

During his military career, President Kreo Fairchild had worked with some of the most ingenious minds within the civilian sector, especially missile defense.

Kreo had grown fond of the missile defense systems that had protected him and his troops, and had drunk several beers and had several conversations with young engineering minds who were on the forefront of missile technology and defense systems.

One of his state-side duties had been overseeing the installation of a new, mobile missile defense system within Washington D.C. itself. It had been codenamed 'GhostEye' and was a mixture of advanced radar technology of the fifth generation, and mobile sidewinder missile launching systems called NASAMS.

He had watched, over a couple of years, as this type of new generation missile and radar defensive and offensive capabilities were perfected and even grew more advanced within its purview.

He had never lost touch with those engineering minds, nor the now-hardened people behind them, and as he took over the presidency, a strategy had developed, with the NASAMS and GhostEye systems at the forefront of it.

He regrated that he'd had to 'black opt' the same people he had drunk so many beers with.

The first year of his administration, and outside the knowledge or approval of his government, he procured every civilian warehouse, manufacturing facility, and engineer in the missile defense sector, and put them all to work using Presidential Emergency Orders.

He could, and did, use his powers extensively, and assured that the strictest and highest clearance for the work would keep it as secret as he could.

He was sorry for the lives lost of several whistleblowers and government workers that tried to blow the secret project.

And he was even more sorry for ordering those deaths.

They were patriots, and were trying to do the right thing, but he needed the programs to remain top secret, and word of the advancements that he had asked for was not released to the outside world.

At the end of the two years after he had initiated the work, several innovative technologies were developed, and prototypes were quickly and securely created, manufactured, tested, and stockpiled.

The biggest advancement within that timeline was the creation of the new US wind-powered nuclear cruise missile.

The sixth-generation cruise missile was like nothing ever seen before. Using a wind turbine engine, slightly modified from what was used to move the largest airplanes around the world, the nuclear-tipped missiles could travel at speeds eight to ten times the speed of sound.

They held radar-defeating stealth technology and could fly the entire circumference of the planet in under five minutes, and land at a pre-determined point the size of a small passenger car.

The other half of the huge and expensive undertaking during those two years was a radar and anti-missile system lightyears beyond the initial GhostEye defense systems.

Under guise of other government earmarks for medical research and deployment of vaccines and medical help for the fake pandemic that the US government had concocted, those missile defense systems were placed strategically around the entirety of the United States mainland and territories.

In two years' time, the US government, under the leadership of President Fairchild, and known to only a very few high-ranking civilians within the defense contracting world, had become not only the most advanced and highly protected country in the world, it had re-ignited the nuclear stockpile that had been depleted, during the Cold War roll down.

The same stockpile that his predecessors had depleted, but refused to fully destroy, regardless of what the rest of the world had been told.

This fact alone made President Fairchild feel justified in what he felt he had to do.

All of that meant that with a single push of a single button within the pocket of President Kreo Fairchild, many things happened all at once, and could not be stopped, in fact were barely seen by every other country in the world.

The first and most decisive thing that happened during the previous two years of secret maneuvers, was that the old forts along the Potomac River, those ancient, crumbling stone edifices of historical battles, had been stocked and filled with mobile NASAM systems.

All up and down the long river, hundreds of thousands of sidewinder missiles, the newest AIM-9X versions, were aimed at the encroaching naval power steaming towards the supposedly deserted capital.

As the last of the naval vessels floated past President Kreo Fairchild's family home, with the pressing of the inauspicious red button those Sidewinder missile platforms opened up volley after volley of explosive-tipped Sidewinder missiles from both sides of the long river.

Being so close to the ships, within mere yards in some instances, the ships had absolutely zero time to not only defend themselves from the missile volleys, but most of them were destroyed and sunk before they even knew what was happening.

Military units assigned to the defense of the capital and stationed now along the very river that Kreo had assured the enemy Navy would travel, mopped up survivors swimming or sinking within the ice-cold river water. Not a single enemy solider survived what would be historically named the "Potomac River Ambush."

Rotting and rusting enemy hulls would remain in the hundred feet of middle channel of the river for generations to come.

Simultaneously, as the Potomac River Ambush was being accomplished, two other defensive maneuvers were taking place, and a single, all-consuming offensive.

On each of the northern and the southern borders of the United States, the enemy forces that assumed the US was weakened to a point of almost zero resistance, suddenly found themselves surrounded on all sides by US Army, Marine, and Special Forces, who had, under cover of darkness, and with stealth and winter maneuvers, outflanked both attackers on both fronts.

Within the waters of both the Pacific and the Atlantic, GhostEye radar systems that could see a robin egg breaking open even through a mile of solid rock, locked onto enemy warships, submarines, and their own missile emplacements hastily erected within the sovereign countries of Mexico and Canada.

Seeing the invaders being massacred by US troops within their own countries, both militaries of Canada and Mexico, along with secretly maneuvered allies of English, French, South American, Australian, and several other Allied countries, had joined in the fight, killing the enemy, while also taking heavy losses themselves.

But within a few hours, the day was won, on both flanks of the ground war.

And as the ground war raged, the Potomac River Ambush succeeded, and the launching of missiles toward enemy emplacements around the US were launched, one last offensive strategy was accomplished.

The very thing that Kreo had kept from the rest of the US population, his own administration, and the very people who would come to suffer from his, and only his choices.

As the ground war, the naval massacre, and the pinpointed killing of enemy targets around the continental United States was accomplished, a very costly offensive was launched toward the rest of the world.

When President Fairchild pressed his single button, over one hundred hypersonic, wind-powered, and nuclear-tipped cruise missiles were launched from every conceivable way known to the US military.

They were launched from miles underwater by nuclear-powered submarines. They were launched from old, Cold War style missile silos.

And they were launched by three separate squadrons of high-flying, radar invisible, and highly trained B-2 bombers, strategically stationed for the greenlight, all around the world, and within every Allied nation.

When those hundreds of hypersonic cruise missiles were launched, all within two minutes of each other, and every single one pointed at a city-center, military depot, or government complex of the United States' most vicious enemies, he truly destroyed the entire globe.

Five minutes after President Fairchild pressed the Doomsday Button within his left pocket, billions of people inside China, Russia, North Korea, North Vietnam, Iran, Afghanistan, Pakistan, India, and all of the smaller countries within the Axis of Evil were killed, their infrastructure destroyed, and the civilizations of thousands of societies obliterated.

Using advanced technology, nuclear weapons, and on a scale never before even thought of, President of the United States Kreo Fairchild had murdered a third of the population of the planet Earth.

And at the same time, using his Powers over Fate, and exhausting his abilities with a global *shifting* of that Fate, he assured not only the sovereignty of the United States on the international stage once again, but he set himself up as the leader of the entire planet.

Never before had a leader who had killed billions been loved universally by the entirety of the survivors.

After the smoke cleared, and the world took stock of what had been done on the morning of January 20th, two years to the day after the assassination of his wife, Kreo Fairchild was raised up as the One World Government Leader, for the rest of his natural and known life.

For the first time in all of human history, the world, which had been divided and at war with each other for millennia, was at peace, and controlled by a single entity.

New World One, the government for the entirety of the human race, was headquartered in a castle in Germany, a year after the decisive victory, and Kreo Fairchild was made to be the figurehead, the leader, the sovereign, the monarch, and the king of the entirety of the planet Earth.

The FateMaker had come into all of his Glory, indeed.

# Chapter 51

Some years later, after the dust had settled, and the world had been put back in order, and his family safely ensconced around him, Kreo was at rest.

In the highest tower of what had once been known as Albrechtsburg Castle in the steppes of the country of Germany, now renamed One World One, King Kreo Fairchild, the FateMaker now known to the entirety of the world, looked out upon a peaceful lake and a serene sunset to the west.

Behind him, books lay open on several desks scattered around the entire library. He had become almost a hermit of a leader, choosing to gather wisdom, knowledge, and understanding, rather than running the day to day needs of the entire planet.

He left that up to his closest advisors and the wisest leaders of the old world.

As an old man, he had not lost any of the vigor or poise he had gained through a lifetime of pain and sacrifice. He had not lost a single step of his strong body, and his even stronger mind.

He had been forged in the fires of oppression, abuse, loss, and pain. And it showed on the craggy, wrinkle-lined face that stared back from the mirror most mornings.

His mind was ever sharp, his powers over the concept of Fate had not wavered, and he ran the world the way he thought it should be, with wisdom, and neutral guidance.

And as he looked down at the world below the castle, he felt that he knew what was to happen next. Like a lone shot in a dark night, a sound reverberated in his skull and a crack appeared behind him in the large, open library room, high within the tallest tower of the castle.

He turned, showing no surprise at what he beheld. A voice spoke from within the Crack, as a figure appeared from it.

*"FateMaker, I am Azazel, the Unmaker, and I am covered in Darkness,"* the creature hissed.

It bent nearly in half in a deep bow. A bow that the god-king was used to receiving from the people around him.

Kreo knew of the proclamation of the Creator, who had caused so much suffering in his own life, against the particular Watcher before him. *And so*, Kreo thought, *it was apt in its words.*

Kreo had expected a visit like this for some time, and therefore, showed no signs of surprise of the appearance of the tall Watcher, nor the green and black movement behind him, where the Crack to the other Existence lay.

The creature bowed lower to Kreo, its cowl brushing the stained wooden floor of the library. And it was, indeed, covered in shadow. Kreo could barely make out the creature's form under the heavy white robe and cowl it wore.

He was fairly sure he did not want to see the creature within the hidden folds of cloth.

It spoke again while Kreo remained silent. And as it spoke, it changed the Fate of all existence.

"Asherah, the Wife of God, and the Mother of Creation, would like a word, FateMaker," it intoned. The voice sounded like a many-voiced choir, all singing off-key.

Kreo nodded toward the darkness before him. He had figured as much from his studies and from the wisdom he had gained as the FateMaker.

"Lead the way," he told the Watcher.

The fallen Watcher did just that, as Kreo, the foretold FateMaker and King of the Earth, followed it into the Crack between Existences.

And shadow swallowed them both as he disappeared within.

Three floors below the large, now-empty library, Emma Fairchild, sprawled out in an over-large beanbag chair, listening to music and drawing pictures of the countryside around the castle, looked to the ceiling above her.

Her brother Charlie was in his corner bed, still not able to move any part of his body, but his mind was working as it always had.

No one had any idea the young man was very much alive within his cocoon of a frozen body.

Emma and Charlie could feel, and hear, the sizzling of the Crack in Existence.

As it winked out around her father, Emma slowly closed her eyes, listening to the sound of the thumping beat in her ears, and the whisperings of the voices around her.

Emma Fairchild opened her eyes suddenly, the blues of her irises glowing softly in the twilight created from the sinking sun outside the large windows in her room, and looked at her pile of CDs haphazardly arranged on a table across the large room.

Without moving, she *willed* her favorite Guns N' Roses CD from the top of the loose pile, and watched as it sailed across the room, touching nothing and being touched by nothing except the *Will* of the young woman.

It landed firmly in her hand. She again *willed* the CD out of its holder, and deposited it, all without touching it, into the boombox in the corner.

She smiled, looked again at the ceiling where her father had disappeared from the world, and turned up the volume on her favorite song on her favorite CD.

The opening lyrics of "November Rain" began, and she moved her head in rhythm with the song.

The siblings, the Children of the FateMaker, both with the powers of *Will*, knew the entire story behind the old song.

As the music played, and Emma listened to the words, several other things around the room began to clean themselves, not being touched by anything. Charlie was cleaning their shared, over-large room, deep in the bowels of the castle.

And so, as the old song played in their ears, Emma helped her brother clean the place. Books, movies, CDs, clothes, and trash zipped by in a crashing cacophony of sound and movement.

But nothing that flew through the air, to alight in their rightful places, was touched by a human hand. Nothing was touched at all.

Not touched by anything except the *Will* of the famous Daughter of the FateMaker, and his supposed vegetable of a son.

Emma Fairchild smiled as the high tempo song played, and her smile lit up the whole world.

And out of the corner of her eyes, hidden from the rest of the world by distance, rumor, and whispered history, she saw Charlie smile just the same.

His smile, more than hers, lit up the whole of the Universe.

# The End

Joshua Loyd Fox
Jan 2022 – Nov 2022

# Epilogue

Two Beings stood looking down on a world that was barely recognizable as such.

The taller Being, the All-Father, God Himself, nodded to the ArchAngel Jeremiel, bidding him to join the fracas below.

And for the first time in all of Creation's History, an ArchAngel's Will was thwarted, as he tried to reach the human, Kreo Fairchild, before the man pushed the auspicious red button.

But the ArchAngel was stopped, and suddenly surrounded by a different type of Host than what he was accustomed to.

As the ArchAngel, resplendent in continuously moving purple armor, flew in what seemed slow motion toward the human at the end of the long, wooden dock, time frozen, and finger poised above the button, the Host of Watchers surrounded the ArchAngel within the space between the Spiritual Plane and the Material, and battle ensued.

The ArchAngel Jeremiel held his own against half a dozen Watchers, their weapons as sharp, and their skills as honed, as the ArchAngel's himself.

And just as the ArchAngel's life was to be spilt within the interim between Planes, his brothers and sisters arrived to rescue him.

No other battle as long, loud, or as arduously well matched and equally tenable had ever been seen before in all of Creation.

At the conclusion of the Stalemate, ArchAngels arrayed on one side, the litany of Watchers on the other, a loud, silver bell sounded in the Heavens, and the earth below was caught in many mightily bright and disastrous mushroom clouds dotting the globe like a rotten fungus-covered head of lettuce.

The Principalities of the Air, the Watchers of another Existence, had slowed and then stopped the ArchAngels from completing their Mission for the first time in all of Time.

As the Watcher horde blinked out of existence between Planes, the Host of Younger Ilk and Older turned to their Father in exasperation, searching for an answer for this Outcome.

But the Father was silent.

He had seen the confrontation between his Heavenly Host and *Antithesis,* and felt the strangest sensation of being watched against the crown of his Celestial Mind.

The Creator of the Heavens and the Earths could not fathom who, or what, could ever watch Him without His knowledge or Will.

He even found himself glancing skyward but saw nothing. He wasn't used to not knowing things, but it was happening increasingly, and uncomfortably, more and more.

God was looking over His shoulder. *What was existence coming to?* he pondered.

A strange notion, indeed.


A million light years away, yet within a whisper of a heartbeat, the All-Father stood with another of His ArchAngels. The most Favored asked but a simple question.

"Gabriel, my Son, is the Mission of *Redemption* prepared?"

The golden, splendidly arrayed ArchAngel leader nodded his golden head.

"Then send my Son, Raguel, Friend of God, to see to its conclusion," He told the golden-auraed Angel standing before Him.

Gabriel nodded his understanding, looking forward to finishing these Missions and getting on with the matter of the ArchAngel War, and all it would consume.

First, however, the Cowboy would need to atone for a lifetime of death and sin.

A burning desire to quelch his sword of Heavenly Diamond Steel into the heart of the Cowboy almost overtook the ArchAngel Gabriel, but the hand of the Almighty on his shoulder tempered down the fires of Retribution within the golden Angel.

"He must be given the chance, like all of my Creation, Gabriel," the Creator said in way of dismissal.

A single, final thought pervaded the mind of the golden Angel before he could leave to instruct the ArchAngel Raguel in his own Mission.

"Remember, my son, the Law must be adhered to, by all. Even your Father," God whispered in Gabriel's mind.

"All must be allowed to seek, and be given, beautiful, merciful… *Redemption*."

Joshua Loyd Fox is the author of five novels to date. *I Won't Be Shaken*, and books I through IV of the Best-Selling ArchAngel Missions Series. All five novels are available on multiple platforms and in several styles from Watertower Hill Publishing, LLC.

He is also the author of one book of poetry, *I Don't Write Poetry: a Collection*, available Summer of 2023, and a short story anthology, *Book of the Tower and Traitor*, available exclusively on Amazon Vella.

All of Joshua Loyd Fox's novels can be found and ordered at <u>www.joshualoydfox.com</u>.

Look for his next installation of the ArchAngel Missions, *Say to This Mountain*, available from Watertower Hill Publishing, arriving Spring, 2024.

This work of fiction was formatted using 12-point Times New Roman font, the author's favorite, with 1.15 line spacing, on 55lb cream stock paper. The page size is 5.06" x 7.81." The custom margins are industry standard, 0.5" all around, and 0.00" inside, with no bleed, and 0.635" gutter, with mirrored pages. Headers and footers are standard.

The cover is full color paperback in a glossy finish.

The binding is 'perfect.'